Wyatt

Susan Fisher-Davis

Men of Clifton, Montana
Book 4

Erotic Romance

Wyatt Men of Clifton, Montana series
Copyright © 2015 Susan Fisher-Davis
First Paperback Publication: July 2015
ISBN: 9798415568444
Cover by Untold Designs Romance and Fantasy Covers

PUBLISHER: Blue Whiskey Publishing
Original Copyright ©2015 Susan Davis

Dedication

To Rob Kristian with Rob Kristian Photography for
the amazing shoot you did for me

https://www.facebook.com/RobKristianPhotography

You are amazing and I treasure your friendship.

To my readers - I do this for you. I love you all.
Thank you.

Chapter One

Rain fell from gray gloomy skies, beating down on his cowboy hat and matching his mood as he rode the fence line separating his property from that of his brother. Wyatt Stone was in a piss ass mood and looking for a fight. Maybe tonight would be a good night to go to Dewey's bar, the local hangout, and get rowdy. He wasn't sure what put him in such a foul mood, but he needed to get rid of it some way, and he figured the only way was with either a good fight or sex. A slow smile lifted his lips. Sex would be good. He shifted in the saddle. Sex would be damn good. It'd been a while.

Wyatt rubbed his hand over his jaw and thought about the last time he'd had any. *Carly Phelps.* She was hot and good. It'd been two weeks since he'd indulged. Suddenly, a pair of amethyst eyes rose before his mind's eye, making him swear. Blinking the vision away, he focused on what he was doing.

He saw a section of fence down, reined Cochise to a stop, and dismounted. The horse stood behind him. He knew he wouldn't go anywhere since Cochise always followed him around like a puppy. Ever since the horse had been born, Wyatt had cared for him. The mare had died giving birth to him and he'd sat up with the colt during the night and fed him. Cochise loved him and no one else.

Wyatt pulled the tools he needed out of the saddlebag and walked toward the downed fence. Cochise nudged him with his nose.

"Give me a minute, will you? It's not like you've never been in the rain before," he muttered. The horse snorted and stepped back from him. Wyatt glanced back at him. "Good boy."

The rain ran down his T-shirt and soaked his back. The shirt stuck to his skin and his boots were sinking into mud. He tugged on the wire with his gloved hands and swore when it slipped from him. He tilted his head down and clenched his jaw. The rain poured off the brim of his hat and splashed onto his boots. He sighed, strode over to where the wire lay on the ground, and pulled it to the post, fastening it tight. Then after putting the tools back in the saddlebag, he mounted Cochise. The horse pranced around. Wyatt nudged him, giving him his head, and Cochise tore off through the pasture. Mud flew up behind horse and rider as they ran full speed through the rain. It seemed Cochise needed to expend some pent up energy too.

He rode Cochise straight into the barn. The drumming of rain on the roof echoed through the building, making it almost impossible to hear. He dismounted and started unhooking the cinch when one of his ranch hands, Ben Collins, came up to him. Wyatt didn't care for him for some reason. There was just something about the man that rubbed him the wrong way. He'd hired Ben because his brother, Kirk, worked for him and Kirk was a hard worker. Ben was a hard worker too, but there was just something...he didn't trust the man.

"Hey boss. Do you want me to do that for you?" Ben asked.

"I got it. Thanks." Wyatt lifted the saddle off Cochise.

"You don't like anyone else touching your horse,

do you?" Ben sneered.

Wyatt turned toward him. "You want to try it? Go right ahead." He stepped away from Cochise.

Ben hesitated then stepped toward the horse and reached for the blanket. Cochise turned and tried to bite him. Ben jumped back.

"Holy hell!" He glanced at Wyatt. "He tried to bite me!"

Wyatt clenched his jaw and bit back a laugh. "I told you I had it. There's a reason no one takes care of him but me." He narrowed his eyes at Ben. "When I tell you something, you listen.

Don't ever take that smart-ass attitude with me again. Understand?"

Ben nodded and strode away. Wyatt was sure he was muttering as he went through the barn, but he didn't give a care about it. He stared after him for a few minutes, and then after wiping Cochise down, led him to his stall. Cochise entered his stall, put his head over the door, and butted his nose against Wyatt's chest. Wyatt rubbed his ears. "I'll see you tomorrow, boy."

He strolled along through the barn, checking on the other horses. Five were his. He was training the other two to be cutting horses before handing them over to clients. Wyatt and his brothers, well known across the United States, were considered some of the best at horse training. Jake, his oldest brother, worked with reining horses, and Gabe, the next oldest, worked with calf-roping or tie-down horses. The brothers were in high demand and stayed busy. Jake recently married Becca Daniels, a spunky redhead who inherited her grandmother's horse ranch and turned it into a lucrative Bed and Breakfast. It was rough going at first because when someone ransacked her home and stole her horses, she blamed Jake, even after she had already fallen in love with him. A man from her past had caused all the problems, but in the end, he died...by Wyatt's skill as an expert shooter. He'd taken him out with one shot after he'd shot Jake in the shoulder, and then took aim at Becca. Wyatt had no choice but to end his life.

His brother, Gabe, married Emma Conner, a beautiful blonde-haired woman they'd grown up with, after he got her pregnant. They now had a beautiful little girl, Sophie. Emma had fallen in love with Gabe when she was much younger but kept it to herself. After they were married, Gabe fell in love with her and they ended up very happy.

Wyatt grunted at the thought. He'd never have that kind of happiness and he was okay with it. Well, now he was but for a long time, he hurt. Stephanie Taylor had broken their engagement off a week before the wedding and it felt like he'd died.

It didn't hurt anymore, but he'd been down so low at one point he didn't think he'd ever get back up. He drank morning, noon, and night until Jake told him to get up and take it like a man or stay the hell away from him. Wyatt got up and stayed up. Stephanie Taylor could go to hell as far as he was concerned. She'd ripped his heart out and left him like the walking dead. At least, that's what he'd thought at the time but now he was glad he hadn't married her. He was sure he'd be even more miserable by now.

He ran from the barn through the rain and headed toward the house, dodging the puddles. Entering through the back door, his German shepherd, Bear, greeted him with a joy he was sure no woman ever would. He took his wet hat off and hung it on a peg by the door.

"Do you need to go out, buddy?" Wyatt asked him as he pulled his wet T-shirt over his head. Bear barked and sat down. "I'll take that as a *no* then. I don't blame you. It's too wet out there even for ducks."

He took his belt off, unzipped his jeans, and peeled them down his legs, the wet material making it difficult. He sat on the bench in the mudroom and removed his boots, pulling the wet jeans off before standing, and then removing his boxer briefs. He headed for the shower with Bear on his heels. He couldn't understand why the dog had to be in the bathroom with him every time Wyatt went in, but he'd gotten used to it. He glanced over his shoulder and grinned as Bear followed him into the bathroom. The dog lay down against the door and closed his eyes.

Wyatt turned on the shower and stepped in. Steam quickly filled the bathroom. Putting his hands against the wall, he moved his head under the spray. Water slid down over his hair, onto his face and dripped into the drain. Straightening up, he washed his hair. He was tired, it'd been a long day, but he had already decided he was going to Dewey's tonight to either find a woman or kick someone's ass.

He grumbled. What was wrong with him? He didn't get into fights anymore, but he just had to get this anger out of him. Hell, he didn't even know why he was angry. It wasn't Ben Collins, although he hadn't helped his mood much. No, Wyatt had felt mad at the world before he went out to check the fence.

He sighed as he soaped up his body and washed. *Son of a bitch!* Why was he feeling like this? Thinking back, he was sure his foul mood had started right after Gabe had left earlier. His brother had teased him about not settling down. Wyatt had told him he was happy the way he was, and he was. Damn it, he was. He didn't need a woman in his life unless it was for sex. He sure as hell didn't need one in his life permanently. Stephanie had ruined that for him. The chance of getting his heart stomped on again was unthinkable. He knew his brothers and their wives hoped he and Olivia would get together but damn, Olivia Roberts had heartbreaker written all over her.

Christ! She made him hard just thinking of her. She was so beautiful...a tall, slim, and breathtakingly beautiful woman. Her long black hair fell like a silk curtain down her back, touching her waist. Her lips were full and lush, and she had a sexy mole at the right top corner.

But it was her eyes which threatened to bring him to his knees if he wasn't careful. They were the color of amethyst. Purple. He'd never before seen eyes like hers, and he'd be damned before he'd let her see she could tie him in knots.

His cock twitched and he groaned. *Damn her!* He couldn't get involved with her, no matter how badly he wanted her under him. He could satisfy himself right here, but he wanted a woman. He loved the way they smelled and the softness of their skin, and the feel of their muscles clenching around his cock when they came. Wyatt groaned again. He needed to stop thinking like this or he'd take care of himself and not be good enough for a woman tonight. He knew how to please a woman. He loved taking them to the edge, watching their skin flush as they tumbled over, and letting their moans of pleasure urge him onto his own orgasm. *Damn!* He seriously needed to get laid tonight. It would be much better than a fight. He switched the water to cold and jumped back when it hit his hot skin.

Sighing, he stepped from the shower and dried off with a fluffy red towel. The entire home was made of log. The interior walls matched the exterior. The bathroom floor was red and white marble tiles. The stand-alone shower was large but there was also a bathtub, which sat against the wall with a skylight above it.

Wyatt walked into the bedroom, got a clean pair of jeans and T-shirt out, and dressed. He sat on the king-size bed and pulled his cowboy boots on. When he stood, Bear barked and ran toward the kitchen. Wyatt followed him and let him out. Once the dog was back inside, Wyatt would leave.

A few minutes later, Bear came back in—soaking wet. Wyatt swore and dried the dog off. Bear rolled to his back, making Wyatt grin. "I think you do that on purpose so I'll rub your belly." He scratched Bear's ears. "I'll see you later, boy. Be good."

He grabbed a dry cowboy hat and ran out the door through the rain to his truck. As he headed for Dewey's Bar, he wondered if maybe Carly would be there. Wyatt grinned at the thought. Yeah, that was a far better way to end the day than punching someone.

* * * *

Olivia Roberts was really getting tired of the man who was hovering nearby hitting on her. He was married and therefore, off limits. It didn't matter how good looking he was, she didn't fool around with married men. She gave him her best *I'm trying to be nice but get lost* smile.

"Look, hon...you're real nice but you're married, so no dice," she told him.

"Aww, come on babe, what she doesn't know won't hurt her," the man slurred. He was so drunk he was weaving. He pulled out a chair and flopped down on it.

She pulled her hand away when he reached for it and narrowed her eyes at him. "Don't do that. Go away. Please."

The man leaned back in his chair and laughed. "You don't even know my wife, so what's it matter?"

"The fact that you have a wife is what matters. Go home to her." Olivia was getting angry and that was never a good thing. She felt Becca lean across her.

"Go home, Jerry. I do know your wife and Carol is a wonderful woman." "Why are you here, Becca? You're married too." Jerry glared at her.

"Girls night out, not that it's any of your business. I'm not here looking to hook up either. I happen to have a man at home I love. Don't do this to Carol."

Jerry folded his arms across his chest and stared at her. He was a good-looking married man who had trouble keeping it in his pants. The entire town of Clifton knew about his wrongdoings. Most women avoided him, though a few took him up on his offers. He signaled for another beer. Olivia glanced over toward the bartender to tell him no and her eyes landed on Wyatt. He was sitting on a barstool with his back to the bar, his elbows resting on the bar behind him. His gaze was roaming the room, but he hadn't spotted her yet. She elbowed

Becca and nodded toward him.

"He's cruising," Olivia said.

Becca glanced at her best friend. "Probably."

Olivia blew out a breath. "There's no 'probably' about it. He is."

Emma, the third member of their party, stood. "I think I'll go say hello." She smiled. "He is my brother-in-law, after all."

Olivia reached out to stop her but Emma moved away from her laughing. Olivia watched as Emma made a beeline for Wyatt. He hadn't seen her yet, but Olivia knew the minute he'd spotted Emma. He straightened up on the stool and smiled at her. Olivia watched as Emma nodded in the direction of their table, and groaned when Wyatt peered around his sister-in-law, his gaze settling on her. She saw his jaw clench and his lips flatten into a flat line. Who in the hell was he to get angry at her being here? *He* was here. She leaned back in her chair and folded her arms across her chest when she saw Emma leading him back to where they were seated. He stood beside it and glared down at Jerry.

"Jerry, you need to leave the women here alone," Wyatt said.

Olivia did everything she could to stop the shiver that ran through her at the sound of his deep, sexy voice. She'd wanted him since the first time she'd laid eyes on him. He stood six foot four with hair as black as a raven's wing. A straight, narrow nose sat over a gorgeous pair of lips, bowed upper lip and a full bottom lip, which screamed, "Suck on me." His eyes were such a dark brown they appeared black. In fact, Olivia was beginning to think they *were* black. She just needed to get close enough to look to be sure. He'd never let her though. For some reason, he kept his distance from her, despite the fact they were constantly thrown together. Her best friend, Becca, was married to his oldest brother, Jake, and her other friend, Emma, was married to the next older brother, Gabe. They were always together, but never *together*. She'd made it clear to him she wanted him and yet he still stayed away. Oh, he was always polite to her but that was as far as it went.

Olivia wanted to lick him all over. Her eyes instinctively went to his crotch. This time the shiver emerged. His jeans fit him like a glove and the soft denim cupped his sex just so that she couldn't pull her attention away. She knew what the backside looked like too. His jeans looked as if they'd been made specifically for him. His black T-shirt hugged his biceps, his chest, and she could make out the six-pack abs under it. She wiggled in her seat. Whoever thought she'd want a cowboy? The black hat sat low on his forehead.

Jerry stood. "I'm not doing anything wrong, Wyatt. You need to butt out."

Wyatt smirked. "Not doing anything wrong, huh? How about the fact you're married and hitting on these women?"

"I'm only hitting on Olivia. The other two are married." He dropped down onto his seat again.

Wyatt laughed. "That's rich. You won't hit on a married woman, but you're a married man hitting on a woman." He pulled Jerry up out of his seat by his shirt collar. "I think it's time you went home to Carol, though why she wants you is beyond me."

"Come on, Wyatt. There isn't a man in this place who doesn't want Olivia."

Wyatt's eyes met hers. "Yes, there is."

Olivia hissed in a breath and stood. "I'll see you two tomorrow," she said to Becca and Emma then strode out the door.

* * * *

Wyatt swore under his breath as she strode past him with her head held high. His gaze shifted to his sisters-in-law to see them glaring at him. He stared at them, waiting for the lecture he was sure was coming. Becca stood and narrowed her eyes at him.

"That, Wyatt Stone, was totally uncalled for."

"I'm just telling it like it is."

Becca laughed. "You're such a bad liar." She sat back down and ordered another drink.

"You're not driving, are you?" Wyatt asked her, feeling protective of the two women.

Becca shook her head. "Nope. Emma is. She's only drinking Coke."

Wyatt swore under his breath. Pissing off either Becca or Emma was not a good idea. His brothers would gang up on him if they learned of it. He smirked as he realized they'd have to gang up on him since he could kick their asses separately and they knew it. Wyatt was a Marine, and a badass sniper, the best in his unit. It didn't matter that he'd been out of the Corp for seven years. Once a Marine, always a Marine.

"Good. I don't want to have to bail you out of jail."

"Go away, Wyatt. I'm pissed at you right now...and take Jerry with you." Becca waved her hand at him dismissively.

Wyatt frowned when he realized he was still holding onto Jerry's collar. He unclenched his fist from the man's shirt. Jerry turned and took a swing at him. Wyatt ducked but Jerry clipped his jaw, sending him backwards. Jerry pounced on him. *Well, here's the fucking fight you were looking for.* Wyatt pulled his fist back to punch Jerry, but a strong grip locked onto his arm. He spun around to see Clifton's Sheriff, Sam Garrett. Sam was staring at him.

"I wouldn't do that if I were you, Wyatt. Don't make me run you in."

Wyatt raised his eyebrows. "Run *me* in? He started it."

"He's also so damn drunk he can barely stay on his feet," Sam said.

Wyatt nodded and Sam released his arm. "I'm leaving anyway. I was just trying to get Jerry to leave them alone."

"I've been here making rounds and I was watching him. Liv was handling it. If it had gotten out of hand, I was going to intervene."

Wyatt put his fingers to the brim of his hat, nodded to Becca and Emma, then headed out the door. Outside, it had stopped raining and he took a deep breath of the late September air. Soon, fall would move in and he knew snow wouldn't be far behind. His eyes roamed the parking lot, and he swore aloud when he saw Olivia sitting on a bench across the street. He headed over toward her and halted in front of her. His breath whooshed out when she raised those gorgeous eyes at him.

"Why do you hate me?" she asked sadly.

"I don't hate you, Olivia."

She snorted. "Well, you sure have a weird way of showing me you like me, cowboy."

He sat down beside her. "I'm not looking for a relationship, Olivia. I've been there and I had my heart torn apart. I sure as hell don't want to go through it again."

"You think you're the only person who's ever had their heart broken? I found my fiancé screwing my college roommate." She sighed.

"I know I'm not but I'm not going through that again," he grumbled.

"I've made it pretty clear how I feel," Olivia whispered.

Wyatt laughed. "Hell, Olivia. You've done everything but lie down and spread your legs for me."

Olivia abruptly stood. "That was a little crude, even for me," she said. "Well, you can bet your ass it will never happen now, cowboy." She marched off across the street.

Wyatt watched her cross the street and only after a slight hesitation, he ran after her and grasped her arm, spun her around to face him and pushed her back against a truck.

"You just don't get it do you?" he said through clenched teeth.

"Let go of me." Olivia jerked away from him, pushing at his chest. Wyatt stepped back and glared at her. He swore under his breath. "What is it I don't get, cowboy?"

He leaned down close so she wouldn't miss a word. "I don't want you."

Olivia laughed. "I don't believe that—not for a minute. I've seen the way you look at me." She poked his chest with her fingertip. "You want me, Wyatt Stone. You just don't want to want me." She gave him a hard shove and strode away from him.

"Son of a bitch," he roared and ran after her, stepping in front of her. "Are you so sure about that?" She nodded. "Wrong. If I wanted you, I'd have you." He stepped back when she stepped closer to him, gazing up at him. She grinned at him.

"I know when a man wants me and you do, cowboy. You just won't go for it for some weird reason."

"You know when a man wants you, eh? So you've been with that many, huh?" He smirked. "Are you telling me you're a slut, Olivia?" Wyatt wasn't ready for the slap she gave him, and his head jerked back and a red-hot heat stung his cheek.

"That's twice you've said something totally uncalled for. What does it matter to you if I am, if you don't want me?"

"Maybe that's why I don't want you," he said then swore when he saw tears fill her eyes, but she quickly blinked them away. *Christ, she has balls.*

"I hate you, Wyatt Stone and I'm so glad I finally see the real you. Now get the fuck out of my way and don't ever speak to me again." She marched around him, got into her vehicle, and drove off. He stood in the street staring after her.

This was just great. How were they going to be around each other now, when she hated him? Their family threw them together constantly. They had no clue about how Wyatt felt. Getting involved with Olivia would tear him apart again. She'd made it clear she wanted him, but he couldn't take the chance. The chance he'd fall and she wouldn't. He groaned. She was so beautiful and he'd love to feel her under him, above him, or any other way he could think of.

Shit! His traitorous body went rock hard. Just thinking of her was all it seemed to take. Anytime he was close to her, his body betrayed him. He loved inhaling her perfume. His cock started to ache just thinking about inhaling her feminine scent. He wanted to bury his face between her legs and taste her.

Jesus Christ! What the fuck was he going to do? Did she really hate him now? Why wouldn't she? *Fool, you implied she was a slut.* He didn't know anything about her, not really. Only that she was Becca's friend, and they'd been together since they were thirteen and before that, Olivia had been in foster homes. But he had no idea why she was. Where were her parents? Were they dead? From what he'd heard, no family had ever adopted her. He'd bet she was a real wild child since she didn't back down from anything now. He smiled when he thought of her glaring at him. She was tough, there was no doubt there. Sighing, he walked back to his truck, climbed in, and headed home. He needed to get some sleep. It didn't look like he was going to get that release he needed from a fight or a woman tonight.

Chapter Two

Olivia sat at the table with her laptop open in front of her, working on next season's reservations. The Clifton Bed and Breakfast was a goldmine for Becca, and Olivia loved working here but for the past week, she couldn't concentrate. A certain dark-eyed cowboy kept invading her thoughts more than usual. *Damn him!* She knew he wanted her and yet he insisted on lying about it. Why would he pretend he didn't want her? He saw other women, she was sure because she'd heard rumors about him with them, so if he just wanted sex, why not her?

Shaking her head, she tried to get back into her work but finally gave up, and closed the laptop. She wasn't going to get anything done today, so she headed for the front desk and smiled at Stacy Miller, who was sitting behind the counter. Olivia took a seat beside her.

"It won't be long and we'll be closing for the season," Olivia said, thinking aloud.

"Wow, hard to believe. The B and B did so well this year. I mean last year was good but this year was amazing. Becca is so proud of herself." Stacy grinned.

Olivia laughed. "Yes, she is and she has every right to be. Now with the cabins on the property, she'll have even more people next year."

Stacy groaned. "I know." She turned toward Olivia. "How are the reservations looking for next season?"

"We're already booked solid."

"We'll be busy for sure with all the rooms and cabins full."

"Poor Evelyn. I'm sure Becca's going to have to hire more help in the kitchen. Evelyn can't cook for so many people alone." Olivia shook her head, truly wondering how Evelyn would do it.

"How is that going to work anyway? All those people won't fit in the dining room here." Stacy frowned.

Olivia was about to answer her when the front door opened, and Becca entered. She smiled at them in greeting.

"What are you doing here, Becs?" Olivia grinned, always happy to see her best friend.

"I was just heading home from town and I wanted to ask you to dinner tomorrow night." She folded her arms across the top of the counter. "How are things going?"

"Great. We're all booked for next season. Stacy and I were wondering how the meals were going to be done. Not everyone will fit in the dining room at the same time."

"Hmm...I suppose the folks in the cabins can call here to let us know they want dinner from here, and then they can come here to pick it up or just like the guests staying here, they can go into town." Becca smiled at her. "Of course, they can always use the little kitchenettes in the cabins since pots and pans are going to be provided and prepare their own meals. As for breakfast, we can do the same or have separate seatings." She turned to Stacy. "You and Josh are more than welcome to come for dinner too."

Stacy smiled at her. "We're going to my mom and dad's for dinner, but thanks for the invite."

"No problem." Becca turned to Olivia. "You'll be there, right?"

Olivia nibbled on her bottom lip. "I suppose so."

"You suppose so? What does that mean Olivia Rene Roberts?"

Olivia shrugged. "Is Wyatt going to be there?"

"Of course he is. Why?"

"I don't want to be around him."

"It never bothered you before. Becca's eyes narrowed as she stared at her.

Olivia blew out a breath. "Never mind, I'll be there."

Becca stared at her, waiting, but Olivia wasn't going to spill her guts to her. She knew, without a doubt, Becca would tell Jake and the shit would hit the fan as a result. Olivia mentally shook her head, deciding she couldn't do it. No matter how rude Wyatt had been, she couldn't bring that kind of tension between everyone. Her eyes met Becca's, and she knew her best friend knew something was up. They'd been friends far too long not to be able to read each other. Becca finally nodded.

"All right. Be there at six. I'll see you then." She turned from the counter and left.

"Since when don't you want to be around Wyatt?" Stacy asked with raised eyebrows.

Olivia groaned. "Is it so obvious?"

Stacy laughed. "That you want him? Yes. Everyone knows it."

Olivia stood and faced Stacy. "Well, I don't anymore. Long story, but I'm past it." *Liar!* She knew she'd never be past wanting Wyatt. "I'll be in my apartment if you need any help. I've got reservations to work on." She knew Stacy didn't believe her but thankfully, she didn't say anything as Olivia walked away.

* * * *

At exactly six o'clock that evening, Olivia pulled her car up by the back door and glanced around. She didn't see Wyatt's truck anywhere. Blowing out a breath, she pushed the car door open and stepped out. As she started toward the porch, she heard a vehicle coming up the drive and when she saw it was Wyatt's truck, she quickly stepped onto the porch, knocked, and entered the kitchen. Becca and Emma both turned and smiled at her. Olivia flashed a quick smile at them.

"Is there anything I can do?" she asked them.

"We just need to set the table. Can you grab some plates? Wyatt's not..." Becca started but then stopped when the back door opened, and Wyatt entered. Olivia turned her back to him.

"I wasn't sure if you were going to make it," Becca's voice held a smile as if his being there surprised her.

"Now why wouldn't I make it?"

Olivia refused to turn and look at him. It was going to be hard enough getting through the evening being at the same table with him, there was no way she could look at him. She pulled the plates down from the cupboard and carried them to the table in the dining room. Walking around the table, she set each plate down at a place.

"Do you really think this is going to work?" Wyatt's voice came from behind her.

"I don't know what you're talking about." She turned to find him leaning against the doorjamb, his arms folded across his broad chest and one hip cocked. The red T-shirt he wore stretched tightly across his pecs and flat stomach. The short sleeves stretched tight around his biceps. Her eyes seemed to have a mind of their own as they skimmed down his body to land on the fly of his jeans. She'd love to know, firsthand, what was behind it. She bit her lip to keep from groaning. She lifted her eyes to meet his, and they held there. His lips rose in a slow smile.

"The hell you don't, Olivia," he muttered, his gaze not wavering.

She stared at him. She loved seeing him with his cowboy hat on, but he looked even sexier without it. His hair was so black it appeared blue under the overhead lights and curled slightly where it touched the collar of his shirt. Her fingers itched to comb through the strands. She took a deep breath and exhaled in an exasperated huff.

"It really doesn't matter if it works or not, does it? We aren't together very often and when we are, we'll just ignore each other."

His soft chuckle ran along her skin, raising goose bumps. "Ignore each other?"

Olivia slammed the last plate down and glared at him. "It shouldn't be too hard for you to ignore me, Wyatt. You've been doing it since the first day we met." She walked forward, halting in front of him.

"Move," she commanded, raising her eyes to meet his. He stared back at her, and then took a deep breath, stepping back from the doorway. When she started to pass him, his fingers wrapped around her arm, stopping her. She narrowed her eyes. "Get your damn hands off me."

"Is something wrong, Liv?" Wyatt's oldest brother, Jake, asked from the doorway leading to the living room.

She tore her gaze away from Wyatt and smiled at Jake as best she could. "No. Wyatt was just giving me a rough time." She gave a half laugh, noticing Jake didn't look as if he believed her, but he gave a nod and left the room anyway. Olivia looked back at Wyatt and growled low. "Don't touch me again." She pushed past him and headed into the kitchen.

* * * *

Wyatt rubbed his hand over his jaw. Damn. His gaze followed her as she headed toward the kitchen. His eyes instinctively went to her ass. The woman sure could fill out a pair of jeans. His groin tightened as he watched the natural sway of her hips. *Fuck!* Striding from the dining room, he headed toward the living room where his brothers were. He flopped down in the recliner. He could feel Jake's eyes on him. Wyatt glanced over to him and raised an eyebrow.

"You have something to say, Jake?"

"What the hell is going on with you and Olivia?" Jake asked him.

Wyatt shrugged. "Just as she said...I was giving her a rough time. Nothing to concern you, or anyone else." Wyatt shifted his eyes to his other brother, Gabe.

"I don't have any idea what either of you are talking about," Gabe muttered.

"They looked like they were having quite a conversation when I interrupted," Jake volunteered.

Wyatt stood and glared at him. "Let it go, Jake."

He knew Jake was about to say something when Becca announced dinner was ready. *Saved by the dinner bell.* Everyone moved into the dining room and took their seats. Just his luck, Wyatt ended up sitting across from Olivia. Biting back a sigh, he knew his family had done this on purpose. He tried his best to keep his eyes cast downward but he happened to glance up, and her gaze captured his eyes. In the years he'd known her, he'd never seen her look at him like she was doing now. It was a look as if she hated him, and it bothered him. It bothered the hell out of him.

* * * *

Olivia had to get through this. With him sitting right across from her, she was finding it difficult to concentrate on the conversation flowing around the table. The food tasted like dirt because she had no appetite. When she heard her name, she quickly looked at Becca.

"Are you all right, Liv? You're not eating and that's not like you," Becca scolded.

"I'm just not..." She glanced at Wyatt. "I'm not real hungry, Becs. I'm fine."

"You're always hungry, Liv." Gabe laughed then grunted when Emma elbowed him.

"Sorry," he muttered.

It was a running joke with all of them how much Olivia ate, but still stayed so slim. She always seemed to be eating and they constantly teased her about it. Now she had no appetite, at least not with Wyatt sitting across from her. Certainly not after the conversation they'd had a while back. He'd practically called her a slut, and then told her he didn't want her for that exact reason. Her gaze ran over him. It didn't look like he'd eaten much either. She'd had enough. She stood quickly, drawing everyone's attention.

"I'm sorry, I...uh, I'm leaving." She quickly

headed toward the back door. Becca and Emma caught up with her in the kitchen. Becca grabbed her arm and spun her around.

"What is going on with you?"

"I told you I didn't want to be here to begin with, Becca. Let it go."

"The hell I will. What happened between you and Wyatt?"

"Something happened between you and Wyatt?" This from Emma.

"We had a...a disagreement and I'd rather not be around him anymore." Olivia picked up her purse. "I'll talk to you later."

"You're damned right you will. This is not over. You will tell me what's going on. Soon." Becca ran her hand up Olivia's arm. "I don't like seeing you like this and I want to know what happened. We've never kept things from each other before and we're not going to start now. I'll let you go for now, but we will talk."

Olivia stared at her best friends wanting to come clean, but knew she couldn't so she nodded. "All right, but not now. I'm going home."

She left without looking back, got into her vehicle, and drove home to the B and B and her little apartment. She could hear her dog, Punkin, barking. Olivia didn't know what she'd do without the little dog. There was no one else waiting for her. If only she could just find a man who was as excited to see her when she came home, she'd be content. Olivia laughed when Punkin tore out of the apartment to head for the back door. Olivia opened the door to let her out and noticed headlights coming up the driveway. Was a guest arriving this late? Closing the back door, she headed toward the desk to check the computer to see if someone hadn't arrived yet.

As she started looking through the reservations, the front door flew open and Wyatt strode in. Olivia let out a gasp. "What are you doing here?"

She knew by the look on his face he was pissed off. "You ran like a scared rabbit and left me to wolves. They all wanted to know what went on between us, and then didn't believe me when I told them nothing." His jaw clenched and a muscle twitched in his cheek.

God! He was so gorgeous and no matter what she told him, she still wanted him.

"I don't want to be around you, Wyatt. You've made it abundantly clear what you think of me." She shrugged. "It was your fault I left the way I did, so it was your place to tell them what is going on. I'm done talking about it. Now get out."

Wyatt stared at her for a few minutes before turning on his boot heel. He strode out the door, slamming it behind him. She blew out a breath she hadn't realized she was holding. It was going to be way too hard to be near Wyatt knowing she'd never have him. Maybe it was time to leave Clifton, Montana.

Olivia sat behind the counter staring at the door Wyatt had just stormed out of in a huff. It wasn't her fault everyone jumped on him about her. She sighed, thinking about Becca coming after her, and she would. Becca wouldn't let it go no matter what Olivia told her—Emma too. They were both stubborn and they'd get it out of her, and then the shit would start. Becca would tell Jake and Emma would tell Gabe, and then the brothers would go after Wyatt. Olivia placed her hands over her face and groaned. Why did he have to be so damn hot?

There were quite a few hot cowboys in Clifton, so why did she have it so bad for Wyatt? She'd even tried going out with Ryder Wolfe but there'd been no spark between them, and so they agreed just to be friends. Ryder was gorgeous too. Why couldn't she want him? Or that sexy sheriff, Sam Garrett? He was drop-dead gorgeous and very sexy but for some reason, he didn't seem interested in her any more than she was in him.

She shut the computer down for the night and headed back to her apartment. It had once been the housekeeper's quarters in the old Colonial style home. Becca inherited the home and ranch from a grandmother she never knew, and turned it into a very lucrative bed and breakfast. Falling in love wasn't in Becca's plans when she came to Clifton but once she met Jake, it all changed. Olivia was happy for her best friend. Becca and Jake were very much in love. Olivia and Becca met Emma in town and quickly added her to the friendship. Emma loved Gabe Stone, and she was so lucky when she became pregnant by him, he did the right thing and married her. They had a beautiful baby girl named Sophie Ann, and Gabe loved and adored them both. Wyatt was the youngest Stone brother and the minute Olivia set eyes on him, she wanted him but he'd always kept his distance from her. He was never rude exactly, but he just didn't go out of his way to talk to her...until the other night, anyway. She still couldn't believe how rude he'd been to her. And it had hurt. It hurt a lot to have him thinking that about her. She was not a slut. Just because she was flirtatious, and had a smart mouth, did not make her a slut. If she thought a man was gorgeous and sexy, she had no problem letting him know. Did that make her a slut? No, she didn't think so. Sighing, she brushed her hair and teeth, undressed, and climbed between the sheets, hoping this was one night a dark-eyed cowboy wouldn't show up in her dreams.

* * * *

The next day, Wyatt worked with one horse for hours. The mare didn't seem to want to do any of the commands he gave her. He was tired, hot, sweaty, and hungry. He nudged the mare to the rail and dismounted.

"I don't get what your problem is today, Candy," Wyatt said in a low tone of voice. "Any other day you're spot on." He shrugged and led her toward the barn. It was then he noticed a hesitation in her gate. Why hadn't he seen it when he was training her? *Damn it!* He lifted her front leg and saw she had a small cut. He slowly led her out and put her in her stall.

Wyatt went to the tack room to get antiseptic. If he couldn't get it to heal, he'd call Doctor Will Carter. He was the best vet in the area and he knew he'd be here in a heartbeat if Wyatt needed him. He couldn't believe he had missed that. *Get your damn mind on your work and off Olivia.* He started back to the stall when he saw Ben coming toward him. Wyatt halted and waited for him to reach him.

"Hey, boss." Ben smiled at him, though it didn't reach his eyes.

Wyatt nodded to him. "Something on your mind, Collins?"

"Could I get off early tonight? I'd like to head over to Dewey's."

"It's not up to me. Ask Lucky."

"You're the boss."

"Lucky's your boss. He knows what's going on and if he needs someone. I only make decisions for you men if Lucky has a problem with one of you or if I want you to do something."

Ben nodded. "I'll ask him then. Goodnight...*boss*."

Wyatt wanted to grab him by his collar and shake him. He wasn't sure what Collins's problem was but he was defiant and it would come to a head eventually, Wyatt *was* sure about that.

He entered the stall to administer the antiseptic. The cut was fresh. His gaze roamed the stall to see on what she could have cut herself. He swore when he saw a rusty nail sticking out from one of the boards making up the stall. Walking over to it, he squatted down and could see blood on it. This never should have happened. The men were supposed to make sure something like this didn't happen. He swore as he stood.

"What's wrong, boss?" Lucky asked as he looked into the stall.

"There's a damn rusty nail sticking out. Who was to check the stalls this week?" Wyatt growled.

"I'll have to check the paperwork, but I think it was Kirk."

"Kirk? He'd never let this happen."

Lucky nodded. "I agree, but I'll make sure and let you know."

Wyatt had to be content with that for now. He couldn't believe Kirk would miss this. Ben yes, but not Kirk. The idea of chewing Kirk out for this held no appeal. Kirk had worked for him for six years, almost since Wyatt started the ranch after he returned from his stint in the Marines at age twenty-six, and that was seven years ago.

Wyatt nodded his appreciation. He turned to leave and saw Kirk standing at the end of the barn.

"Kirk," Wyatt called out to him. He saw Kirk lift his head, glance his way, and then began heading his way.

"Yeah?" Kirk put his hands on his hips, but his body language was anything but casual.

Wyatt frowned. "Is there something wrong?"

Kirk glanced away. When he looked at Wyatt, he had a profound sadness in his eyes.

"Come into the office." Wyatt led the way. He motioned for Kirk to have a seat while he took a seat behind the scarred oak desk. "What's going on?"

"Nothing..."

"Bullshit." Wyatt sat forward and folded his arms on the desk. "Did you repair the stalls this week?" At Kirk's nod, he went on. "There was a nail that was missed and it cut Candy's leg." He raised his hand up when Kirk opened his mouth to speak. "It wasn't bad but the fact that it happened at all is unforgivable. Candy isn't my horse. If a client finds out a horse's leg has been cut due to negligence, it could ruin me, and all of you would be out of jobs. I'd still have a problem if the horse were one of mine, but being a client's is something that we can't allow to happen—ever. You're a good ranch hand, Kirk and you'd never make this kind of mistake if something wasn't bothering you."

"Nothing's wrong. I fucked up. That's all."

Wyatt sprang to his feet. "That's all?" he yelled. "I can't have you fucking up. I can't have any of you fucking up. We'd all be out of jobs if shit like this gets out."

Kirk gazed up at him with guilt in his eyes. "I'm

sorry, Wyatt," he mumbled.

"Go home. Take the rest of the weekend off—without pay."

Wyatt strode from the office. He stopped to explain the situation to Lucky, and then headed back to the house. He mentally shook his head. What in the hell was the problem? He never yelled at his men like this. Damn. He knew exactly what the problem was or rather he should say he knew *who* the problem was. He headed for a shower. It had been a long, drawn out day and he was tired. He just wanted to sit in his recliner in his living room, have a beer, and watch some television. Most of the hands would be heading out tonight since it was Saturday night. They would head for Dewey's. Wyatt just didn't feel like going out tonight. He didn't need to run into Olivia again.

He sighed. It would happen again though. They were family so there would always be gatherings. Emma and Gabe put on a big Thanksgiving dinner every year, and Wyatt only missed one year of attending since Jake and Becca first got together. Stephanie's father had invited him to his home so they could discuss business. He couldn't turn down an invitation from Blake Taylor, since it was Blake who had gotten Wyatt his start with training. It had been damned uncomfortable with Stephanie sitting there across from him at the table. She stared at him all day and he knew she wanted him back, but there was no way. Wyatt even wondered what he ever saw in her. She was beautiful, yes, but she was also a spoiled rich bitch and he knew now it never would have worked between them.

Stephanie Taylor had her eye on Wyatt the minute her father introduced them and like a fool, he had fallen for the blonde haired beauty. *God!* What a fool he was. He fell hard for her, and then she broke him apart. Jake kept telling him she wasn't the woman for him but Wyatt refused to see it. All he saw was Stephanie and he believed she wanted him too. She wanted him all right, until he wanted her. Why she said yes when he asked her to marry him was anyone's guess. She only wanted him because of his money. He had a lot of it and even though her family was rich, she couldn't seem to get enough. But a week before the wedding, she decided he wasn't the man she wanted to spend the rest of her life with. He was a firm believer in everything happening for a reason. Wyatt knew he never would have been happy with her. The only thing was that she had ruined his trust of women. Throwing his heart out there again just wasn't going to happen. He had no problem being with a woman for sex but the minute she started getting ideas of roping him in, he bolted.

Olivia popped into his head. *Holy shit!* He sure as hell wanted her. He had lied to her when he told her he didn't, but he was never going to let her know the truth. If there was ever a woman he was afraid of, it was Olivia Roberts. The woman should have the word *heartbreaker* tattooed across her forehead. He may be a *love 'em and leave 'em* kind of man but he had a feeling he wouldn't want to leave her and that just wouldn't do. Wyatt didn't know what to think as he headed toward the bathroom to shower. A night in was sounding better all the time.

Chapter Three

Olivia sat in her apartment working on the website for the B and B when she heard a knock on her door. She set the computer aside and answered the door. Becca stood there.

"Hi, Becs. Come on in." Olivia sighed, opening the door wider.

Becca waltzed in and took a seat on the sofa. "It's time you told me what's going on with you and Wyatt."

Olivia nibbled on her bottom lip. With any other person, she'd tell them to butt out but she couldn't do that with Becca. They'd been friends far too long.

Becca patted the cushion beside her and after taking a deep breath, Olivia took a seat beside her and proceeded to tell her about Wyatt.

Becca jumped up quickly. "Jake will kill him."

"No. This is why I didn't want to tell you. I don't want the brothers at odds with each other. It's over. Please forget it. I have," Olivia said but knew it was a lie. It would never be over in any way, shape, or form. She'd always want Wyatt, no matter how he treated her.

Becca sighed. "All right." She hugged Olivia. "But if anything like this happens again, I will not hesitate to tell Jake about it. He'd be as appalled by Wyatt's actions as I am." Becca sighed and hugged her. "I love you, Liv. I'm here for you."

Olivia could do no more than nod her head as Becca strode out the door. Olivia closed the door and leaned back against it. How much longer would it be before she could wake up and not think of him? Or go to sleep without seeing him in her dreams? Dear God, how was she to survive around him? She'd done a lot of thinking on whether to stay in Montana or move on. Leaving wouldn't make her forget him, but she wouldn't see him either, and that was the most important thing. Not seeing him. Because every time she saw him, she'd never be able to keep herself from wanting him. Becca was right, though. They were family. Becca was her family, and Becca married into the Stone family. Becca wouldn't have everyone to dinner and not invite Olivia but she would always include Wyatt. Olivia put her hands over her face. *God, what a mess.*

Three days later, early in the morning, Olivia sat at her kitchen table answering emails with her headphones in listening to music. The song, *'Lost'* by Anouk came on and made her pause. The song was a reminder of how she wanted a man she couldn't have.

She ripped the headphones out and tossed them onto the table. She needed to get out for a while. This sitting around and trying to work was going to slowly drive her insane. She stood and stretched. After grabbing her keys, she ran out the door, leaving Punkin gazing after her.

"I'll be back later, girl," Olivia shouted over her shoulder.

Cold weather was moving in from the Glacier Mountains. She gazed at them for a few minutes before getting into her car. They were already snowcapped, and she'd learned how snow came early and swiftly in Clifton. She shivered at the thought. Being from Maryland, she was used to snow but what they got in Montana was downright ridiculous. Pulling out of the driveway, she turned left with no destination in mind, just driving. She passed Jake's ranch, then Gabe's, and then slowed when she came to the entrance of Wyatt's ranch.

Olivia chewed on her bottom lip. Should she, she wondered. He wasn't home because she knew he was in Butte. Becca told her the brothers had made the trip and anytime they went to the sale, it was always a three-day trip. One to get there, one for the sale, and one to travel back home. It was almost unheard of to return home the night of the sale. She was sure he wasn't home and she'd love to see Cochise again. Although she was terrified of horses, Cochise was the most gorgeous horse she'd ever seen. To her, he looked as if someone had tossed a can of black paint over a white horse. He had gorgeous blue eyes too.

Shrugging, she pulled into the drive and stopped at the barn. She glanced around and didn't see anyone. Where were the ranch hands? The place looked deserted. The large log home resembled a ski chalet with rows of windows on the front. A wraparound porch beckoned with rocking chairs. Olivia opened her car door, got out, and strolled into the barn. The smell of horses, hay, leather, and manure hit her. It wasn't too long ago when she thought the smell offensive, but now it wasn't as unpleasant to her. She strolled down the center aisle, glancing at the horses in the stalls. None of them was Cochise. Where was he? Heading out the back of the barn, she entered the huge metal building where she knew Wyatt did his training. Jake and Gabe had the same type of buildings at their places.

Olivia went inside and sighed at the feeling of the warm air. The buildings stayed heated for winter and air-conditioned for summer since the men spent so much time in them. As she moved closer to the stalls, she noticed a wooden sign with the silhouette of a woman riding a horse with the words, THERE IS NO BETTER FEELING THAN SEVENTEEN HANDS BETWEEN YOUR LEGS scrolled on it. What in the hell did that mean? Olivia shrugged and moved on.

Sitting on the floor next to a stall was a basket of apples. She picked one up and used her penknife on her keychain to cut it into quarters. Not that she'd actually put her hand out to a horse. Their teeth were too big. She shuddered at the thought. There were three stalls along the back wall, so she headed toward them. The first two were empty, but the third one was where she found the beautiful beast.

"Hello gorgeous," Olivia whispered to Cochise. She frowned when he backed away from her, tossing his head and kicking at the wood shavings on the floor of his stall.

"Come here, Cochise. I have an apple for you." She held her hand out and tried to keep it steady. She wondered if horses smell fear like dogs did. If so, then Cochise was getting a hell of a dose of it. He stood in the back corner, his ears pinned back. She gulped. "I won't hurt you, and hopefully, you won't hurt me. Come on. Come and get this apple. You'll love it."

Cochise stared at her, and then whinnied. He pawed at the shavings. If a horse could glare, he was doing it. Olivia held her hand out again.

"Listen, Cochise. I'm not a fan of horses. It's

nothing personal. I've just never been around them until lately and the thought of being on one terrifies the shit out of me but you see, I think you're perfect. Just like your master. Is that right? Is he your master, like a dog owner is?" She chewed on her bottom lip. "I really have no idea."

She smiled when Cochise moved closer to her but he still didn't take the apple. His ears were up and he wasn't stomping anymore. He seemed to be looking past her. She glanced over her shoulder and gasped. Wyatt stood in the doorway. He just stood there leaning against the doorjamb with his arms folded across his chest and his booted feet crossed at the ankles. His hat sat low on his forehead, but she knew his eyes were on her. *Shit!* Could the floor just open up and swallow her now?

* * * *

Wyatt stared at her. Why was she here? *Son of a bitch.* He pushed himself away from the doorjamb and sauntered toward her. He halted in front of her.

"What are you doing here?" he asked.

"What are you doing here?" She threw back at him.

He raised his eyebrow. "I live here."

"I meant, you're supposed to be in Butte." Olivia glanced away from him.

"I came home last night."

"I didn't see your truck."

Wyatt grunted. "So, if you had seen it, you wouldn't have stayed?"

"I...yes. I mean, no." She waved her hand. "I wouldn't have stayed."

"You still haven't told me why you're here."

"I was so bored at home and so I went for a drive. I ended up here. I wanted to see Cochise again. He won't even come to me." Olivia shifted her eyes toward the horse.

Wyatt took the apple from her hand and held it out to Cochise. The horse gently took it from him. Wyatt rubbed his velvet nose. Cochise butted his head against him.

"He's a Paint, isn't he?" Olivia asked.

Wyatt glanced at her. "He's an American Quarter Horse."

Olivia frowned. "I thought if they were spotted like this, they were Paints or pintos."

"Paints are a breed of horse, like a Quarter Horse is a breed. Pinto is a coloring." He jerked his chin at Cochise. "His coloring is pinto."

"You lost me." Olivia frowned at him.

"Not all pintos are Paints, but most Paints are pinto." Wyatt rubbed the horse's nose. "Hey, buddy. Looks like that ride's going to have to wait." Wyatt glanced at Olivia. He heard her sigh.

"I'll go so you can go for your ride." She turned to leave but Wyatt grasped her arm, and turned her to face him.

"I'd rather go for a ride with you, Olivia," he said in a low voice.

Olivia stared at him. "What?"

Wyatt huffed. "I can't get you out of my damn head."

"Really?" Olivia murmured.

"Yes."

She smiled up at him and his heart slammed into his ribs. This was not a good idea but he had to have her. Maybe once he had, he'd get over this obsession with her. He mentally shook his head. He seriously doubted that. Her hand slipped behind his neck as he leaned down to kiss her. Both of them groaned when their lips met. Wyatt's arms slipped around her waist. He lifted her up. Her arms wrapped around his neck, knocking his hat to the floor. Her hands fisted in his hair as he deepened the kiss, and Olivia's legs wrapped around his waist. Wyatt knew it would be like this. She tasted so good, and he wanted to taste every inch of her soft skin.

She pulled back from him and looked at him with those amazing eyes. "Tell me again how you don't want me, cowboy," she whispered, her voice suddenly husky sounding.

Wyatt gazed into her eyes. Olivia was so beautiful, she took his breath away. He carried her into an empty stall and leaned her against the wall. His lips trailed down her neck and back to her ear. He felt her shiver when he took the lobe between his teeth. Her moans were setting him on fire. He set her down and pulled her jacket off, then her shirt over her head. He groaned when he saw her breasts popping out the top of her demi-cup bra.

"Dear God, you're perfect," he whispered as he unhooked the front clasp and her breasts fell free. They were beautiful, just as he knew they would be. Her nipples were a rosy hue and already peaked. His hands cupped them and he rubbed the pads of his thumbs over the nipples, making them harden more. He leaned down and took one into his mouth. He lapped at it with his tongue, and then pulled at it gently with his teeth. Her hands clenched in his hair. He ran his hands down her sides until he encountered the snap of her jeans. He slowly unzipped them, before moving his hand inside, dipping inside her panties to what he'd only imagined. Wyatt moved his finger up and down between her wet slit.

"You're so wet, darlin'. You're killing me," he growled.

Olivia's hands went to his belt, unhooking it before she unsnapped his jeans and lowered the zipper. His hard cock strained against the material. When her hand wrapped around him, he almost came.

"*Very* impressive, cowboy. But then, I knew you would be," she whispered against his lips.

Wyatt stepped back from her and she whimpered. He grinned. "I'm not done with you yet." He shoved her jeans down and pulled her boots off. He slung the jeans across the stall and turned to gaze down at her. Dear God, the woman had a hell of a body. She stood before him in nothing but black boy-cut panties. He almost fell to his knees to praise God for her. She stepped toward him, pushed his jeans down, and then stared up at him.

"Condom?"

Wyatt reached behind him, pulled his wallet out of his jeans, and retrieved a condom. He handed it to her. She smiled at him, and after tearing the packet open, she slowly rolled the condom down over him. He growled. "You're doing that on purpose."

She laughed. "Maybe." Then she glanced up at him with a sexy tilt to her head. "Show me what you got, cowboy."

Wyatt grinned. "You've seen what I've got."

"Please show me you know how to use every delectable inch of it."

He picked her up, carried her toward the wall, and leaned into her. He moved his arms under her knees, opening her wide for him, before slowly inching into her. When he could go no deeper, they both groaned.

"You feel so fucking good," Wyatt whispered against her lips. He started pumping into her and she moved her hips with him. When she took his bottom lip between her teeth and sucked it into her mouth, he almost lost it. "Jesus, I'm not going to last," he growled.

He felt her tighten around him right before she cried out. He moved harder, faster, and deeper into her. His orgasm ripped him to shreds. It had never felt like this with anyone. Not even Stephanie. *Son of a bitch!* He knew right then, he'd never get enough of Olivia. He leaned his forehead against hers. She opened her eyes, gazed up, and smiled at him.

"Hi," she whispered between breaths.

He smiled. "Hi yourself, darlin'."

Olivia laughed. "Wow."

Wyatt chuckled. "Yeah. Wow is right."

She stared into his eyes. "They are black," she said in awe.

"Yes," he said, knowing exactly to what she was referring.

* * * *

Olivia stared at him. It had finally happened and it had been well worth the wait. She'd never get enough of him now. She blinked at the tears in her eyes. Sighing, she started to lower her legs and he let her down. She watched as he zipped his jeans. To say he had one hell of a body would be an understatement. She sighed. Now what? After picking up her clothes, she dressed then glanced around.

"Was that considered a roll in the hay?" She laughed.

"Not really. A roll in the hay is just that, doing it in the hay. It's not all it's cracked up to be either. Damn straw pokes you in spots that don't need poking."

She snorted. "The voice of experience, huh?"

Wyatt grinned. "No comment."

A stab of jealousy went through her. Had it been Stephanie? The woman he was engaged to and who called off their engagement a week before the wedding. Olivia didn't like her. She'd met her and thought Stephanie was a piece of fluff, nothing of any real importance. Stephanie had no liking for Olivia either, obvious since the first time they met. Stephanie was tall, blonde, and beautiful and she'd told Olivia she wanted Wyatt back. That was months ago and as far as

Olivia could tell, Wyatt hadn't been seeing Stephanie. It didn't mean she wouldn't be around eventually, especially if she found out Olivia and Wyatt had been together. Of course, his roll in the hay could have been with any woman, not just Stephanie. Olivia knew he saw his fair share of them. She glanced at Wyatt. He was staring at her.

"What's going through that gorgeous head of yours, Olivia?"

"You can call me Liv, ya know." Wyatt shook his head.

"You don't like Liv?" She pouted.

"I like Olivia," Wyatt told her.

She grinned. "Aww, Olivia likes you too."

"You always have a smart-ass answer, don't you?"

"What does the sign in the barn mean?"

Wyatt frowned. "What sign?"

"The one about having seventeen hands between your legs."

Wyatt burst out laughing. "Not what you're thinking, that's for sure."

Olivia swatted at him. "What's it mean then?"

"A horse is measured in hands. A horse can be up to eighteen hands tall, some are taller, not many though. A Quarter Horse is average at seventeen hands." When she continued to frown at him, he grinned. "A hand measures four inches across the palm, the horse is measured from the highest point of the withers, which is the base of the horse's neck at its back. If a horse measures sixty inches, it's divided by four, which is fifteen." He shrugged. "The horse is said to be fifteen hands tall. The sign means there's nothing like having a horse that stands seventeen hands tall between your legs."

"Oh, that's as easy to remember as that pinto Paint thing. Why not just say the horse is sixty inches tall?"

Wyatt shrugged. "Cowboy way, I guess."

She laughed. "I love the cowboy way." Then she squealed when he picked her up, tossed her over his shoulder, and carried her out of the arena and into his house. He set her on one of the stools at the center island. She gazed around the kitchen. The white appliances sat nestled between black marble countertops. The mahogany cabinets matched the hardwood floors. A large window brought natural light in above the sink.

"This is a gorgeous kitchen. Too bad I don't cook." She grinned.

"You should since you eat all the time."

"I like to eat, what can I say? You could always

help me work the calories off," she told him.

"I could." Wyatt sighed. "What are we doing here, Olivia?"

She tilted her head. "What do you mean?"

"I mean, I didn't want this to happen," he grumbled.

She slid down from the stool. "You should have thought of that before you fucked me, not after!"

He ran his hand down his face. "It will get complicated."

"Again...*before* we had sex."

"Damn it! We have to be together for family functions. What if we keep seeing each other, and then one of us wants to end things? Don't you think that will make it complicated?"

"We agree to let it go." When he huffed, she went on. "We're adults, Wyatt—consenting adults. When the time comes one of us wants to walk away, we let them." God, it was killing her to talk about him walking away, because he would be the one who did. She'd never leave him given the chance. She heard him swear as he turned away from her. She clutched his arm. "Is once enough for you? Because I'll be honest here and tell you I already want you again." Wyatt stared at her then shook his head.

"No. Once isn't enough," he whispered as he stepped closer to her. He cupped her face in his hands and lowered his lips to hers. She loved the way he kissed. When his tongue entered her mouth, she groaned and touched hers to his, making him growl deep in his throat. He slowly raised his head and stared down at her.

* * * *

"No. Once would never be enough," he said as he picked her up and carried her toward the bedroom, where he laid her on the bed. His hand moved down over her breasts, then down her stomach to her jeans. He cupped her through the fabric. She moaned low in her throat as he moved his hand up and down between her legs. When he moved his hand to the snap of her jeans, he slowly unfastened it, lowered the zipper, and slipped his hand inside of her panties. His finger moved down between her slit, making her squirm. Wyatt moaned at how wet she was.

"God, sweetheart, you're still so wet and I need you so much." He shoved her jeans down as her hand went to the snap on his. She lowered the zipper slowly. He was so hard he thought he was going to explode when her hand gripped him. Wyatt shoved his jeans down and moved between her legs.

"I want you too much, Olivia. I can't wait," he whispered against her lips.

"I can't either, Wyatt. Please..."

Wyatt reached into the bedside table and retrieved a condom. After sheathing himself, he groaned as he moved into her. He kissed her deep and hard when he buried himself deep inside her. When her legs wrapped around his waist, he rode her hard, and then rolled to his back for her to straddle him. Gazing up at her was amazing. His hands went to her bra.

"Take this off. I have to see you," he told her. He watched as she reached for the clasp and unhooked her bra. He groaned when they spilled free. His hands went to them and he ran his palms over them, making her nipples hardened into peaks. He then ran his hands down her ribcage to her hips. He sat up, wrapping his arms around her and pressed his lips to hers. His tongue entered her mouth as she started to moan. Wyatt gazed into her face. It was amazing in the throes of her orgasm. He felt her tighten around him as she rocked her hips, grinding against him.

"Wyatt," she cried out. He rolled her to her back and thrust into her hard. His orgasm shook him to the core, making him moan her name against her neck before he lightly bit her shoulder. Olivia moaned as she came again. He collapsed on top of her. Her arms tightened around him. He raised his head to look at her. God, she looked so gorgeous with her cheeks flushed, her sexy lips parted, and sweat on her temples. He traced her mole with his fingertip.

"This is so fucking sexy," he whispered, and then he kissed her quickly rolling off her, and over to the edge of the bed, where he reached for his jeans. "How about something to eat?"

Olivia nodded. "I am hungry now that you mention it."

"You're always hungry. You should weigh three hundred pounds the way you eat." He chuckled.

She threw a pillow at him. "Emma said the same thing. I know how to burn calories off, cowboy." She grinned.

"I'll say. Come into the kitchen after you get dressed. I'll have some food for you, and then we'll burn off more calories." Wyatt winked and headed toward the kitchen.

* * * *

Olivia made a quick visit to the bathroom, and then joined him in the kitchen. He had his back to her as he made up sandwiches. She glided up behind him, wrapped her arms around his waist, and laid her cheek against his strong back. He felt amazing to her.

"I thought you were hungry?" Wyatt murmured.

She laughed. "I am." She kissed his back. "Just not for food."

Wyatt spun around. "That's a first." He laughed when she swatted at him. "Here." He handed her a plate with a sandwich and chips on it.

Olivia smiled, carried her plate to the center island, and took a seat on a stool. The kitchen was a chef's dream. Above the island, there hung shiny copper pots and pans. There were no curtains or blinds on any of the windows so sunlight poured in with tiny dust motes dancing in the beams. The house was beautiful. The living room was a large open area with a stone fireplace centered on an outside wall. Windows on each side of it ran from the floor up to the ceiling. The front windows faced the pine tree lined driveway. She loved it.

Wyatt sat down across from her after setting a glass of tea in front of her. She took a bite of her sandwich and glanced around, looking everywhere but at him. Her eyes swiftly shifted back to him when she heard him chuckle. She narrowed her eyes.

"Something funny, cowboy?"

Wyatt nodded. "You. I never figured you to be shy. We've seen each other naked now, and I have to say, it was way beyond my fantasies."

"You fantasized about me?"

"Almost every damn night since the first day I saw you." He swallowed hard. "You got into my head, Olivia and I didn't like it."

"You still don't," she said in a whisper.

"You're right. I don't but it's done."

"What's done?" Her heart hit her stomach.

"You're in my head. Not much I can do about it," he mumbled.

She slid off the stool. "Jesus! Don't make it sound like it's my fault. You're the one who said you wanted to *ride* me!"

Wyatt stood slowly and glared at her. "You didn't say no."

"I've been honest from the start about how much I wanted you. Why in the hell would I say no? At least I own up to it! You still can't admit you want me," she exclaimed, her voice rising with each word.

"Obviously I do, or I would have walked away in the barn."

She picked up her jacket and put it on. "Well, I'm the one walking away now." Olivia ran from the house, got into her car, and drove home.

Chapter Four

"Son of a bitch," Wyatt roared as he heard her driving away. He knew it wouldn't be easy if he got involved with her, but he already wanted her again. His groin tightened as he thought of her clenching around him. Sex with her was amazing. Just as he had suspected it would be. It was one reason he had stayed away from her for as long as he had. Olivia wouldn't be easy to walk away from, and now he had to walk away. He wasn't interested in a long-term relationship with anyone, and he knew if he tried with her, she could break his heart.

Fuck! You need to learn to think with your head, not your dick.

He sat back on the stool again and ran his hand over his face. When he saw her in the barn, he thought he was seeing things. She'd let him know from the beginning how much she wanted him and he was the one who had lied about not wanting her. He had wanted her from the instant those amethyst eyes met his.

He ran his hand along his jaw. *Shit! Now what?*

Sighing, he stood and put his coat on. He had to see her again and tell her this couldn't go any further. It just couldn't, and that bothered the hell out of him because he knew there wasn't another woman out there, anywhere, who could compete with Olivia—in or out of bed. Wyatt wasn't looking forward to having this conversation. Blowing out a breath, he got into his truck and drove toward the B and B.

Pulling up to the front door, he glanced around.

There were a few people in the yard and some sitting in the rocking chairs on the porch, the cooler weather not seeming to bother them. The B and B would close next month. Becca only kept it open from May until mid-October.

He hopped out and headed toward the porch. A few women sitting on the porch smiled at him. He put his fingers to the brim of his hat, and nodded at them. He grinned when they laughed. He strode into the foyer to see Stacy Miller sitting at the desk. She grinned at him in welcome.

"Hi Wyatt," she said.

"Hey, Stacy," he said glancing around. "Is Olivia around?"

"Hello handsome," a woman's voice said from behind him.

Wyatt turned to see a tall, beautiful redhead smiling at him. He nodded at her. She stepped closer.

"A real cowboy, huh?" she purred.

"Yes, ma'am," Wyatt answered politely. He glanced back to Stacy, who sat grinning at him.

"Olivia?"

"I'll get her, Wyatt. I'll be right back," Stacy told him as she left the foyer and headed toward the kitchen.

"Wyatt, huh? I like your name." The woman smiled up at him.

"Thank you." Wyatt felt damned uncomfortable. He was used to women coming on to him but this woman was doing more than coming on to him. He knew he could have her right here and now if he wanted to.

"What are you doing here, Wyatt?" Olivia's voice had him turning away from the woman.

"Can we talk?"

"I think we said all we need to..." Olivia started.

"Honey, if you don't want to *talk* with him, I will," the woman said with a sly grin.

Wyatt spun around and narrowed his eyes. "No."

The woman laughed. "Playing hard to get?"

"I'm not playing," Wyatt said through slightly clenched teeth.

The woman finally took the hint and walked back toward the living room with a last glance over her shoulder, her eyes going to his crotch.

"Holy hell," he muttered, and then looked to where Olivia had stood, but she was gone. Wyatt headed toward the kitchen. He knew the B and B like the back of his hand. He knocked on the door of her apartment. She opened it and glared at him. "Can I come in?"

Olivia sighed with obvious annoyance, but opened the door wider to let him enter. He strode past her and turned to look at her. She closed the door and leaned back against it. He closed his eyes for a few seconds then opened them to look at her, hopefully, with something other than desire. He saw her blink her eyes quickly.

"Olivia..."

"If you've come here to tell me we won't see each other, I get it. Now you can go."

"I..." He swallowed hard. "Damn it, I did come here to tell you that but now that I'm here, I want you..." He stepped closer to her and kissed her.

Without hesitation, her arms snaked around his neck as he lifted her legs around him. He rubbed his crotch against the apex of her legs. She moaned deep in her throat. When Wyatt reached to lift her T-shirt off over her head, she dropped her feet to the floor. He groaned when he saw she wasn't wearing a bra. Her breasts were perfect and fit just right in his hands. He hooked his thumbs into the top of her flannel pajama pants and shoved them down. She stepped out of them. Wyatt's hand went between her legs. He growled low in his throat as he rubbed the pad of his thumb against her clitoris, making her jerk against him.

Her hands went to his fly. She unzipped his jeans and slipped her hand inside, wrapping her fingers around him. He pushed his erection into her hand, and then lifted her up so her legs encircled his waist.

"Shit! I don't have a condom," Wyatt grumbled.

"I'm on the pill and I'm safe. Please, Wyatt."

"I'm safe too, but I don't have sex without a condom." Her hips moved against him, making him groan. He put his forehead against hers. "I can't...stop. I have to have you." He thrust into her. Both of them groaned. Wyatt pounded into her hard and fast. He pressed his lips to hers and kissed her, moving his tongue deep into her mouth. Wyatt felt her muscles tightening around him as his orgasm started crashing over him.

"Wyatt...please," she whispered.

"Now, Olivia...*now*," he growled as he came. She was right there with him and he felt her shiver against him as she cried out his name. After a few more thrusts, Wyatt stared into her heavy-lidded eyes.

"Believe it or not, I didn't come over here for this." He lightly kissed her. "Are you all right?"

"I don't think I have any splinters in my ass, if that's what you're asking."

Wyatt chuckled. "I'm sorry to hear that. I would

have enjoyed removing them for you."

She stared up at him. "You really did come to tell me you didn't want to continue seeing me, didn't you?"

He stepped back from her. "Yes."

"So what was that?" She waved toward the door. "You have a weird way of breaking things off, cowboy."

He sighed and walked toward the couch and took a seat. "Could you dress, please?"

Olivia pulled her pants up and put her T-shirt on over her head. She took a seat in the chair opposite him. "What do you want to do, Wyatt? Because if you really don't want to do this anymore, I get it, but I won't be someone you'll just have sex with when you feel like it. I have feelings too. If you want to continue this, then we do it the right way."

"What do you mean?"

"We see each other and no one else. I won't share you with other women. We go out—"

"Out? As in date?" She nodded. "I don't date," he told her shaking his head.

"You will with me or it's not at all. I won't be some fucking booty call for you when you're horny."

He stared at her. She was actually serious. "Date?"

Olivia nodded. "Date."

He ran his hand down his face and swore. "No. I don't date. That requires a relationship and

I've told you I'm not interested in any kind at all, other than just sex." "So, you do sexual relationships?" Olivia asked. Wyatt nodded.

"Then don't tell me you don't do any kind of relationships. I think you need to go." She walked to the door and opened it for him to leave. As he walked past her, she smiled up at him.

"Who knows? Maybe I'll be the one to walk away first and you'll be angry it wasn't you." The door closed behind him and not too gently.

Wyatt stood in the kitchen wondering what the fuck just happened. Did she really think he'd agree to *date?* He groaned as he headed back toward the foyer and walked past Stacy without saying a word. The woman who came on to him earlier was standing on the porch. She smiled at him and started toward him but he shook his head at her, stopping her in her tracks.

He climbed into his truck, spun the tires when he tore out of the driveway, and headed home. He pulled up to his house, turned off the engine but just sat there behind the wheel.

No, there was no way it would ever work. Yes, he wanted her, but to go out on dates. What was she thinking? *No way.* He slammed his fist into the roof of the truck and swore when he hurt his knuckles. He got out and entered the house, swearing the entire time.

Bear ran toward the back door and Wyatt let him out. As he headed toward his bedroom to shower, he swore the entire time. He entered the bedroom, glanced toward the bed, and saw the messed up covers from their earlier lovemaking. Hell no! They hadn't made love. It was sex. Pure and simple. Just sex. His body ached thinking about how good it had been with her. Could he stay away from her or would he have to succumb to her terms.

"Damn you," he shouted. Thing was, it wouldn't just make him angry if she was the one who walked away first, it would kill him. It was going to be a long fucking night.

* * * *

Olivia had slammed the door behind him, and then blinked back the tears stinging her eyes. She refused to cry over him. No tears would fall for Wyatt Stone. A sob tore from her as a tear slid down her cheek. She marched over to the couch and lay down on it. Grabbing a pillow, she put it over her face and sobbed. Once the tears subsided, she screamed into the pillow, and then tossed it across the room. She sat up and stared at the door. The sex was fantastic, as she knew it would be. How could she ever see him casually now? He'd been right when he said it would make things complicated. *Great! Just fucking great!* It would be even harder to be around him now. If it had been hard before, it would be nothing compared to what it was going to be like now. Seeing him at family functions was going to be harder than ever. After being with him, how could she ever see another man? It was time to admit she was in love with him. She'd denied it long enough.

Olivia groaned as she continued to stare at the door. She fell in love with him the minute she first set eyes on him. When he'd walked into the feed store and Becca introduced them, she fell right then, and all he'd ever done was ignore her. Speaking to her only when she spoke to him, and then it was always small talk. At times, it was like pulling teeth just getting him to say anything to her...until this morning in the barn. That was the most he'd ever talked to her. She couldn't believe it and then amazing sex with him three times in one day. Damn. And she'd do it again if he were here right now.

If she couldn't convince him to be with her for

more than sex, she'd have to move away. It would be for the best. He would forever be in her heart so the longer and further she was away from him, the better. She stood and headed toward the bathroom for a shower. She was just going to have to do her best to get him interested enough to spend time with her for something other than sex.

She laughed without humor. *Just how do you plan to do that when all you'll want is sex too?* No, she realized it wasn't all she wanted. She wanted his love and that was going to be a long hard climb. With his heart all locked up in chains, she'd have to do her best to break it free. Nodding, Olivia stepped into the shower and began working on a plan to get Wyatt Stone to fall in love with her.

* * * *

Her chance to see him again came sooner than she expected when Emma invited her to dinner, along with everyone else in the family. Olivia dressed in skinny jeans and a tight purple sweater, which matched her eyes, and on her feet were matching stilettos. With her make-up perfect, she headed out the door to drive to Emma and Gabe's ranch. She parked beside Jake's truck and glanced around. She smiled when she spotted Wyatt's truck. Taking a deep breath, she pushed open her car door, walked up the steps, and entered the kitchen. Her heart stopped when she spotted Wyatt leaning back against the counter. He wore a blue and white checkered flannel shirt over a blue T-shirt, soft denim jeans, and he was eating an apple.

"You're going to ruin your appetite, Wyatt Stone," Emma was scolding him.

"My appetite's fine," he said as his eyes moved over Olivia.

She took her coat off and hung it up before hugging Emma. "He seems to have a very healthy appetite," she said and watched as Wyatt's lips rose in a smile.

Emma's gaze shifted back and forth between them. "I suppose," she murmured and headed toward the living room, leaving Wyatt and Olivia alone.

Wyatt stared at her. Olivia moved toward him and took the apple from him then took a bite of it, and handed it back. His eyebrows shot up.

"Why do I get the feeling you're tempting me like Eve tempted Adam?" he said in a low voice.

Olivia grinned. "You tell me, cowboy."

Wyatt glanced away from her then back. "You do tempt me, Olivia."

"Is that so? Well, what are you going to do about it?"

"Damn it. I don't date," he muttered.

"Your loss," she said stepping away from him. He wrapped his fingers around her arm and pulled her back to him. She watched as his eyes roamed over her face and landed on her lips. He swore under his breath.

"All right," he growled.

Olivia raised her eyebrows. "All right?"

"Yes, damn it."

Olivia burst out laughing. "Gee, you make me feel so special. Since tomorrow's Saturday, we can go out tomorrow night."

"Son of a bitch," he swore. "I'll pick you up at six."

"Six it is, cowboy." She started to move away when he pulled her back again.

"Wear sexy underwear," he whispered into her

ear making her shiver.

"Oh, I always do, but don't think we're going to have sex every time we go out. You'll have to work for it, Wyatt." She headed toward the living room and grinned when she heard him muttering to himself behind her.

* * * *

Wyatt watched her walking away. She had him by the balls and she knew it. He'd do anything she wanted now. Since having her, he couldn't get enough of her. He'd made up his mind today that he was going to get her back into his bed one way or another. Then she throws this dating shit in his face again. He sighed. If he had to date Olivia to have her, he'd do it but if he started falling, he was out of it with lightning speed. There was no way he was going to fall for her. He was too damn close now. He wouldn't allow her to break his heart. It was just sex— great sex but just sex. At least that's what he told himself as he headed toward the living room.

He took a seat on the sofa next to Becca.

"Are you going to the sale tomorrow, Wyatt?" she asked.

"Uh, I don't think so," he told her.

"You don't think so? What kind of answer is that, Wyatt?" Gabe asked.

"I forgot about it." Wyatt shrugged. "I don't need to go this time."

Wyatt noticed Jake and Gabe frowning at him, while Becca and Emma wore confused expressions, but Olivia was smiling at him. *Shit!*

"Maybe he has other plans," Olivia volunteered. "Do you, Wyatt?"

Wyatt clenched his jaw and glared at her. She

might be gorgeous, but she was such a pain in the ass. "I might. What's it to you?" At Emma and Becca's gasps, he swore.

"Sorry," he muttered.

Jake stood and glared at him. "Come with me," he said to Wyatt.

Wyatt rolled his eyes as he stood and followed his brother to the kitchen. He knew he was in for an ass chewing. He sighed in exasperation as he took up the spot against the counter he'd just vacated. Jake pulled a ladder back chair out from the table, spun it around and straddled it. He raised an eyebrow at him.

"What the fuck is your problem? I know you've always been an ass around Liv but that was uncalled for."

"You know Jake, I've been telling you this for years, you're not my father," Wyatt growled.

"No, I'm not but when you act like an ass, someone needs to call you on it."

Wyatt groaned when Gabe entered the kitchen. "Don't even start, Gabe."

Gabe grinned at him and leaned against the doorjamb. "I'm not starting anything. I just wanted to see this."

Wyatt straightened up. "Fuck you both. I'm not a child..."

"Then quit acting like one," Jake said through clenched teeth. "We love Liv and don't like seeing her hurt and whether you want to admit it or not, you hurt her every time you ignore her. And this shit of talking to her like you just did stops now."

Wyatt glared at Jake, and then walked toward the door where Gabe stood. When Gabe didn't move, he glared at him. "Don't make me move you,

Gabe."

Gabe smiled at him. "You can try it, little brother, but with two of us here, you don't have a snowball's chance in hell."

"You two need to back off. Wyatt didn't mean anything by it," Olivia said from behind Gabe. All three brothers looked at her. She shrugged. "It didn't bother me. Really," she said smiling at Jake and Gabe.

"See? It didn't bother her. Now move, Gabe." Wyatt narrowed his eyes at his brother. Gabe kept grinning but stepped back to let him pass. Wyatt walked into the living room and took a seat in one of the recliners. He raised his eyebrow at Becca and Emma because they continued to stare at him.

"I don't understand you, Wyatt." Becca shook her head.

Wyatt didn't say anything. He just sat in the chair and hoped the night would pass by quickly. As soon as possible, he was out of here. He glanced up when Jake, Gabe, and Olivia reentered the room. He watched her take a seat beside Becca and Emma on the sofa. When she looked over at him, she winked. He quickly glanced around at everyone but no one seemed to notice. His gaze shifted back to her and he stared at her. She kept a smile on her face. Wyatt wiped his hand over his face to hide a grin. Damn, she was nothing but trouble with a capital T and he couldn't wait to get her into bed again.

* * * *

Later sitting beside him at the table, Olivia joined in the conversation going on around the table. Wyatt remained quiet, only joining in when someone directed a question at him.

She leaned toward him slightly and whispered. "Are you pouting, cowboy?"

His head snapped up and he glanced around the table. "Stop it," he muttered.

She laughed. "Stop what? No one is noticing a thing. You know, eventually they'll know we're dating. They're not stupid."

"You got that shit, right. They're too damn smart," Wyatt said in a low growl.

Olivia moved her hand to his knee and he jerked. "What are you doing after dinner?" Her hand moved slowly up his thigh.

"Jesus Christ, Olivia. Stop it," he hissed squirming a bit.

She laughed low in her throat and inched her hand up higher to his fly. Her hand cupped him through the denim. She smiled when she felt him grow hard. His hand wrapped around her wrist but when she thought he was going to remove it, he moved her hand up and down his hard length through his jeans. Her fingers slowly lowered his zipper and her hand snaked inside to his hard shaft. When he groaned and covered it with a cough, she almost burst out laughing, but it soon backfired on her. Feeling his smooth, hard cock under her fingers had her squirming in her seat. She slowly removed her hand. The house suddenly seemed too hot. She glanced up at him from under her lashes only to find him staring at her.

"I'll get you back for that," he said quietly.

"I can't wait," Olivia whispered. She laughed when he growled.

"Did you say something, Wyatt?" Jake asked.

"Nope, didn't say a thing, Jake."

"We're just talking, Jake. Everything's fine,"

Olivia said, and then almost burst out laughing at the surprised looks on their faces. They seemed shocked to hear she and Wyatt were talking.

She was startled when she felt Wyatt's hand on her knee.

"Yeah, we're just...talking," Wyatt added.

Olivia turned her head slightly toward him. "Move it or lose it, cowboy," she said in a low menacing tone.

Wyatt chuckled. "Payback's a bitch, darlin'."

"Oh, you can pay me back, Wyatt, just not now." Olivia smiled at him.

Wyatt leaned toward her as he removed his hand. "I'm going to pay you back from head to toe, darlin', and everywhere in between. You can bet your sweet ass on that." His eyes moved over her from her head to her butt. "And I know it's a sweet ass for sure."

Olivia groaned. She was in so much trouble here, but she couldn't wait to get out of here and be with him.

Chapter Five

An hour later, Wyatt was ready to go. He'd sat through the rest of dinner as well as after dinner conversation, but now he was getting antsy...or maybe he was just horny. He glanced over toward Olivia, and almost groaned. The woman was so hot and he wanted her now. He quickly stood, drawing everyone's attention.

"I'm heading home. I'm tired," he told them.

"It's too early to call it a night, little brother. We're getting up early and we're not ready to call it a night yet," Jake told him.

Wyatt shrugged. "I've had a long day. A problem with a horse and I'm beat." He nodded at Emma. "Thank you for dinner, Em. It was great as usual." He glanced around to the others.

"Goodnight everyone." He practically ran from the room and out to his truck.

When he pulled up to his house, he wondered how long it would be before Olivia arrived. He entered the house and let Bear out then took his coat and hat off. He walked toward the living room and after settling into his recliner, he picked up the remote and turned on the television. He glanced over to where his grandfather clock sat in the corner. *Shit!* He'd only been home five minutes. Where in the hell was she? She should have been right behind him. He sighed as he flipped through the channels. There wasn't a damn thing on he was interested in watching.

Damn it! He should have gotten her cell phone number. He'd be calling her right now, that's for sure.

He stood and walked toward the kitchen when he heard Bear barking. Opening the back door, he peered out into the yard but saw nothing out of the ordinary and he especially didn't see Olivia's sports utility vehicle. Where was she?

He whistled for Bear. The dog leaped onto the porch and entered the house. Wyatt stared down his driveway and only saw darkness. Shaking his head, he entered the house and headed toward his bedroom. Maybe he'd read her signals wrong and she wasn't going to show up.

Shit! She wanted to go out on a date. Was that what she'd expected? Wyatt groaned as he thought about it again. The small town of Clifton would have a field day once they saw Olivia and him out together. He supposed he could take her to dinner in Hartland. There was a nice restaurant there. He swore at the thought. He hated dating. Women expected too much with dating. They started thinking in terms of long term relationships. Surely, Olivia didn't want that, did she?

He took his flannel shirt off then pulled his T-shirt over his head. He sat on the bed to remove his boots when Bear started barking again. Wyatt walked toward the kitchen.

"Damn it, Bear. What is it?" He walked to the door and looked out. Headlights were coming toward the house. He opened the back door, stepped onto the porch, and leaned against a column when he saw Olivia's SUV stop by the steps, and then she hopped out. She leaned back against her vehicle.

"A little chilly to be out without a shirt on, isn't it, cowboy?" She smiled up at him.

"I was heading to bed," he told her.

Olivia walked up the steps and past him, going inside the house. "I'm just in time then," she threw over her shoulder.

He sighed and shook his head. She was going to be the death of him. He turned to follow her inside. She smiled at him as she took her jacket off. Wyatt walked toward her, took her jacket, and hung it on the back of a stool. When he turned to face her again, he almost groaned. She was the most exquisite woman he'd ever set eyes on. He folded his arms to keep himself from pulling her into his arms.

"What took you so long?" he asked.

Olivia sighed. "Becca and Emma kept talking. I had a hard time getting out of there. Even Jake wanted to go and I know Gabe was ready for bed." She stepped closer to him. "Did you think I wasn't going to show?"

Wyatt shrugged. "Didn't matter."

Olivia burst out laughing. "Really? So...if I decide to leave now, it wouldn't matter to you?" He shrugged again but when she reached for her jacket, he pulled her into his arms.

"Hell yes, it would matter," he said before pressing his lips to hers. Olivia moaned as her arms wrapped around his neck. He pulled her tighter against him, but then she leaned back from him.

"I can feel how much it would matter. Now, what do you want to do about this?" She pressed against him.

Wyatt picked her up and tossed her over his shoulder. "I'll show you what I want to do about this."

After entering his bedroom, he carried her to the

bed and dropped her down on it. He sat on the edge of the bed and took his boots off then stood and removed his jeans before stretching out beside her.

"You are so beautiful, Olivia," he whispered against her lips. Olivia smiled at him before pressing her lips against his, and that fast, he was lost. He was on a downward spiral and there wasn't a damn thing he could do about it.

* * * *

Olivia ran her hands over his whiskered cheeks. If she lived to be one hundred years old, she'd never get enough of this man. Her fingers sifted through his thick, black hair as she slowly moved her tongue into his mouth. When he moaned, she smiled against his mouth.

"What are you smiling about, sweetheart?" Wyatt asked pulling back to look at her.

"I like hearing you moan for me," she whispered. Wyatt chuckled. "I like the noises you make too."

"I don't make noises," she said.

"The hell you don't." He pressed his lips to hers and when his tongue entered her mouth, she moaned low and sexy. Wyatt raised his head. "Right there," he said.

She laughed. "Oh, those noises."

Wyatt's kiss cut her laughter off and she felt his hands go to the snap of her jeans. She raised her hips for him. He pulled her jeans and panties down, and off together. He then lifted her sweater off over her head and removed her bra. Although she was completely naked in front of him, she felt no embarrassment. He'd already seen her this way, so there was no sense in being shy now. Besides, being shy wasn't something she usually felt. She reached for his boxer briefs and pushed them off him then pushed him to his back.

Wyatt stared up at her. She grinned as her hand wrapped around his hard shaft and she pumped her hand up and down his hard length, slowly. His head went back and his eyes closed. She leaned down, kissed the swollen head, and then ran her tongue along the length of him. Wyatt's hands plunged into her hair, and when she moved her mouth down over him as far as she could, she heard him hiss in a harsh breath. Her hand wrapped around the base as her mouth moved up and down his length. With her other hand, she cupped his balls and gently caressed them. His groans were turning her on. He reached for her, but she pushed his hands away. She raised her head and looked at him.

"Don't make me handcuff you," she told him.

Wyatt's breath whooshed out. "It wouldn't surprise me a bit if you had handcuffs."

"Oh, I do, cowboy, and I'm not afraid to use them. Now just relax and let me take care of you." She put her mouth back over him and smiled when he groaned again. Her hand pumped his length as she sucked on him. She ran her tongue up and down his length, and then took him into her mouth again. His cock seemed to grow harder, and she knew he was close.

"Olivia...*Christ!* You have to stop now..."

She laughed. "You really don't want me to stop, cowboy. Relax."

"Relax? Who the fuck can relax?" Wyatt groaned low in his chest.

She took him deep in her mouth and felt him stiffen. His hands fisted in her hair as a long, low growl tore from his chest, and he came. Olivia continued to suck on him until he lay spent and breathless. She crawled up his body and gently kissed his lips.

"You okay?"

Wyatt raised his head and looked at her. "Yes. That was fantastic. Thank you." Olivia laughed. "You're welcome." She lay down beside him.

Wyatt rolled toward her and pressed his lips to hers. "You have got to be the sexiest woman I know." His lips moved to her ear. He took the lobe between his teeth and sucked it into his mouth. She shivered and felt him grin.

"Something funny, cowboy?"

Wyatt chuckled. "No ma'am."

She smiled with a sigh when he moved down her neck to her breasts. He palmed one in his hand and ran his tongue over the other one to her nipple. Taking it into his mouth, he sucked on it, and pulled it into a tight peak. She pulled his head tighter against her.

* * * *

Wyatt moved to her other breast and gave it the same attention. He could spend all night just on her breasts, but he had a certain destination in mind as he kissed his way down her flat stomach to her belly button. He dipped his tongue into it, and then moved down toward her feminine curls. He grinned when he saw that small patch. He spread her legs wide, running his tongue along her slit, and then lapped at her.

"You're wet, darlin'."

"I enjoyed what I did for you," she whispered then gasped when he moved his tongue over her clitoris.

"I knew you'd taste this good," he murmured

against her. He settled his mouth over her and sucked on her. She pulled his hair making him chuckle. He dipped his tongue inside her before sliding his tongue back up to her clitoris—again, and again. He inserted two fingers as he sucked on her and felt her inner muscles clenching. She screamed as she came. Wyatt slowly kissed his way back up her body to her lips.

"Can you taste yourself on my lips?" he whispered against her lips.

Olivia groaned. "Yes," she hissed.

He reached down between them, ran his finger up and down her slit, and then ran his finger over her lips. "You taste fantastic, Olivia, don't you?"

"Wyatt..."

"Don't you?" he asked again.

"Yes. Yes," she whispered.

He pressed his lips to hers just as he inched into her. She gasped against his lips. He lifted her legs over his shoulders and rode her hard, and deep. Wyatt sat back on his heels and thrust into her. It wasn't long before he heard her breathing change, and cry out as she came. Her orgasm sent him over the edge and he growled her name out as he tumbled over too.

He fell to the bed beside her and tried to catch his breath. Sex with Olivia was...ah hell...he had no words for it. It had never been better. With anyone. Ever.

He glanced over at her.

"You all right?"

Olivia started laughing. "To use your words...that was fantastic. Thank you."

Wyatt chuckled and rolled toward her. "You're welcome, darlin'."

He pulled her close to him and as their bodies began to cool, he reached down and pulled the quilt over them. He would just close his eyes for a few minutes.

* * * *

The sunlight streaming in through the window woke Olivia. She stretched and opened her eyes. After glancing around the room, she realized she wasn't in her apartment but still at Wyatt's home. She sat up quickly and glanced toward the other side of the bed. He was gone. She ran her hand over where he'd slept. It felt cool so he'd been gone a while. She glanced around for a clock and saw the one on the bedside table. She gasped when she saw it was ten o'clock. Getting up quickly, she looked for her clothes. Not having time for a shower, she dressed and practically ran through the house. The smell of coffee stopped her for a few seconds, but she kept going. She had to get to the B and B, shower, and get to work. Stacy was probably wondering where she was. Olivia never stayed out all night.

As she ran out the back door, she looked toward the barn but didn't see anyone. Shrugging, she hopped into her SUV and tore out of the driveway. Why had he let her sleep so late? She groaned remembering the night before.

Dear God! That man was hot. Not only could he kiss but also he knew how to make a woman feel special, and he certainly knew his way around one. She shivered remembering. He was a fantastic lover.

She pulled around to the back door of the B and B then ran inside. Evelyn Robinson, the cook, turned from the stove and stared at her. Then with a knowing grin, she wiped her hands on a towel.

"Late night, Liv?"

Olivia groaned, and suddenly wished her apartment had a private entrance.

"I, uh...overslept," she mumbled and headed toward her apartment. She could hear Evelyn chuckling behind her. Evelyn was a short, slim widow in her early sixties. Olivia adored her but knew she'd never hear the end of this now.

After taking a quick shower, she headed to the front desk to help Stacy with the guests, but her mind stayed on Wyatt the entire time. Her body trembled again with arousal just thinking about what he'd done to her.

"Are you cold?" Stacy asked from the stool beside her.

"Uh, yes," Olivia lied.

"I think it's hot in here," Stacy murmured.

"I just felt a chill for a second."

Stacy smiled at her, and then turned toward the door to greet some guests coming in. Olivia smiled too, but she wanted to be somewhere else with someone else. She wondered what he was doing now and she sighed, her thoughts drifting off as she imagined what she'd like to be doing with him right now.

* * * *

Wyatt strode from the barn and stopped in his tracks when he saw Olivia's vehicle was gone. *Damn, she left. Just like that?* Pulling his leather heavy work gloves off, he walked toward the house and entered. He glanced around but didn't see a note or anything. Why would she leave a note? He knew where she'd gone—back to the B and B. She probably had to get to work.

Damn. He was hoping to find her still in bed.

Wyatt swore aloud when he felt himself growing hard. He ran his hand down his face. *Christ!* What amazing sex. If he concentrated hard enough, he could still taste her and smell her scent. He wanted her again and muttered under his breath. How was that even possible? He woke her up two times last night and still wanted her. *Shit!* He stormed out of the house and back to the barn. There was plenty of work to do, and he'd see her tonight. He smiled as he thought about being with her again.

He strolled into the barn and saw Ben standing by a stall. Clenching his jaw, Wyatt headed toward him and stopped beside him.

"What are you doing?"

"I'm taking a break," Collins told him. "I'm entitled."

"Really? Who told you that? From what I can hear, the men are having a problem with a horse and yet here you stand, doing nothing." Wyatt stepped closer.

Collins shrugged. "There are plenty of men to help out."

Wyatt fisted his hands at his sides. "Did you ask Lucky if you could take a break?"

Collins huffed and started walking away. "I'll go back and help."

"See that you do," Wyatt said. He watched him stroll away as if he had all the time in the world. There was something about the guy he just didn't trust, so Wyatt followed him to the corral.

Ben jumped over the wooden rail and walked slowly toward the horse to help hold the rope. The other men had a rope around the horse's neck trying to calm it down. Wyatt not only trained cutting horses, he also broke horses before training them to be cutting horses. It was a hard, tedious job but he loved every minute of it. He had two ranch hands, other than himself, who could break the horses, and he never asked anything of them he wouldn't do himself. They were a lot younger than he was though, so he let them do it more often. At thirty-four, his body wasn't what it used to be. He was still in great physical condition, he worked out and worked hard on his ranch but being thrown from a horse gets old, and he'd hate to see how he felt in another ten years.

The two ranch hands, Ethan White and Mason Wright, were only twenty-three and young enough to believe they could do anything. They were good though, and Wyatt paid them highly for doing what they did. He smiled as he watched Mason grab the saddle horn and hoist himself onto the horse. The horse had worn himself out but Wyatt knew once the rider mounted, the horse would get its energy back and do all it could to dismount the rider. The men started cheering when the horse began to buck trying to dislodge Mason, but he held on. The next thing Wyatt knew, Mason was flying through the air and all five men standing along the rails groaned when he hit the ground, hard.

Wyatt jumped the fence and ran toward him. Just as he got there, Mason sat up and grinned up at him. Wyatt shook his head.

"You crazy son of a bitch." He put his hand out to help him up. Mason stood and dusted himself off.

"Let me at him again," Mason said.

"Are you sure? Ethan can try," Wyatt told him with a grin, but he knew Mason wouldn't let Ethan take this one.

"Hell no. I got this," Mason said as he walked back toward the horse and once again, hoisted himself onto the horse. The horse jumped and bucked around the corral again. All the men were shouting encouragement—except Ben Collins. Wyatt glanced over at him and saw him staring at him. Wyatt raised an eyebrow at him and Collins turned away. Wyatt sighed. He knew it was just a matter of time before he'd be firing the man. He was just waiting for him to fuck up big time.

"Hey, boss," Kirk Collins said from beside him.

"Kirk. How's it going?" Wyatt nodded.

"Fine...can we talk?" Wyatt stared at him then nodded for him to follow him to his office in the barn. He closed the door, Kirk took a seat, and Wyatt leaned against the desk. Kirk took a deep breath. "Ava's leaving me," he said quietly.

Wyatt was shocked. "What? Why?" He held his hand up. "No. It's none of my business. Are you going to be all right?"

Kirk shook his head. "I'm trying. I'm staying with Ben for now, but she's moving to Texas. She has family there." He ran his hand down his face. "I don't know what happened to be honest. One day we were fine, the next, she wants to leave me."

"I'm sorry Kirk. That's why you were preoccupied the day Candy's leg was cut."

"Yeah, I'm real sorry about that, Wyatt. If my mind had been on my work instead of my wife leaving me, I would have caught it," Kirk told him.

"I wish you would have told me. I wouldn't have sent you home for the weekend without pay."

Kirk shrugged. "I deserved it."

"Yes, but you didn't need to be sitting at home

alone. I know. I've been there." Wyatt sighed. "I try to rotate the weekends so you guys have family time but if you had told me, I would have let you work."

Kirk stood. "I fucked up and it was the right thing to do. I do understand about being home alone so I'll work any hours you want me to."

Wyatt nodded. "Check with Lucky and the men. Some of them will be more than happy to let you work their hours." He put his hand on Kirk's shoulder. "I'm real sorry to hear this, Kirk."

Kirk gave a terse nod and strode from the office. Wyatt stared at the door, and then grunted. This was what love does to a man—brings him to his knees. It was why he wasn't going through it again. He glanced down at his watch and swore. He had to pick Olivia up in a few hours and he hadn't even told her where they were going. He pulled out his cell phone and called the B and B.

"Clifton Bed and Breakfast. How may I help you?"

"You sure sound professional, darlin'.."

"How did you know it was me, cowboy?"

Wyatt chuckled. "I'd know that sexy voice in my ear any day." He laughed outright when she groaned into the phone.

Olivia laughed. "You're not breaking our *date* are you?"

"Nope. I'll pick you up at six. We'll go into Hartland for dinner."

"You ashamed to be seen here with me?"

"Christ, you're suspicious. No, I'm not. I just thought you'd like to go to a nice restaurant since all we have is the diner. Up to you though. We can go to the diner."

"I'd like to go to Hartland. I'll wear a dress. I just

might wear underwear." Wyatt growled. "I knew this was a mistake," he muttered.

Olivia laughed. "I'll be your favorite mistake, cowboy. See you later." She hung up.

Wyatt stared at the phone in his hand. Damn. He should have canceled the date. This was going to go south fast, he could feel it in his gut. *What were you thinking?* He snorted. The thing was he hadn't been thinking, not with the head on his shoulders anyway. It was so good with her though that he wanted her again. Right now, but he'd wait. Tonight would be soon enough. He hoped.

* * * *

Olivia smiled as she hung the phone up. She couldn't wait until tonight because if he thought they were going to have sex, he had another think coming. She chuckled when she thought of his reaction when she told him no.

"What are you grinning about?" Evelyn asked from the doorway to the foyer.

Olivia jerked. "Don't sneak up on me for God's sake, Evelyn."

Evelyn laughed. "You look guilty, Liv. What are you up to?"

Olivia stood and faced her. "Why, not a thing." She fluttered her eyelashes.

Evelyn burst out laughing. "I don't know why I don't believe you."

Olivia walked toward her and headed to the kitchen with Evelyn behind her. She took a seat at the table and stared out the window. The sky was beginning to darken and the wind was picking up. The temperatures had been dropping all day. It was going to be a cold night and she was going to be alone in her bed when she could have a hot cowboy next to her keeping her warm. Olivia snorted. *Warm? Try hotter than hell.*

She wiggled in her seat just thinking of the things he'd done and said to her in bed. It shouldn't have surprised her since she'd been pretty sure he was going to be like that way back when she first met him, and he'd looked at her like he couldn't stand her. He wouldn't even shake her hand. For almost two years, she'd let him know in every way she could just how much she wanted him and he never took her up on it. She was glad now she'd gone to his place to see Cochise, otherwise they'd still be dancing around each other. Now they were dancing between the sheets, and against walls, doors...

"Earth to Liv," Evelyn said.

Olivia glanced over to her and grinned. "Just doing some day dreaming."

"About a man?"

"What makes you say that?" Olivia tilted her head.

"You come home in the morning and you have a shit-eating grin on your face all day.

Sounds like a man to me."

"Oh, yeah, you mean like you look when Stan comes around or talks to you," Olivia teased.

Evelyn huffed. "I certainly do not."

Olivia laughed. "Yes, you do. You've got the hots for Stan, Evelyn Robinson."

Stan Watson was the foreman at the B and B. He'd worked for Becca's grandmother for years. When Becca inherited the ranch, he had stayed on. He still took care of the horses for the riding trails. Olivia was certain Evelyn had a crush on the man and if she was right, Stan felt the same in return.

"The hots? What a way to put it, Liv." Evelyn sighed. "Although he does make me feel like I'm having hot flashes, even though they've been gone for years."

Olivia burst out laughing. "Go for it. I've seen the way he looks at you."

"What? Oh no. I see what you're doing. You're trying to change the subject from your man. Who is it?"

Olivia shook her head. "My lips are sealed."

"I'll find out eventually, you know. If he comes here to pick you up for a date, or do you two just *hook-up*?"

Olivia nibbled on her bottom lip. "He's going to pick me up."

Evelyn folded her arms across her chest. "When?"

"In a few hours," Olivia mumbled.

Evelyn cackled. "I can't wait."

Damn it! Why hadn't she thought of this? Wait. Why should she have? She wasn't trying to hide anything and if Wyatt was, he had better get over it real quick. The grapevine in Clifton would be in full swing by tomorrow. She was also sure some people from Clifton would probably be at the restaurant in Hartland since it was a Saturday night. Sighing, she smiled at Evelyn and headed toward her apartment.

"I need to figure out what to wear."

"You get real sexy for him, ya hear me?"

Olivia stopped in her tracks. "Him who?" She narrowed her eyes at Evelyn.

Evelyn grinned. "Wyatt, of course."

Olivia gasped. "How...?"

"Because I know how much you like him and

seeing you this excited about going out can only mean one thing...you're going out with him." Evelyn tilted her head. "Tell me I'm wrong."

Olivia sighed. "I can't because you're not."

Evelyn nodded. "I'm glad he finally came to his senses. I'm happy for you. Now, you go figure out what to wear, honey. I hope you have a great time." She entered the pantry, leaving Olivia to stare after her.

She sighed heavily. If Evelyn only knew the truth about it, she'd laugh. The only reason Wyatt was taking her out was that she'd practically blackmailed him into it. She closeted herself in her apartment to get ready for her date.

Chapter Six

At six o'clock, Wyatt pulled his truck up alongside the back porch of the B and B. He blew out a breath trying to calm his insides, opened the door, and hopped out. After taking a deep breath, he walked up the porch steps, knocked on the back door, and then walked in. He watched as Evelyn turned toward him and smiled at him.

"Hello Wyatt, how are you?" she asked.

He smiled. "I'm fine, Evelyn. How are you?"

Evelyn grinned at him. "Just fine, honey."

Wyatt cleared his throat when she kept staring at him. He gave her a nod and started toward Olivia's apartment door when it opened, and she stepped out. He suddenly forgot how to breathe and his heart forgot how to beat, because she looked amazing. She wore a short skintight black dress, which showed every one of her sexy curves. His mouth started to water as his gaze moved over her silky black hair, down over her breasts, flat stomach, and took in every inch of her long legs. On her feet were black stilettos. He swallowed hard, and then looked into her eyes. She stood there simply smiling at him.

"Hi cowboy," she said in a low sultry voice.

"Hi," he murmured, and then he cleared his throat again because it sounded kind of creaky.

"You look beautiful."

"Thank you. Are you ready to go?"

Wyatt nodded. "Are you?"

"Oh, I'm ready all right." Olivia grinned at him. *Shit!* "Let's go then."

Wyatt smiled at Evelyn, who still hadn't taken her eyes off him, and put his hand out toward Olivia. When she placed her hand in his, he felt a shock and quickly glanced at her. She continued to smile up at him as he held her jacket for her. After he lifted the soft strands of her hair from inside the jacket, he jerked his chin for her to go out the door ahead of him, and then wanted to kick himself as his eyes strayed to her ass. The dress barely covered it.

"That's some dress you're almost wearing," Wyatt muttered. Her throaty laugh washed over him. "You wore it on purpose," he mumbled, silently cursing her.

Olivia stepped around the truck to the passenger side. Wyatt followed and opened the door for her. He held out his hand to help her in. She grinned at him. "You *do* remember how to date, cowboy."

"Just good manners," Wyatt whispered as he leaned toward her and pressed his lips to hers.

"Are you hungry?"

"Yes. What about you?"

His lips moved across her cheek to her ear. "Starving."

He grinned when he felt her shiver. He moved back from her, closed the door, walked around the truck, feeling a little more in control, and got in behind the wheel. Glancing at her one more time, he turned to the front and started the engine. They drove in silence to the restaurant. Once there, Wyatt walked around the vehicle to open her door and help her down.

"Jesus, Wyatt. Can it be any harder to get in and out of this damn truck? My dress keeps riding up."

Wyatt laughed. "I can't help it if you wore a dress

that barely covers your ass."

"Well, the people here in the parking lot will get one hell of an eyeful if it rides up too much more," Olivia muttered.

"Are you telling me you're not wearing panties?"

Olivia put her hands on his shoulders and gazed up at him. "I'm telling you there is nothing between me and this dress."

"How the hell am I supposed to get through dinner knowing that?" Wyatt growled.

Olivia laughed. "You weren't supposed to find out. I can't wear underwear with this dress. Every line would show."

"Damn it, come on. Let's get this dinner over with." Wyatt took her hand in his and led her into the restaurant.

"Could you please slow down? I can't run in these fuck me shoes."

Wyatt stopped and narrowed his eyes. "Did you say *fuck me shoes*?"

Olivia shrugged giving him an innocent look, which he knew wasn't so. "It's what women call them."

"Jesus H. Christ. I'm dying here," Wyatt said as they walked into the restaurant.

The hostess smiled at both of them, but her eyes kept going back to him. She led them to a table and they took their seats. After handing them menus, the hostess left them and a waitress came over to take their orders.

"Do you want to see a movie after dinner?" Olivia asked him after they ordered.

Wyatt stared at her. "No."

"Go for a drive?"

"No."

"I'd ask what you want to do but I think I know," Olivia whispered.

"You know exactly what I want to do. You." Wyatt didn't take his eyes from her.

Olivia leaned across the table and smiled at him. "Not happening tonight, cowboy."

Wyatt raised his eyebrows. "What?"

"I told you we were going to date and you had to work for it." "Work for it?" Wyatt asked between clenched teeth.

Olivia sat back and nodded. "Yes."

"I'm not some fucking dog you have on a leash, Olivia."

"No one said you were, but I'm not some slut you think you can hop into bed with at every opportunity." She shrugged. "Even though you think I am."

Wyatt sat back in his chair and folded his arms. "I shouldn't have—"

"You're right...you shouldn't have." Olivia leaned forward in her chair. "The thing is Wyatt, you don't know me. Not really. You just assumed, for some reason, that I'm a slut." She reached toward her wine glass and ran her fingertip around the top of it. "How many men have you seen me go out with since I've lived here?"

He leaned forward. "I haven't paid attention."

Olivia laughed quietly. "Liar." She held her hand up when he started to speak. "I can count on one hand how many times I've gone out with someone. How many women have you been with since we've met?"

"I'm not having this conversation," he muttered.

Olivia grinned at him. "So...who's the slut?"

Wyatt took a deep breath. "I'm sorry I said it.

Now, tell me why you think I have to work for it when we've already been to bed together—several times."

The waitress, who had just arrived with their food, almost dropped it when she overheard his remark. She quickly glanced at Wyatt, and then Olivia. "Do you need anything else?"

"We're fine, thank you," Wyatt told her but kept his eyes on Olivia.

"Because this is how we do it or we don't do it at all. I like to be wined and dined. Granted, we had sex first but if you want to continue being with me, then we go out on dates. I'm not a slut and refuse to be treated like one. If you think you can just call me or come by for sex anytime you feel like it, we need to end this right here and now."

Wyatt ran his hand over his mouth. *Fuck!* He stared at her and she stared right back. If this *date* had happened before the sex, he'd say fuck it, take her straight home, and say good riddance. But the sex had come first and he knew how damn incredible it was with her. He glanced away from her and swore under his breath.

"Why is it all right for you to make demands, but I can't? Why is it I have to take you out on dates but yet I can't take you to bed?" He picked up his knife and fork, and began cutting into his steak. "Sounds to me like you're getting everything you want, sweetheart, but I'm not."

Olivia cut into her steak, and then stared at him. "Seems to me that you already got what you wanted, cowboy."

Wyatt grunted. "Are you telling me you didn't want it?"

"I've wanted you since the first time I saw you,

Wyatt. I like to go out and have a good time with a man. I enjoy dating and I haven't been on a date since..." She chewed on her bottom lip.

"Ryder," Wyatt muttered.

Olivia's eyebrows shot up. "I thought you said you haven't been paying attention."

"Gabe and Emma made sure I heard about it."

Olivia stared at him and then burst out laughing. "I love those two."

Wyatt chuckled. "It was the night Jake and Becca made their engagement official. You left early."

"I remember. You were ignoring me as usual and I wanted to get away from you," Olivia said.

"I always knew when you were around, Olivia." He shrugged. "I just didn't want you knowing."

Olivia grinned. "Nice to hear you finally admit it." She stood. "Excuse me."

Wyatt stood and watched her stride across the restaurant, turning heads as she went. He wanted to punch every guy whose gaze followed her, but he couldn't blame them. She was beautiful, confident, and sexy as hell. He was going to get her into bed tonight despite what she said. She might not believe that but he did. He could be very persuasive.

Sitting back down, he reached for his soda, took a sip, and almost spit it out when he saw Stephanie barreling down on him. *Damn it!* Good manners had him standing when she reached the table. She smiled up at him.

"Hello, Wyatt," she said her hand touching his arm. It took everything he had not to jerk away from her.

Wyatt gave a terse nod. "Stephanie."

"You should come and join us," she said.

"No, thank you."

Stephanie stuck her bottom lip out into a pout. He'd always hated when she did that. He never thought it was cute and it never worked on him.

"At least come over and say *hi* to daddy." She looped her arm through his and tried to pull him along.

Wyatt took his arm from hers. "I will on my way out. Now, if you'll excuse me..." He closed his eyes briefly when he heard Olivia clear her throat behind him. He turned toward her and saw her smiling. Wyatt took her hand and pulled her around him to sit at the table as he heard Stephanie gasp.

"You're here with *her?*" Stephanie remarked through clenched teeth.

"Nice to see you too...fluffy," Olivia said as she took her seat.

Wyatt laughed, and then covered it with a cough when Stephanie glared at him.

"Have a nice dinner, Stephanie," he told her.

Stephanie sputtered before spinning on her heel and marching across the restaurant. Olivia chuckled, making Wyatt look at her as he took his seat.

"It's a bitch running into the ex when you're on a date, isn't it?"

He narrowed his eyes. "Why do I get the feeling you enjoyed that?"

"Because I did. She's such a bitch." Olivia shrugged. "Sorry, but she is."

"You're not telling me anything I don't already know," he mumbled.

Olivia narrowed her eyes as she watched Stephanie walk away, and then she glanced back to him. "What did you ever see in that piece of fluff anyway?"

Wyatt chuckled. "I really don't know anymore. But what's your problem with her?"

"She made me angry with a remark she made to Emma one day."

"What did she say?"

"Something to the effect that Emma got pregnant on purpose so Gabe would marry her."

"That's bullshit," Wyatt growled.

"I agree and I told Stephanie Gabe married Emma because he loved her."

Wyatt laughed. "Well, not really, but he loves her now."

"I think Gabe loved her, he just didn't realize it."

"I'm surprised you think that way."

"What do you mean? Just because I had a rough childhood doesn't mean I don't believe in love. I want that all-consuming love too. Like Becca and Jake, Emma and Gabe, and Brody and Madilyn. I want to find that kind."

Wyatt stared at her. "You won't find it with me."

He watched as she glanced away from him, blinked her eyes quickly, and then turned back to face him.

"You're just a stop along the way, cowboy."

He clenched his jaw as he stared at her, and then he nodded. "Good. We're on the same page." He signaled for the waitress. "Are you ready to get out of here or do you want dessert?"

"Nothing for me, but you go right ahead."

Wyatt grinned. "I'll have dessert when we get to your place."

"No."

"To my place?"

"You can have dessert alone at your place."

"Olivia..." he growled.

"Just think how much sweeter it'll be the next time." Olivia winked.

Wyatt stood and sighed. "Fine. Let's go."

He took her elbow in his hand and led her from the restaurant without stopping to speak to Blake Taylor. He just wanted to get out of there. They walked across the parking lot and Wyatt opened the truck door but when she started to climb in, he pulled her to him and spun her around to face him. He cupped her face in his hands and pressed his lips to hers. When she moaned, he slipped his tongue inside to taste her. *God!* She tasted so good. Everywhere. He leaned into her, letting her feel how much he wanted her. Her arms encircled his neck. He slid his hand down her side to the hem of her dress and moved his hand under it. He lifted his lips from hers.

"You weren't lying. There *is* only you under this dress," he groaned.

Olivia laughed low in her throat and ran her lips along his whiskered jaw to his ear. "And you're making me wet, Wyatt."

He groaned. "Don't tell me that shit. I want you, Olivia."

"I want you too, but we're going to go to our separate beds tonight."

He leaned his forehead against hers. "Sure?"

"Yes."

He blew out a breath and nodded. Once he helped her into the truck, he strode around it and got in. Christ, she was killing him. Slowly but surely, she was killing him. They rode to the B and B in silence. When he stopped the truck at the back door, he got out and walked around to her side. He opened the door and put his hand out to her. She placed her hand in his and stepped out. She started toward the porch steps when he grasped her bicep in his fingers and spun her to face him.

"I did a lot of thinking on the way here. This shit of not having sex until you want to... well, it's bullshit and I'm not going along with it."

"What do you mean?"

"What I mean is you're not calling the shots. At least not all of them. If we're dating, you know damn well, it will only be on weekends. So you're expecting to go out to dinner, a movie or whatever, but only have sex when you say. No way. I won't go along with that."

Olivia jerked her arm from him. "So, what are you suggesting? Sex whenever you want it? How many times do I have to tell you I won't be someone you hop into bed with only when *you* feel like it?" She folded her arms across her chest and stared up at him.

Wyatt ran his hand over his mouth and sighed. "Look, I'll be honest here. Sex with you is great and I want to be with you every chance I get. How is that wrong? We can go out on Saturday nights, but you spend the night at my place." He held his hand up when she started to interrupt. "We'll spend all day Sunday together until I bring you home that evening." He shrugged. "If we end up in bed on Sunday, it'll be because we both want it. If not, that's fine. We'll get to know each other better, but don't expect me to go for however long you decide without sex, because I won't. I'll see someone else."

Those beautiful amethyst eyes stared up at him.

"I told you, if we see each other we see no one else."

"Then you'd better make up your fucking mind," Wyatt said through clenched teeth.

"You'd want to spend Sundays together?"

Wyatt shrugged. "Why not? We could go for a horseback...oh, that's right, you're afraid of horses." He threw the challenge out there.

"You know I am, so what would we do?"

"Just have a lazy day around the house. I can't believe I'm even suggesting this," he muttered.

Olivia chuckled. "I can't believe you are either. What about Friday nights? We can do what we want on our own?"

"As long as it doesn't involve seeing someone else, yes."

"I'll think about it," she told him, spun on her heel and entered the house.

Wyatt stood staring at the spot where she'd been standing, and then swore aloud. He started up the steps but stopped himself. It was what she wanted him to do. *No. Damn it, no.*

He got into his truck and headed home. He wasn't sure who the hell she thought she was fooling with, but he wasn't going to let her do this to him. If he didn't hear from her in a few days, he'd say the hell with her, and find someone else to take to bed. Someone probably not as good or as hot as Olivia, but that was the way it would have to be. *Son of a bitch!* He knew she had him by the balls but she didn't need to know she did.

* * * *

Olivia couldn't believe he left. Didn't he know he was supposed to follow her inside? Damn. If he weren't so damn hot, she'd say the hell with him and find someone else. She snorted. *Yeah, right.* The man was entirely too sexy for his own good, and to say he was only good in bed would be a huge understatement.

She let Punkin out to do her business and once she was back in, Olivia retreated to her apartment where she undressed and took a shower. After putting lounging pants and a T-shirt on, she plopped down on the sofa to watch TV. She couldn't believe she was sitting here at ten o'clock on a Saturday night. The lug head should have at least taken her to a movie.

Wyatt definitely needed some lessons in the dating department. She knew she was going to agree to his terms. The thought of spending the night with him every weekend was mind blowing. She never thought he'd suggest such a thing, but he was right when he said she couldn't call all the shots. He was going to take her out as she wanted and she'd stay with him just as he wanted. It was a win-win situation. Did he realize she'd have to have some of her clothes there? She still couldn't believe he just left.

Sighing, she headed to her bedroom with Punkin on her heels and crawled between the sheets. She wasn't sleepy, but sitting around watching TV held absolutely no appeal.

Why did you have to be so adamant about not sleeping with him tonight? Olivia groaned.

They could be lying in bed together right now.

"Stupid. Stupid. Stupid," she chastised herself. She rolled over and punched the pillow.

"You've never been stupid over a man before, Olivia. What the fuck is wrong with you?"

Sitting up, she reached for the sleeping pills on her bedside table and took two. Punkin jumped up on the bed with her and settled in among the covers. She let out a big sigh, making Olivia laugh.

"Yeah, girl, I know how you feel." She turned the light out and hoped sleep would come soon.

Sunlight streaming through the sheer curtains woke her up. She glanced at the clock to see it was seven in the morning. Olivia yawned and stretched. Once she had fallen asleep, she slept well. After dressing, she wandered into the kitchen of the B and B. Evelyn was standing by the stove preparing breakfast. She glanced over her shoulder and smiled at Olivia.

"How was your date?" Evelyn asked.

"We had a good time. Dinner was nice." Olivia poured a cup of coffee and leaned against the counter.

"I wasn't sure you were here."

"Wyatt brought me home before ten." She sipped her coffee waiting for it.

Evelyn's eyebrows shot up. "Ten? That's awfully early, isn't it?"

"We had a little disagreement." Olivia pulled a chair out at the table and sat down.

"Really? Are you going to see him again?"

Olivia grinned. "Every chance I get."

Evelyn burst out laughing. "Good girl. He really is a gorgeous man. All the Stones are."

"I agree. I remember when I first came here and met them. I thought this must be where all the gorgeous men were hiding."

"Somethin' special about a cowboy, honey." Evelyn laughed.

"Something about a sheriff too," Olivia said, laughing.

"You got that right. Sheriff Sam Garrett is gorgeous too."

"Yes. If I'd never met Wyatt, I'd have gone after Sam."

Evelyn laughed. "My good friend, Betty Lou Harper, is his dispatcher. She told me he gets calls from women all day for one reason or other. Sam's a good man though."

"I like him but he never showed any interest in me. I went out with Ryder Wolfe one time, but we both knew there was nothing there so we decided to be friends."

"Now, there's another gorgeous man. Where were all these men when I was your age?" Evelyn shook her head. "I've lived here all my life and watched them all grow up. They were hellions, all eight of them."

"Eight?"

"Jake, Gabe, Wyatt, Ryder, Brody, Trick, Riley, and Sam," Evelyn called them out as she ticked off their names on her fingers.

"I've met Trick but don't know him real well. I don't think I know Riley." Olivia frowned.

"Riley Madison. He left here, well, close to nine years ago I'd say. His dad is a real bastard. Used to beat Riley, I suppose once he'd had enough, he left. Roscoe Madison will die alone just like he deserves, for treating Riley the way he did. Ryder's parents were just as bad."

Olivia shook her head. "How can someone beat their own child? Where's his mother?"

"She left here when Riley was six. I never could understand how she could leave her child behind with Roscoe." Evelyn shook her head.

The back door opened and Stan walked in. His eyes went straight to Evelyn and he nodded at her. He shifted his eyes to Olivia and flashed a grin.

"Good morning, ladies."

"Good morning, Stan. What's up?' Olivia asked.

"I'm going to take a few riders out this morning. I wanted to let you know in case you need me for something."

"That's fine. Carl's still here, right?"

"Yes, ma'am." He glanced toward Evelyn but Olivia noticed she had turned her back to him.

"I'll, uh...see you later." Stan left pulling the door closed behind him.

Olivia cleared her throat. "I never took you for being shy, Evelyn."

Evelyn spun around and sighed. "I'm not, except when it comes to that man. He gets me all flustered."

Olivia laughed. "I think you do the same to him."

Evelyn shook her head. "No, I don't."

"He couldn't keep his eyes off you, and you wouldn't even look at him."

"If I look at him and he looks at me, I blush. I know a woman my age shouldn't still blush, but I do."

"A woman your age? Evelyn, no matter what age a woman is, if the man she's interested in looks at her in a certain way, she blushes—whether you're a teenager or ninety. I honestly believe that."

Evelyn stared at her. "You think so?"

Olivia stood and hugged her. "Of course. A man has a certain way he looks at a woman he's interested in, and if she's interested in him too, then there's this electricity between them. Sexual attraction is very powerful. It doesn't matter what age you are. We all feel it. Wyatt told me he wasn't interested in me, but I knew he was lying. I could tell by the way he looked at me that he wanted me."

"I just don't know what to say to Stan. We rarely speak." Evelyn sighed. "I just don't know what to say," she said again.

"Talk about the B and B, the weather, what his day was like. Just start a conversation. You know we close soon and you'll be going back to your apartment in town. You won't be here every day. Evelyn, my girl, you need to make a move."

Evelyn burst out laughing. "I'll think about it. Now, what do you want for breakfast? I can whip something up for you quick before the guests come down."

Olivia grinned and told her what she wanted. After she ate, she decided she was going to call Wyatt, give him her decision, and tell him how much she couldn't wait for next Saturday night.

Chapter Seven

Saturday night finally arrived and Wyatt picked her up at six just as he had before. This time, they were heading into town to the diner.

"Are you sure you want to go to the diner? I mean, the whole town will know then."

"I don't care. Unless you do?" Wyatt glanced over at her.

"Do you seriously think I care what these people think of me? Remember, I'm the one who picked up the pregnancy test for Emma. I was pregnant by at least five different men."

Wyatt chuckled. "I remember. Okay, so the diner it is."

Olivia smiled. After she'd called him to tell him her decision, he had teased her mercilessly on the phone. He kept whispering what he'd do to her if she were there and she was hoping he planned to do those promised things to her tonight. She wiggled in her seat and glanced over to see him watching at her. He grinned as if he could tell what she was thinking. Damn the man. He probably could.

"Are you hungry?" he asked.

"Aren't I always?"

Wyatt smiled at her. "Good to hear."

She knew he didn't mean for food and she didn't either. She was starving for him. It'd been a week and she wanted him so much she was tempted to say to hell with dinner, and just go straight to bed. Olivia glanced over at him.

"We could skip dinner," she suggested.

"No. I'll need my strength," he told her then laughed when she groaned. He pulled the truck into the parking lot, found a spot, and then he got out, strolling around to her side while watching her through the windshield. Once there, he helped her out, only to push her back against the truck, put his lips to hers, and nibble them. "You have no idea how much I want you but we're going to go inside, have dinner, and then we're going to see a movie."

"Are you fucking serious?" Olivia growled.

"It's what you wanted, isn't it?"

"Damn you, Wyatt Stone."

She pushed against his shoulders, moved past him, and headed toward the diner. He caught up to her and took her hand in his as they entered the restaurant. It seemed like everyone in the place stopped what they were doing to look at them. Olivia raised her eyebrow and everybody quickly went back to his or her meals. She felt Wyatt squeeze her fingers as he led her to a booth.

After taking their seats, Connie, the owner, came over and gave them menus. She couldn't seem to keep the smile off her face. Olivia grinned when Connie winked at her.

"You'd think they'd never seen people on a date before," Wyatt muttered.

Olivia laughed. "They just haven't seen *you* on one."

Wyatt huffed. "I guess. They'll get used to it. I'm sure we'll be the main topic of conversation tomorrow."

She nodded, and then glanced toward the door when the bell above the door rang. She smiled when she saw Becca and Jake walk in.

"Your brother just walked in."

"Which one?"

"Jake. And Becca is with him."

"That's just fucking great."

Olivia raised her hand at them and gave Wyatt an innocent look when he glared at her.

"You're the one who said we'd be the main topic of conversation tomorrow."

"You two are eating together?" Jake asked as they reached the booth.

"Looks that way, don't it?" Olivia smiled.

Wyatt stood and kissed Becca's cheek then he nodded at Jake. "Actually, we're on a date."

The silence in the place was deafening. It seemed the entire restaurant had heard. Becca stared at her, and then glanced to Wyatt.

"A...a date?"

"You haven't been married so long that you've forgotten what a date is, have you, Becca?" Wyatt teased.

Becca swatted her hand at him. "No, but..."

"What she's trying to say is you two barely speak to each other and now you say you're on a *date,*" Jake said.

Olivia smiled. "Shocking, huh?"

"It sure as hell is." Jake smiled at them. "Have a good time, you two. Come on, Red. Let's get a table." He started to lead Becca away.

"Would you like to join us?" Olivia asked and saw Wyatt whip his head toward her.

"Hell no! This has been a long time coming. You two have a good time," Jake told them, smiling as he led Becca to a table.

Wyatt sat back down and sighed. "Damn. Is it really so shocking?" he growled.

Olivia laughed. "Yes. Everyone knows how you've been avoiding me since I arrived in Clifton. What do you expect them to think, Wyatt?"

He blew out a breath. "I have no idea." He shook his head. "They'll just have to get used to it."

Olivia sat back and stared at him. "You make it sound like it's going to happen quite a bit."

Wyatt's eyes narrowed. "Why shouldn't it? You in a hurry to move on to the next cowboy?"

She leaned across the table and pointed her finger at him. "Do not piss me off with that shit again, Wyatt. I told you I am not a slut. I haven't been with a man since I met you."

"What? You can't be serious."

"As a heart attack," she growled.

They stared at each other for a few seconds before his lips lifted in a smile. "Glad to hear it."

Olivia shook her head. "I don't understand you at all."

"What's not to understand?"

"You call me a slut in one breath, and then in the next breath, you're glad I'm not but want me. Make up your damn mind."

"We're here, aren't we? It looks to me like I've made up my mind and I did not call you a slut just now. Just because I asked if you were ready to move on, did not mean I was saying you're going to jump in bed with another man. In fact the thought of you in bed with another man really pisses me off."

Olivia laughed. "Glad to hear it."

"Christ, you're such a fucking smart ass."

Just then, Olivia saw Becca get up and head toward the restroom. She sent a glance Olivia's way and she knew Becca wanted her to follow so she scooched out of the booth.

"I'll be right back. Don't miss me too much."

She winked at him, and then chuckled when she heard him grumbling. She entered the restroom and saw Becca standing by the sinks with her arms folded. Olivia mentally groaned. *Here we go.*

"Spit it out, Becs," Olivia told her, squelching the desire to roll her eyes.

"Are you sure this is a good idea? I mean, I know you're in love with him but I don't want to see you hurt."

"I'll be fine."

"Really? When he breaks your heart, you'll be fine?"

"Gee, you have a lot of confidence in me," Olivia said through clenched teeth.

Becca sighed. "I love you and I don't want you hurt, and Wyatt is not looking for a long term relationship. You know that, Liv."

"I do know it but I'm not denying myself being with him because of it. He's an amazing man and I know there's a good chance I'll be hurt...but Becs, what if I'm not? Isn't there a chance he could fall too? Don't I have the right to find out?"

"I suppose you do. I'm just afraid for you. I swear if he hurts you, I will cut his balls off."

Olivia burst out laughing. "I know you will."

"So...how is it?" Becca grinned at her.

"Oh. My. God. Fanfuckingtastic. He's an amazing lover. It was well worth the wait."

Becca nodded. "I'm happy for you, but please be careful. I'm here for you if you need me."

Olivia hugged her. "I know and I love you for it. Don't worry about me, I can handle myself."

"I hope so. Let's get back out there before they

send someone in after us." Becca smiled at her.

* * * *

Wyatt sat down and waited for Olivia to come back when he saw Jake heading toward him.

Shit! This won't be good. Wyatt sighed as Jake slid into the booth across from him.

"Don't hurt her," Jake told him.

"Back the fuck off, Jake."

"I will not. Liv is family and for almost two years, you've ignored her and now you're dating. What the fuck is going on?"

Wyatt shrugged. "I really don't see where it's any of your business—"

"The hell it's not," Jake growled. "We all love her and if you hurt her, I will take great pleasure in kicking your ass, and Gabe will help me."

"He'd have to, it's the only way you could," Wyatt said through clenched teeth.

Jake sat back and sighed. "Look, I'm happy you're finally coming to your senses where Liv's concerned but I also know you're not looking for a relationship, so don't hurt her," he repeated.

"We're both adults and what we do is our business. We both went into this with our eyes wide open."

"Into what? Dating? You don't date, Wyatt. You fuck around."

"No matter what I do, or who I do it with, it isn't your business. Olivia knows what this is.

We're dating..."

"Are you sleeping with her?"

Wyatt grinned. "Not much sleeping is involved, actually."

"*Jesus Christ!*"

Jake slid out of the booth. "I'm not going to say

it again...don't hurt her, little brother." He strode back to his table as Olivia arrived at the booth. She slid in and smiled at Wyatt.

"You got the talk too, huh?"

Wyatt ran his hand over his jaw and nodded. "Apparently, you and I don't know what we're doing."

Olivia leaned over the table. "I know what I'd like to be doing, cowboy."

Wyatt burst out laughing, causing the patrons in the diner to look their way. They smiled at them. Olivia laughed too.

"After the movie, we're going to my house and you can tell me about it."

"Deal." Olivia smiled at him.

Connie brought their dinners. Wyatt had chosen the steak and baked potato, and Olivia had ordered the trout with a salad. As they ate, the conversation flowed easily between them. When they'd finished with dinner, they left and drove to the theatre where they decided on an action movie. Olivia ordered buttered popcorn, making Wyatt shake his head in wonder. She grinned up at him.

"I love theatre popcorn."

"You just ate."

"I'll need my strength," she whispered, throwing his words back at him.

Wyatt groaned. "We could go now."

Olivia laughed. "Nope. I want to see this. We have all night, cowboy. All night."

Wyatt stared at her. She was exquisite. The dark purple blouse she wore matched her eyes and her jeans hugged her curves. She wore very little make-up, but she didn't need much with her porcelain skin.

"What?" she asked him.

"You're so beautiful," he whispered and watched a blush stain her cheeks. He smiled. "I can't believe a woman who could make a sailor blush with her language actually blushes herself."

"Stop..." she groaned.

Wyatt chuckled. "Just sayin', sweetheart."

When the lights went down, she laid her head on his shoulder, and watched the movie. Wyatt held her hand and leaned his cheek against her hair. This wasn't so bad. Actually, it was rather nice. He didn't mind doing this if it meant she was going to be in his bed later and spend all day with him tomorrow. They'd go for a walk or just stay in the house and relax. He didn't work Sundays unless he absolutely had to. He had enough men to do the work that needed doing and if someone couldn't make it in for one reason or another, Wyatt called someone in or covered for them himself.

When the movie ended, they drove to his place. He took her suitcase from behind the seat and grasped her hand. As he opened the back door, Bear ran out, stopping long enough for Olivia to pet him, and then took off down the steps to find a tree.

"What about Punkin? What did you do with her while you're here?"

"Evelyn's going to take care of her for me," Olivia told him.

He nodded. "That's nice."

"I love that woman. She's a wonderful person."

"Yes, she is. Becca did well in hiring her." Wyatt took Olivia's coat off and hung it up then removed his. He picked her suitcase up, carried it toward the bedroom, and set it inside the door.

He turned and bumped into Olivia.

"I'm sorry. I didn't know you were behind me." He caught her arms to keep her from falling.

"It's okay." She stared up at him. "Kiss me, cowboy. I've been waiting all night."

Wyatt pulled her closer and lowered his head. His lips brushed hers. Once. Twice, and then he sipped at her lips until she fisted her hands in his hair, and pressed her lips to his. He grinned.

"You love to tease me," she whispered with a smile.

He chuckled. "Oh, and you don't love to tease me?" His lips trailed across her cheek to her ear. "Cockteaser," he whispered against her ear before taking the lobe between his teeth, making her shiver.

"Kiss me," she groaned.

Wyatt pressed his lips to hers and slowly moved his tongue into her mouth. He cupped her face in his hands and tilted her head back to deepen the kiss. He slowly raised his head, taking her bottom lip between his teeth and running his tongue along it.

Olivia groaned. "Wyatt...please..."

"Please, what?" he murmured.

She grinned up at him. "Me. Please me."

Wyatt chuckled. "Oh, I will for sure, darlin'."

He picked her up and carried her to the bed where he laid her down, and he was about to lie down beside her when he heard Bear barking. "I'll be right back. I need to let him in."

"I'll be right here, waiting for you."

Wyatt groaned. "I'll only be a minute. Do you want me to bring you anything? Water? Soda?"

"Water and...you," she whispered.

He nodded. "All right."

He quickly left the room to let Bear in and get her a glass of water. Bear ran into the kitchen and settled down while Wyatt filled a glass with ice, and then water. As he walked back toward the bedroom, he looked at the glass and grinned. He entered the bedroom to see her already under the sheet.

"Here's your water," he told her handing it to her. She took the glass, sipped from it, and then set the glass on the bedside table. She lay back and stared up at him.

"Come on, cowboy," she said to him, crooking a finger at him.

Wyatt quickly stripped and got under the sheet with her, rolling to face her. His hand cupped her cheek.

"You're so gorgeous." He moved his hand down her neck, to her shoulder, around her back and settled on her ass. "You have such a great ass." He grinned.

Olivia laughed. "So do you. All muscle," she said as her hand moved down his back.

* * * *

She watched as Wyatt reached into the glass she'd placed on the table, and pulled out an ice cube. He grinned at her while he ran it along her lips and down her chin following it with his mouth, down along her neck, the cold making her hiss in a breath. He moved the ice cube to her breast and encircled her nipple, making it tighten into a stiff peak. His tongue moved over it before he sucked it into his mouth while moving the ice cube to her other breast. His lips moved along her chest to her other breast where he pulled on her nipple with his teeth.

She clutched at the pillow as he moved the ice

cube down along her flat stomach, around her belly button only to stop above her curls, making her whimper. His tongue followed every wet trail the ice cube made. When he moved the ice to touch her clitoris, she almost sprang off the bed and she heard him chuckle. Then he moved the ice cube down between her heat and back to her clitoris, where he kept it rubbing it against her. As one ice cube would melt, he'd reach for another one.

Olivia began panting in anticipation as he pushed her legs further apart and replaced the ice cube with his mouth. Her body was so sensitive due to the cold ice that she screamed out as she came hard against his lips. When Wyatt moved up her body, she could do nothing to stop him from doing anything he wanted to her. She lay spent. The next thing she knew, he thrust into her hard and fast. When he pressed his lips to hers, she tasted herself there and thought it the most erotic thing ever when he pushed the ice cube from his mouth into hers. She moaned against his lips.

"God, what you do to me, Wyatt," she whispered.

"Hold on tight, darlin'. It's going to be a hard ride," he said against her lips as he started moving his hips. Slowly at first, then he picked up the pace and thrust hard into her.

Her legs locked tight around his waist as he pressed his lips to hers. She felt the waves start to crash over her again and she plummeted over the edge, biting his shoulder as she did. Wyatt went rigid and groaned out her name before collapsing on her. She ran her fingers through his thick hair.

"That was fantastic," she said.

Wyatt raised his head and stared at her. "Yeah, it was." He kissed her and rolled off her.

"Do you mind if I take a shower?" she asked.

He waved his hand. "Have at it. I'll be here...sleeping."

Olivia laughed and headed toward the bathroom. "Thought you had more in you than that, cowboy."

She smiled as she closed the door and turned the shower on. The bathroom quickly filled with steam. Stepping inside the shower, she closed the glass doors, picked up the soap, and lathered it up. She began to wash and grinned with satisfaction when she heard the bathroom door open. "Did you decide on a shower after all?'

The glass doors slid open and Wyatt stepped in. "Woman, I never back down from a challenge."

"Oh, really? Well, I'll just have to toss a few more out there then."

He chuckled. "Just try not to kill me."

Olivia put her hands on his chest and rubbed soap on him. Her hands slowly lowered to his cock and her fingers wrapped around him, making him groan. He grew thick and hard in her hands. He picked her up, set her back against the wall, and slid into her. She moaned deep in her throat. "You feel fantastic."

"Not as good as you feel, sweetheart. Damn, am I ever going to get enough of you?" he murmured.

She locked her legs around his waist and held on as he pounded into her. Sex had never been this good before. This man knew how to please her. She never wanted to let go and she was going to do everything in her power to keep him. Her orgasm ripped through her, making her shudder and cry out. She felt him stiffen as his own orgasm engulfed through him. Wyatt kissed her and leaned his forehead against hers.

"Damn."

Olivia laughed. "Yeah...damn."

"I do need to sleep now."

"Why are men like that?"

Wyatt laughed. "Because we wear ourselves out, and in case you hadn't noticed, we just did it twice within a few minutes."

"Oh, please...like women don't get worn out from it?"

"I'm smart enough not to have this conversation. Let's wash up and go to bed."

"Now you're talking." Olivia grinned.

"To sleep," he growled.

"Sure. Whatever." She laughed.

She took the soap from him and washed him again but when her hand started to stray downward, he grasped her wrist. She gazed up at him and laughed.

"Behave. I have an idea. You wash you and I'll wash me," Wyatt told her.

"Spoil sport." She sighed. "All right but I don't want any grumbling from you if I wake you up during the night. I'll challenge you to that."

Wyatt groaned. "You're going to kill me."

Olivia burst out laughing. "What a way to go."

She squealed when he picked her up and carried her out of the shower. Setting her down, he grabbed a towel and rubbed her dry, and then quickly ran the towel over his damp body. He leaned down, kissing her hard and quick, and then tossed her over his shoulder, carrying her back to the bed. He had accepted her challenge.

Chapter Eight

A week later, Olivia sat at the front counter with Stacy and watched several of the guests leaving. Some of them even hugged her and Stacy before leaving. As she sat there watching them going out the door, she saw Wyatt walking in. Women stopped to stare at him but he didn't seem to notice. She bit back a grin when one woman ran into the doorjamb. Wyatt turned toward her and Olivia heard him ask if she was all right. The woman nodded as she continued to stare up at him. He touched the brim of his hat and turned back toward the foyer. Olivia and Stacy burst out laughing. Wyatt frowned at them.

"Was she all right?" Olivia asked.

"She said she was." Wyatt shrugged.

"She was totally in awe of you." Olivia laughed.

"What? No." Wyatt shook his head.

"Oh yeah, she was staring at you. It's why she ran into the door," Stacy told him.

Wyatt screwed up his face as if in disbelief before turning serious and looking at Olivia.

"Can you take a break for a few minutes?"

"Sure. I'll be right back, Stace." Olivia led Wyatt to the kitchen. She stopped by the kitchen table and stared at him. "What's up?"

"I know it's our date night, but is it all right if we just stay in tonight? I'm beat, sweetheart."

She stared at him in surprise. She figured he was there to cancel the date, not have a night in. "I'd love a night in, cowboy. You could have just called me though. You didn't have to drive over here."

"I was heading back from town. I'll make some steaks. Do you want me to come back and pick you up or do you want to drive over?"

"I'll drive over. Can I bring Punkin? Evelyn can't watch her this weekend."

"That's fine." Wyatt kissed her gently. "I'll see you later, darlin'," he whispered against her lips, and then he left through the back door.

Olivia headed back to the front desk and took her seat beside Stacy again. Together, they helped the guests check out, and Olivia hoped the day went quickly so she could soon be with Wyatt.

Later as she pulled up to his place, it began to flurry. Snow came early in Clifton. Being in northern Montana and close to the Glacier Mountains, it wasn't a stretch to have it snow in October. She'd lived in Clifton long enough now to be used to it and to recognize that the way the snow was beginning to come down, it was going to start accumulating. She parked and hopped out. After retrieving her suitcase from the back, she let Punkin out and they headed toward the steps. The back door opened and Wyatt stepped out. He did look tired and her heart went out to him. He reached for her suitcase and gave her a quick kiss before turning to hold the door open. He motioned for her to enter, which she did with Punkin on her heels. As soon as Punkin entered the house, she and Bear took off running toward the living room. Wyatt carried her suitcase to the bedroom while she stayed in the kitchen.

After taking her coat off, she walked to the counter and picked up the package of steaks. She about jumped out of her skin when Wyatt's arms wrapped around her from behind. She leaned back against him.

"You do look tired, cowboy," she whispered.

"I'm beat. It was a long day." He rested his chin on her shoulder.

"Are you even hungry?"

Wyatt sighed. "No. I'm too tired to be hungry, but I can make dinner. I just hope I don't fall asleep while trying to eat."

Olivia put the steaks in the fridge then took his hand and led him toward the bedroom. "I think we'll just go to bed. You sleep and I'll watch TV."

"Not much of a date." He yawned.

She laughed. "You can make it up to me next weekend or tomorrow."

"Deal," he said as he yawned again. He stood by the bed and removed his jeans, boxer briefs, and shirt. Then, without hesitation, he crawled between the sheets.

"I'm just going to brush my teeth and get into my comfy clothes. I'll be right back." She smiled when she saw him simply nod. She bet he was asleep before she got back.

* * * *

The next morning, the sunlight danced across her face, waking her. She stretched and looked toward Wyatt's side of the bed. Seeing it empty, she got up and headed to the kitchen. There were no sounds in the house. Olivia yawned as she reached for a cup for coffee. Her hand stopped in mid-air when she glanced out the window above the sink. Snow was everywhere she looked. After pouring her coffee, she headed toward the back door, where she glanced out before opening it, and stepped out onto the porch. The sun glistened on the snow, making it appear as if diamonds lay sprinkled upon it. She shaded her eyes as she looked toward the barn, but she didn't see anyone. Shivering, she sighed, closing the door against the cold, and headed toward the living room. She decided she'd watch TV until Wyatt made a trip back inside the house. Glancing out the front window, she shook her head. She was still amazed at the amount of snow Montana got. She heard the back door open and waited for him to come into the living room. When he strolled in and stopped at the doorway, she almost groaned. If someone had told her a few years ago she'd fall in love with a cowboy, she would've scoffed at the mention. But seeing him standing there, with snow on his hat and on the shoulders of his coat, she couldn't imagine not loving him.

"We got some snow. Did you see it?" he asked her.

"You call that *some* snow?"

He grinned at her and her heart slammed against her ribs. "Okay, I may have fibbed a little on that."

"I hope it's gone by tomorrow." *Liar!*

"In a hurry to get out of here, darlin'?"

"We only agreed on Saturday nights and Sunday days. I don't want to overstay my welcome, cowboy."

He chuckled. "Did you get something to eat?"

She noticed he didn't say anything about her overstaying her welcome. She sighed. "Not yet. I haven't been up long. Did you sleep well? You were out like a light when I came back from the bathroom last night."

Wyatt nodded and took a seat in the recliner. "I did. I'm sorry about dinner. I'm sure you're starving. I can make you something."

"Are you hungry?"

He stood. Then grinning, he moved toward her, stopped in front of her, and cupped her cheek in his gloved hand. "Not for food, sweetheart."

Olivia grinned up at him. "What are you going to do about it?"

"Nothing right now. I have to get back to work. Two men didn't make it in." He leaned down and kissed her. "I'll make it up to you later though."

"Can you make a fire first?" She nodded toward the fireplace.

"Just needs to be lit and the flue opened." He moved to the hearth, crouched down, and reaching inside, opened the flue. He then lit a match and set the wood ablaze. The flames crackled and snapped as they wrapped around the logs. Wyatt stood and glanced over at her. "I'll be back later. I only came in to see if you were awake yet."

"I'll be right here," she said.

He gave a terse nod and left the room. She heard the door close behind him. The two dogs came running into the living room and greeted her.

"You two must have been outside somewhere, huh? Where were you when I was on the porch? In the barn with Wyatt? I bet that's where you were. You both feel cold." She laughed and walked toward the kitchen with the dogs at her heels. She decided to make herself some toast and hope it didn't take Wyatt all day to come back to her.

* * * *

After the snow stranded Olivia at Wyatt's place for three days, she knew she needed to head back to the B and B as soon as possible. Stacy needed help these last couple of weeks, and Olivia knew she couldn't leave her stranded. It seemed the closer it got to closing for the season, the crazier it got. There were no vacancies but someone still had to operate the phones, and help with the guests.

Having gathered her things, with a sigh Olivia went in search of Wyatt to tell him she had to leave. She walked out onto the porch and shaded her eyes against the brightness. The sun shining down on the snow made it almost impossible to see and her eyes had trouble adjusting at first. Then she saw him exiting the barn with one of the ranch hands. They were laughing about something. She loved his laugh.

Good Lord! He looked so sexy. Who ever thought that a man who wore a damn cowboy hat could look so sexy? His jeans and boots were dusty with bits of hay clinging to them from working in the stalls. He was in need of a shave and haircut but neither took anything away from his dark good looks. His sheepskin coat was open, allowing her eyes to roam down over his hard chest to the fly of his jeans. She closed her eyes. All too aware that what was behind it was pure temptation, and...nope, she shook her head because she couldn't think of a good enough word to describe it. Mouthwatering? Wonderful? Magnificent? Yes, yes, and yes.

Olivia knew the instant he caught sight of her. He grinned and his white teeth flashed in his dirty face. He said something to the ranch hand then walked toward her on a path through the snow. He stopped at the bottom of the steps and gazed up at her.

"Hi, darlin'." He smiled up at her.

Olivia took her bottom lip between her teeth to bite back a moan. He slowly climbed the steps until he was even with her. Wyatt reached a hand out and cupped her hip in his gloved hand. She smiled. He grinned at her and put his other hand on her cheek. The leather from the work glove was soft and worn. He kissed her.

"I need a shower, want to join me?" He nibbled along her jaw.

Olivia moaned. "I'd love to, but I have to leave."

Wyatt pulled back. "What do you mean you have to leave?"

Olivia sighed. "Stacy's going to need help and I can't leave her stranded."

Wyatt swore. "Do you have to go right now?" When she nodded, he swore again.

"I wish I didn't but there's no one else to help out."

Wyatt nodded, stepped up onto the porch, hesitated, and then entered the house. Olivia stared after him and after taking a deep breath, she followed behind him. He was standing in the kitchen staring at her suitcase where she'd left it on the floor. He glanced at her and frowned.

"Find someone else to help her."

Olivia's mouth dropped open. "There is no one and you know it." She folded her arms across her chest. "What is wrong with you? You knew I'd have to go back sooner or later."

"I don't want you to go back yet," Wyatt growled.

"Tough," she said and then gasped when he picked up her suitcase and left the kitchen with it. After a slight hesitation, she ran after him. "Wyatt. Give me my suitcase."

"You don't have to go back yet. Becca can cover until you get back."

Olivia grabbed his arm. "You can't be serious.

Becca is married. She has a husband to take care of, and don't even think of suggesting Emma."

Wyatt spun around to face her. "Becca needs to hire more people. It can't be that hard sitting at the desk and checking people in or out."

Olivia could feel the heat pouring into her face. She clenched her fists to keep from punching him. "It's not as easy as it looks, cowboy." Her jaw hurt from gritting her teeth. "Give me my damn suitcase."

Wyatt headed into the bedroom. Olivia stood rooted to the spot.

"Fine." She turned and headed back into the kitchen. "I have more clothes at home." She called over her shoulder as she went out the backdoor with Punkin on her heels. She put Punkin in the back of her vehicle and was about to get in when he came down the steps with her suitcase.

"Olivia, why are you doing this?"

"I'm not doing anything. I just have to go. I'm just down the road for God's sake, Wyatt." She got into her car and put the window down. He folded his arms atop the car and stared at her. It took every ounce of her willpower not to get back out. She took a deep breath. "Please don't be angry with me."

Wyatt swore. "With one of us being able to walk away whenever we want, shouldn't we take advantage of it while we can?"

Dear God. She suddenly wanted to cry.

"It sounds to me you know exactly how long this is going to last, which means you're just stringing me along until you decide to walk away." She jumped when the palm of his hand slapped the top of her car.

"I have no idea how long anything's going to last

but all the same, why shouldn't we make the most of it?" When she didn't answer, he put her suitcase in the back and then stepped back from the car. He put his hands on his hips and didn't look at her. "Go."

Olivia blinked back tears, put the car in gear, and drove off. She glanced in the rearview mirror and saw him standing there staring after her. A tear rolled down her cheek. *Damn it!* She drove back to the B and B and entered through the back door. Evelyn smiled at her until she saw the tears.

"Oh, honey. What's wrong?" She pulled Olivia into her arms.

Olivia wrapped her arms around her and sobbed. She didn't know anyone else was there until she felt another pair of arms go around her. She raised her head and saw Emma.

"Come on, Liv. Let's sit down and talk." With an arm around her shoulders, Emma led Olivia to her apartment. Once inside, Emma took a seat on the sofa and patted the cushion beside her for Olivia to sit down with her. She flopped down beside Emma.

"Tell me," Emma murmured and listened as Olivia told her what had happened with Wyatt.

"I don't know how you did it, Emma. Loving Gabe as you did and not giving up."

Emma shrugged. "I knew I'd never love anyone the way I love Gabe. I decided that I'd take him any way I could get him. Now look at us, we're very happy."

"But Wyatt doesn't want any of that," Olivia admitted, her voice cracking.

Emma snorted. "You think Gabe did? He was just like Wyatt. He only wanted sex."

Olivia blinked back new tears. "I can't give up on

Wyatt. I'm so in love with him." She shook her head. "I knew this was going to break my heart."

Emma smiled at her. "I think he cares more than he's letting on, Liv. Don't give up. Not yet."

Olivia wiped at her eyes. "I miss him already."

* * * *

Wyatt watched her drive away. It was probably for the best anyway. He was getting in way over his head. He went to bed thinking of her and woke up thinking about her. It couldn't be this way. Wanting her the way he did wasn't good, but the sex was amazing with her. He turned, heading back toward the barn to get some work done. *Damn it!* He slammed his gloved hand against the barn door when he reached it.

He entered the barn to find Ben Collins watching him. Wyatt raised his eyebrow at him.

"Don't you have something to do, Collins?"

"I'm taking a quick break. I already asked Lucky about it."

Wyatt nodded. "All right."

He walked past him to go to his office. As he opened the door, he glanced back over his shoulder to see Collins staring at him. Mentally shaking his head, he entered the office and closed the door. He moved behind his desk and took a seat. After booting up the computer, he began working on the sales and payroll, but Olivia kept popping into his head. He sat back in his chair and glanced toward the window to see more snow coming down from the Glacier Mountains. It was too bad she left when she did or she might have been stuck with him for a few more days.

How was this going to end? Should he just go ahead and end it now before he got in too deep or before she had a chance to end it? He'd been through enough heartache, he wasn't looking forward to more, and the way he was starting to feel about Olivia, he knew he was heading for it. It would be best just to break it off now and get it over with before he got in too deep. Sighing, he stood and walked out of the office to see Collins still standing where he'd been earlier. Wyatt clenched his jaw as he strode toward him.

"Why aren't you working?"

"I'm heading back now," Collins told him.

"You've been standing here for almost thirty minutes. At least, since I went into my office."

Collins narrowed his eyes. "I thought you said you weren't my boss."

Wyatt stepped closer toward him. "I'm your boss when I think you're fucking around," he growled.

"I'm not fucking around. I didn't get a lunch break today..."

"Not my problem. If you have a problem with the way things are around here, then maybe you should look for another job." Wyatt glared at him.

"I'm fine with it. I'll get back to work," he muttered as he stepped around Wyatt and walked down the center of the barn.

Wyatt took a deep breath and left the barn. He didn't know what to do about the man. He was belligerent and did what he wanted. It didn't work that way on this ranch. The other ranch hands had no problem following orders. They liked their jobs. Wyatt was about at his rope's end with Collins but until he had a real reason to fire him, he'd have to let him stay on. He couldn't fire him just because he didn't care for him and being Kirk's brother, he'd let him stay. Kirk practically begged Wyatt to hire

Ben, and now he wished he hadn't.

He entered the house with Bear on his heels. The dog ran the ranch freely every day but always seemed to show up when it was time to quit work for the day. Wyatt fed him, and then headed to the bathroom for a shower. Leaving the door open, he undressed and stepped inside the shower. The hot water felt so good on his tired body. The only thing missing was Olivia. His cock started to harden just thinking of her.

Fuck! You just decided to quit seeing her but your damn dick has other ideas.

Turning on the cold water full blast, he jumped back when it hit his skin but it did the trick. He shut it off and stepped out. After drying off, he pulled on a T-shirt and sweatpants. He'd see her tomorrow and end it. That was going to be the real problem. Seeing her and breaking it off because he knew once he saw her, he'd want her again.

* * * *

The next day, Olivia sat at the counter watching people come and go. She hadn't heard from Wyatt and she was afraid when she did, he was going to end it between them. After the way he had acted when she left, she was sure of it and her heart was breaking. Why had she ever thought this could work? She just had to have him, and now she was going to lose him. She snorted.

Idiot, he was never yours to lose. Olivia put her hands over her face and fought back tears while wondering why she had allowed herself to get in this deep. She was surprised when someone touched her arm. She glanced over to see Stacy sitting beside her.

"Are you all right?" Stacy asked.

"Yes," Olivia said, and then shook her head. "Not really, but I will be."

"I'm here if you need to talk, Liv," Stacy told her.

Olivia nodded. "I appreciate that but I'll be fine." She stood. "I'll be back in a few minutes."

She didn't wait to see if Stacy responded. She practically ran from the foyer and headed toward the kitchen. Without giving Evelyn a chance to ask her anything, she passed through straight to her apartment, where she flopped down onto her couch, and sobbed.

What was she going to do? How could she stay here once this ended? How could she see him and know she'd never have him again?

She pulled a pillow over her face and cried into it, only crying just pissed her off. She wasn't a crier, and never over a man. She wouldn't break down when he broke it off but she would leave Clifton. It was the only smart thing to do. Get far away from him so eventually she'd forget him. Maybe. She was startled when someone knocked on her door. Sitting up, she wiped the tears from her face and opened the door to see Evelyn standing there, smiling at her.

"Wyatt's here to see you," she told her.

And so it begins. Olivia stepped through the doorway and headed toward the foyer.

Chapter Nine

Wyatt stood leaning against the counter waiting for Olivia and watched people coming and going. Most of the women smiled at him and he'd touch the brim of his hat in a proper greeting. He straightened up when Olivia entered the foyer. She stopped and stared at him. He could tell she'd been crying and he frowned.

"What's wrong?" he asked.

"Nothing. What are you doing here?"

"I wanted to talk to you. Do you have a few minutes?"

Olivia nodded and jerked her chin for him to follow her. They walked back the way she'd just come to her apartment where, once inside, she took a seat on the sofa and he sat in the chair opposite her. He couldn't sit close to her. If he did, he'd never be able to do this. He noticed she wouldn't look at him.

"Olivia..." he began.

"Just spit it out, cowboy, I have things to do." She folded her arms and narrowed her eyes at him.

Wyatt blew out a breath. "I don't think this is going to work..." He stopped when she abruptly stood.

"Fine. I have to get back to work." She walked toward the door.

Wyatt leaped up, grasped her arm in his hand, and spun her around.

"That's it?" he growled.

She jerked away from him. "What do you want me to say? We agreed we could walk away whenever we wanted. Apparently, you want to."

"Jesus, Olivia. I don't know what the fuck I want. I did come here with the intention of ending this but all I have to do is see you, and I want you again." He ran his hand down his face and sighed.

"Make up your mind," she practically shouted at him. Well, at least she was reacting.

He moved away from her and sat back down in the chair. "I...damn it! I don't know."

"Was it so bad? Us going out together? I enjoyed it."

"I don't date."

She snorted. "What is it we've been doing?"

"You know damn well what I mean."

"And you know what I mean. We date or we don't have sex. Simple as that. I won't be a slut for you or any man. A woman likes a little romance before hopping into bed."

"Not all."

"Well, I do!" Olivia took a seat on the couch again. "We're both getting what we want if we go out."

Wyatt raised his eyebrow. "Really? It seems to me you're getting more."

"Why do you say that?"

"You're getting your date of dinner, a movie, and sex."

"You get those things too, cowboy."

"I don't need the fucking dinner or movie, for Christ's sake."

"Not too long ago, you told me you didn't want me because you thought I was a slut, but yet you want to treat me like one. Well, I won't be one for you. I won't be someone you can just jump into bed with when your dick gets hard."

"I don't date," Wyatt repeated.

"Then I guess we're at an impasse."

Wyatt stood and moved to the door where he paused. "I guess we are."

Without looking at her again, he opened the door and walked out. He saw Evelyn watching him as he stormed through the kitchen, but he didn't care. He walked out of the B and B, heading to his truck. It was what he wanted. Wasn't it?

* * * *

Olivia stared at the door as if what had just happened wasn't real, but then she felt a tear roll down her face. It was real...he'd done it. He'd ended it and her heart was literally breaking. She could feel it crumbling as she collapsed onto the couch and stared at the door. Picking up a pillow, she threw it at the door. *Damn him!*

That had to be the fastest relationship on record. *That's where you're wrong, Olivia.* There was no *relationship.* It was only sex—amazing, hot sex. She curled her legs up under her and continued to stare at the door. Now what? What should she do now? Not much she could do. It looked like the time to leave Clifton had arrived sooner than she'd hoped. She sighed when someone knocked at her door. She really wasn't in the mood to talk to anyone right now. She stood, crossing the room to open the door and silently cursing whoever was on the other side for bothering her. Opening it, she was shocked to see Wyatt standing there.

Back to rub salt in my wounds?

"Forget something, cowboy?" She raised an impatient eyebrow at him.

He moved into the room past her and stopped in the middle of the room before he spun around to stare at her. "Damn it, Olivia. I don't like this."

Olivia closed the door, returned to the couch and flopped down, arms folded across her chest. "What is it you don't like?"

"You having me by the damn balls," he growled. She sputtered. "What?"

"I was only halfway to my truck and I came back because I don't want this to end. If you didn't have me by the balls, I could've gone on home," he said with an angry scowl.

"I'm not holding you here, Wyatt, and you know it. If you want to continue this, we do it as before." She lifted her chin defying him to object and glared at him.

He moved to stand over her and stared down at her. "The hell you're not holding me here. Get up."

Surprising herself, Olivia did as he commanded. She stood in front of him and raised her eyes to meet his. He leaned down and pressed his lips to hers. When her arms went around his neck, he jerked her hard against him.

"I have to have you. Now," he said against her lips. He picked her up and carried her to her bedroom where he laid her on the bed before stretching out beside her. "You're in my head and I can't get you out of it. I know no other woman is going to set me on fire like you do and that scares the hell out of me."

"You think I'm not scared too? I'm terrified, Wyatt. For so many reasons and I don't know what to do about it, other than be with you as much as I can. As much as you want me to be."

* * * *

Wyatt pressed his lips to hers and forced her lips apart to let him inside. He couldn't get enough of her. His heart wouldn't be able to take it if she broke it. It would hurt so much more than when Stephanie had broken it. Looking back now, he knew he'd only been hurt she'd broken the engagement, not his heart. No one ever held his heart, not like Olivia and if he were being honest with himself, he knew he'd never love another woman. But he couldn't let her know because she didn't love him, she only wanted him and for now, it would have to be enough. He lifted her T-shirt over her head and unclasped her bra. Groaning, he moved his lips down over her chin, her chest, and to the nearest nipple. He sucked it deeply into his mouth while Olivia's hands fisted in his hair as she pulled him closer. Wyatt moved his hand down her stomach to the snap of her jeans, unsnapped them, and then slowly lowered the zipper. His hand snaked inside of her panties to her core. Moving his finger up and down her cleft, he smiled when she moaned and arched her hips against his hand.

"You're getting so wet, darlin'. I love how wet you get for me," he whispered.

"Wyatt..." she whispered as she tugged on his T-shirt. He sat up, pulled it over his head, and then lay back down.

"Get those jeans off, cowboy," she growled.

He chuckled as he toed off his boots. Olivia sat up, unbuckled his belt, and lowered the zipper. His cock was so hard it made it difficult to lower the zipper. He raised his hips and shoved his jeans down then he removed hers and tossed them across the room. He groaned when he saw her black lace, boy-cut panties.

"You're fucking killing me. You're so damn beautiful," he murmured against her lips before taking them in a deep kiss. He hissed in a breath when she wrapped her hand around his hard shaft. He wrapped his fingers around her wrist. "It'll be over before it begins if you keep that up."

She lightly laughed. "Oh, I plan on keeping it up, cowboy."

"I never knew you were so evil, Olivia." He stared into her eyes, and then grinned. "I like it." He rolled to his back, pulling her on top of him. "Ride me, darlin'."

Olivia leaned down and ran her tongue along his lips. He growled and cupped her face in his palms, kissing her until she moaned. He felt her hand move down over his chest to his stomach and her fingers wrapped around him again. Her hips lifted and she inched down over him. Wyatt clenched his teeth, and then groaned when she settled on him, pulling him deep inside. When she sat up, he stared up at her. She smiled down at him as she began rocking her hips and lifting herself up. Each time she inched back down, he groaned. Her nails scraped his chest. He put his hands on her hips and tried to make her move faster. She laughed deep in her throat.

"My ride...my way, cowboy." She leaned down, capturing his bottom lip between her teeth before sucking it into her mouth. When she sat back up, he put his hands over her breasts and rubbed her nipples with his thumbs, making them stiffen. Olivia moaned and tilted her head back. Wyatt felt her long hair touching his thighs and it made him even hotter. Her hips moved harder and faster against him, and he could feel her inner muscles start clenching around him as her orgasm hit her hard. Her breasts rose and fell as her breathing quickened. Wyatt sat up, wrapped his arms around her, and flipped her to her back, making her gasp as he started pummeling into her. A guttural growl tore from deep in his chest when he felt his orgasm sweeping over him. He hooked his arms under her knees and opened her more to his thrusts. He watched the flush move across her cheeks as she took her lower lip between her teeth, and then tilted her head back on the pillow and cried out as another orgasm had her gasping and shaking.

Wyatt collapsed on top of her, breathing hard. "You're going to kill me."

Olivia laughed. "It was supposed to be my way, not yours. I would still be riding you, as you asked, if you hadn't had to take over."

He glanced over toward her. "Are you complaining?"

"Pffft." She waved her hand. "You'll never hear me complain about sex that good."

Wyatt laughed. "Me neither. How about a shower?"

"I'd rather soak in the tub. You shower. I'll soak."

Wyatt stood and put his hand out toward her. "All right. Then we can go get some dinner."

"I'm working, cowboy, in case you forgot. In fact, I'm sure Stacy's wondering where I am."

Wyatt grinned. "I have a feeling she knows exactly where you are and what you've been doing."

Olivia put her hands over her face. "You're probably right." She sighed. "I really have to get back to the front counter."

Wyatt pulled his jeans and shirt on then sat down and pulled his boots on. "All right. So I'll pick you up Saturday at six." It wasn't a question.

He leaned down, kissed her quickly, and then

left her to clean up and get dressed. As he headed toward the foyer, he passed Stacy heading into the kitchen. She smiled at him. He smiled back at her.

"She'll be out in a few minutes."

He chuckled when he heard Stacy snicker as he headed out the door to go home.

* * * *

Olivia took a quick shower. Her long soak would have to wait, but she couldn't keep the smile off her face. What a fantastic lover he was. She shivered just thinking of him. When she stepped into the kitchen, Evelyn and Stacy both turned toward her. Both of them were wearing silly grins on their faces.

"What?" she asked with as much innocence as she could muster.

They started laughing. Olivia couldn't help but laugh with them.

"You sure look happier now than you were earlier," Evelyn told her.

"Maybe." Olivia smiled.

"Wyatt seemed to look happy too. Don't you think, Stacy?" Evelyn glanced at Stacy.

"For sure. I wonder why? Did you have a nice...conversation, Olivia?"

Olivia stuck her tongue out at them. "I hate you both."

She headed toward the foyer with their laughter trailing behind her. She was still smiling as she took a seat behind the counter and talked with guests. The B and B would close in two weeks and although she would continue to work on the books and reservations, she couldn't help but wonder how much more often she would get together with Wyatt. She could easily do all of her work on her laptop from his place, but only if he wanted her there. She knew she'd be bored to tears if she had to sit around here with no one else was around. Shaking her head, she knew there was no sense in worrying about it yet. She'd cross that bridge when she came to it. Maybe she could try to bring it up casually when they saw each other again.

* * * *

Two days had passed since he saw Olivia. Wyatt was in the arena working Cochise when the door opened. He glanced over, groaning when he saw who it was, and then dismounted. Cochise's ears went back making Wyatt rub them in understanding.

"I know how you feel buddy," he whispered to the horse while glancing over at Stephanie and wondering what she was doing here. Cochise whinnied and shifted around. Wyatt calmed him down and wrapped the reins on the saddle. Taking a deep breath, he walked toward Stephanie. She smiled at him then climbed up on the fence rail and perched there. He glared at her and stopped in front of her.

"What are you doing here?" Wyatt asked.

"I came to see you." She grinned at him.

"Well, now you've seen me, you can go."

"Wyatt..." She reached out, grabbed the front of his T-shirt, and tugged him toward her. It caught him off guard causing him to stumble and fall against her. She pressed her lips to his. He jerked back in response.

"Stop it," he growled.

Stephanie blinked her eyes at him and pouted. "Why? I want you back. We were good together." She narrowed her eyes. "I'm sure we were better together than you and your slut are."

Wyatt's jaw tightened and he flattened his lips. "If you mean Olivia, she's not a slut."

Stephanie waved her hand. "Oh, please. Why would a single woman be on birth control pills if she doesn't whore around?"

"Get out," Wyatt told her between clenched teeth.

Stephanie's eyes widened and she hopped off the fence. "I'm just telling it like it is."

"Why is that any of your business?"

"I'm just saying that Olivia must like to sleep around."

Wyatt leaned his face down to hers. "You weren't a virgin, either."

Stephanie gasped. "No, I wasn't but I've only been with two men. How many has your slut been with?"

Wyatt straightened to his full height, took her bicep in his hand, and tugged her toward the door. "I'm not going to tell you again. Get out." He practically shoved her out the door. She pulled away from him and fled out the door. He took deep breaths to calm himself. The anger was coming off him in waves. His fists clenched and he gritted his teeth. Cochise butted his head against Wyatt's back as if in sympathy.

Wyatt turned and rubbed the horse's nose. The day was a complete waste since Stephanie had shown up. *Damn her.* But he knew what would make it better. He smiled as he led Cochise out of the arena and mounted the horse. Cochise pranced around, excited about a run, and was ready to go. Wyatt nudged him and the horse bolted out of the yard toward the north pasture. He was going full speed, passing through Gabe's land, and then

Jake's, until they finally got to the B and B's land. He reined the horse in at the top of the hill and gazed down at the house and barns. Cochise shifted under him. He nudged him gently to walk down the hill. He needed to see Olivia.

* * * *

Olivia sat at the kitchen table working on the website. Evelyn was preparing the lunch meal and bustling around the kitchen. Olivia smiled as she listened to the woman talking to herself. She was adding pictures of the new riding horses to the site. She shuddered at their size. She still had no desire to get on one of those big animals. No matter how beautiful they were.

"Oh my," Evelyn muttered as she looked out the door.

Olivia glanced over to her. "Is Stan out there again?" She teased.

Evelyn slapped a kitchen towel at her. "He is, but I was talking about the other gorgeous hunk out there."

Olivia frowned then got up and went to the door to look out. She gasped when she saw Wyatt talking to Stan. Cochise stood beside him. Had he ridden that horse all the way here from his ranch? She looked around the yard, but didn't see his truck anywhere. Her eyes went back to him and she bit back a groan. He looked so good. His coat hung open, showing his T-shirt hugging his pecs and rippled stomach. His jeans were so faded they were almost white. The crotch cupped his sex alluringly. She looked over her shoulder at Evelyn.

"He's one fine looking young man," Evelyn said with a grin.

Olivia watched until she saw him heading

toward the door. She quickly moved back to her seat at the table since she didn't want him to know she'd been watching him. Evelyn stood at the stove stirring a huge pot of stew. The door opened and he stepped in. He closed the door and leaned back against it, folding his arms. She glanced up and her eyes met his. She leaned back in her chair and folded her arms. He tipped his head down so his hat covered his eyes. When he raised his head back up, she could see he was trying not to grin. His lips twitched as he walked toward her. He placed one hand on the table in front of her and one on the chair back. He took his hat off, put it on her head, and leaned in close to her. Right before his lips touched hers, he whispered.

"Hi, sweetheart." Then he pressed his lips to hers. "I've missed you."

"Not as much as I've missed you," Olivia said against his lips.

"Want to bet?" He smiled.

"What's the bet?" Olivia nibbled her bottom lip.

Wyatt straightened up. "If I win, you come home with me."

"And if I win?" She gazed up at him.

Wyatt turned a chair around, straddled it, and laid his arms across the top of it. "If you win, you come home with me."

Olivia narrowed her eyes at him. "How is that fair?"

"Who said it had to be fair?" Wyatt shrugged.

Olivia stood, not breaking his stare as she closed her laptop, and then walked to her apartment. She came back a few minutes later to find him gone. She glanced at Evelyn.

"Where did he go?"

Evelyn nodded her head toward the door. "Out."

Olivia called for Punkin and walked out onto the porch. Wyatt was talking to Stan again. He glanced over to her and after seeing the suitcase, strode over to her. She took his hat from her head and placed it on his.

"Let's go." She walked to her car and let Punkin in. She was about to get in when she saw that Wyatt was still standing in the same spot. Olivia put her hands on her hips.

"Well, cowboy, what are you waiting on?"

She laughed when she saw him run to Cochise and leap into the saddle. He nudged the horse and took off through the deep snow in the pasture.

Chapter Ten

Olivia arrived at his ranch before he did. She walked into the house and took her suitcase to the bedroom. Going back outside, she watched Punkin and Bear chase each other around the yard. When one of the ranch hands came toward her, she waited. He tipped his hat at her.

"Do you need some help ma'am?" He smiled at her.

"No, thank you. I'm waiting for Wyatt."

"He's sure been busy today. You're the second female who's been here to see him." He grinned and walked away.

Second female? Who was the first? Had he lied about not seeing anyone else? Why would he ask her to come here then? She was about to go back inside and wait for him in the kitchen when he rode into the yard. Her breath caught. He looked incredible on that horse. She watched him jump out of the saddle and saunter toward her. He halted when she glared at him.

"Who was here earlier?"

Wyatt frowned. "Huh? What do you mean?"

"One of your ranch hands found it necessary to tell me there was another female here to see you today."

"Son of a bitch," Wyatt muttered.

"Who?" Olivia asked again.

Wyatt reached for her hand. She stepped back from him. He sighed, took her elbow, and led her toward the house. She glanced in the direction of Cochise, but he grumbled something about him not going anywhere. Once inside the house, she jerked her arm from him.

"Stephanie was here..." Wyatt began when she started back toward the door. He stepped in front of her. "You need to listen to me before you throw a hissy fit."

Olivia put her hands on his chest and shoved him. "I *do not* throw hissy fits. I told you I wasn't going to be with you if you were seeing someone else." She tried to walk around him but he grabbed her by the waist.

"I'm not with anyone else and there's no way in hell I'd be with Stephanie. I can promise you that, she's only coming around because she knows I'm seeing you." He spun her around to face him. "I don't want anyone but you, sweetheart."

The fight went out of her and she leaned into him. She looked up at him and felt a huge blast of satisfaction when he groaned.

"Those eyes of yours are going to do me in." He lowered his head and kissed her. She threw her arms around his neck and kissed him back.

Wyatt raised his head. "I'm telling you the truth, Olivia. After she kissed me..."

"You kissed her?" Olivia said, punching his arm and cringing slightly when it hurt her hand.

It was like hitting a steel beam.

"You're not listening. I said *she* kissed me." He softly swore. "I don't want anything to do with her and you have to believe that or there's no sense in us being together." He took her hands in his. "I told you I wouldn't see anyone else while I'm seeing you. I'm not a liar, Olivia."

"I bet she had some things to say about me though, didn't she?" Olivia knew by the look on his face that she was right. "What did she say?"

"It doesn't matter." She continued to glare at him. He sighed and so told her.

"I'm not a slut," Olivia exclaimed after hearing the account.

"I know that," Wyatt said kissing the palm of her hand.

Olivia took his hand and led him to the living room. "I want to tell you about my life."

"You don't have to do that."

"I want to...please." She gazed up at him. When he nodded, together they sat on the sofa.

She cleared her throat and took a deep breath.

"My mother abandoned me when I was two years old. She took me to a police station, pinned a note to my coat, and walked out. Since no one could find her, I ended up in an orphanage, and then I went to foster homes but no one ever adopted me. I was a hellion and did whatever I could to get attention. I was rebellious and no matter what home I went to, they sent me back to the orphanage." She blew out a breath. "I wasn't a good person. I had sex when I was fifteen and that was even after I went to live with Becca and her parents." She sighed. "I still can't believe they loved me the way they did. I was a bitch for the first two years but deep inside, I knew it was wrong acting as I did. At sixteen, I decided to turn my life around and be the person they thought I could be. Becca's parents became *my* parents. They disciplined me and for once in my life, I listened to someone trying to straighten me out. I grieved right alongside Becca when they died." Olivia blinked back sudden tears. "When I was twenty-one, I fell in love with a boy in college. I thought he was the one, until I caught him screwing my roommate. Trust me, if Becca hadn't been with me, he'd no longer be among the living."

She saw Wyatt's mouth twitch but he nodded for her to go on. She gave him a sad smile.

"I had a hard time trusting men after that. I figured they were all the same, especially when married men would hit on me. I'd tell them what I thought of them screwing around on their wives. You wouldn't believe their excuses." She gazed into those black eyes. "I grew up tough and until I met Becca and her parents, I didn't give a shit about anyone. I love Becca as a sister. We may not share blood but I'd do anything for her." She took a deep breath. "I've been with four men. One, if you don't count the three who were actually boys, and had no idea what they were doing. I was in relationships with each one of them. The relationships didn't last long, but then it wasn't really love I felt for any of them. I am on the pill but not because I screw around. It's because I have menorrhagia, which means I have very difficult and nasty periods." She shrugged. "The pills help some. I always made my partners wear condoms—until you. That's it. The Olivia Rene Roberts story."

"That's it?" Wyatt asked.

"Yes. I understand if you don't want to see me anymore."

"Do you now?"

She glanced at him and nodded. "I do."

Wyatt huffed. "As far as I'm concerned, none of that matters, Olivia. What matters is the here and now."

She gasped in surprise. "Are you sure?"

Wyatt chuckled. "Do you think I've been squeaky clean?"

"You mean you haven't?" She narrowed her eyes and grinned.

"No. You wouldn't believe how Jake, Gabe, and I tore up this town when we were teenagers. A lot of our friends too." He laughed. "You think Sam was always a good guy? He was one of the worst."

Olivia laughed. "Sam? Well, now that you mention it, there's something about a bad boy turned sheriff." She gazed at Wyatt through her lashes. He growled at her and stood up. She laughed then squealed when he picked her up and tossed her over his shoulder.

"I'll show you a bad boy." He carried her down the hall.

Olivia ran her hands over his butt in those tight jeans. "Please do, cowboy. Please do."

* * * *

Wyatt lay on his back with Olivia draped across his chest while he tried to catch his breath. She amazed him, always giving as good as she got. He absentmindedly played with a few strands of her hair. She sighed and her warm breath blew across his chest. He tightened his arm around her and knew he had fallen hard into a pit of trouble.

Olivia rose up on her elbows to look at him. "Kiss me," she told him.

He flipped her onto her back and leaned over her. He kissed her chin, her nose, and across her cheek but kept away from her lips. She moaned and his groin twitched. How was that even possible? They had just had mind-blowing sex but he was ready to go again already. He ran his tongue along her collarbone.

"Wyatt, kiss me," she begged but then whimpered when he kissed her lips quickly, and moved to her ear. She grabbed a fistful of his hair. "Wyatt Stone, if you don't kiss me, there will be hell to pay."

He chuckled and then pressed his lips to hers, moving his tongue inside her mouth. She moaned and moved her tongue against his, making him groan. He pressed his erection against her leg. She pulled back from him and gazed up at him in surprise.

"Yeah, tell me about it." Wyatt grinned as he moved on top of her.

Olivia reached between them, wrapped her fingers around his hard cock, and moved the head between her hot, wet heat.

"Jesus, Olivia." Wyatt groaned. She laughed, and then gasped when he reached between them and guided himself into her, making them both sigh.

"Wrap your legs around me, darlin'," he whispered and groaned when she clasped him tight. He gazed into her eyes and what he saw there couldn't be what he thought it was, but only his wishful thinking. She moved her hips to his rhythm. Wyatt kissed her hard and deep.

Olivia tore her lips from his. "Please…faster…harder," she pleaded with him.

He complied.

He tried to hold back but when he felt her inner muscles tighten, he lost it. "Now, darlin'. You with me?"

"Yes," she cried out.

A little later, they lay in each other's arms. Olivia's fingers were trailing over his pecs and rippled stomach. He knew she wanted to say something.

"Spit it out, Olivia. I can hear the wheels turning." He chuckled when she blew out an exasperated breath.

"Tell me about Stephanie."

Wyatt sighed, wishing it was something other than that. "I was engaged to her, she broke the engagement a week before the wedding. What else is there?"

"Tell me how you met her, and how you fell in love with her so much so that you wanted to marry her."

"I met her years ago. She's five years younger so we didn't run in the same circles. I was twenty-eight when I met her through her dad. Blake and I had become acquainted through me training cutting horses. I thought she was beautiful..."

He felt Olivia stiffen beside him. "Are you going to listen or just get pissed?"

When she relaxed, he continued. "Anytime I was at Blake's to talk with him, she was there. We started seeing each other and we fell in love...well, I fell in love. I'm not really sure about her now. I'd been out of the Marines for two years and looking into law school..."

"You wanted to attend law school?" Olivia asked in surprise.

"Yes. She talked me out of it. I kick myself every day for listening to her but in a way it was the best thing that happened. I love what I'm doing now. I was training horses part time and the more I did it, the more I loved it." He shrugged. "So, I guess it was for the best. I only hate that I let her talk me out of it instead of making it my own decision."

"Why did she break the engagement?" Olivia asked.

Wyatt grunted. "She told me I was spending too much time working the horses and if I had gone on to law school, we'd have more time together."

Olivia sat up and glared at him. "Are you serious? She's the one who talked you out of going."

"That's what I said, but it didn't matter to her. She gave me the ring back and that was it." He shrugged.

"Were you deeply in love with her?"

"When I think back, I don't think I loved her enough. I was more interested in combining my business with her father's. Stephanie was just a bonus. As I said, I thought she was beautiful but it didn't take too long to realize she wasn't a nice person. I'm glad now that I didn't marry her."

"Was she good in bed?" Olivia asked.

Wyatt burst out laughing and she swatted him in response. "You want to tell me what's so funny, cowboy?"

He rolled on top of her and kissed her. "If you like having sex with a block of ice, she was great. She doesn't compare to you, darlin', and never will." He kissed her again.

Olivia moaned against his mouth while wrapping her arms around his neck. All was good with the world—for now.

* * * *

The next morning, Olivia woke up alone. She dressed and walked to the kitchen looking for Wyatt. He wasn't in the house so she headed out the back door in search of him. Her breath whooshed out of her chest in amazement when she saw him ride Cochise into the yard and head toward her. He smiled and her knees almost gave out.

"It's about time you got up," he said gazing down

at her.

"You should have gotten me up." She grinned up at him, waggling her eyebrows.

Wyatt shifted on the horse. He moved the horse closer to her but she backed up.

"Is he going to bite me?"

"No. Come here." He put his hand out to her. She shook her head.

"Olivia, do you trust me?"

"Yes...but..."

"No buts. Give me your hand."

Olivia was terrified, but she put her hand in his anyway. He lifted her onto the horse as if she weighed no more than a feather. She put her hands over her face and closed her eyes.

"You can open your eyes," Wyatt whispered in her ear. "I've got you, darlin'."

She opened her eyes and glanced down. "I can't believe you got me on a horse."

Wyatt grinned at her as he nudged Cochise into a walk. She clung to him. Her arms wrapped tightly around his waist. After a few minutes of walking Cochise around the yard, he halted the horse and let her down. He grinned down at her with smug satisfaction.

"That wasn't so bad, was it?" he asked her.

"No, but you know my motto."

"I don't. What is it?"

Olivia grinned. "Save a horse, ride a cowboy."

Wyatt laughed. "Let me put Cochise up and we'll talk about your motto."

"Oh, we're going to do more than talk about it, cowboy."

Olivia spun on her heel and sauntered away from him with a little more sway in her hips. She went inside just as the phone started ringing. She checked the caller ID and saw it was Gabe. She wondered if she should answer it. She shrugged. It could be important.

"Hello?"

"Uh, who's this?" Gabe asked.

Olivia laughed.

"Liv? What are you doing answering the phone at Wyatt's? Are you living there now?" He chuckled.

"Not quite. Wyatt's in the barn. Do you want him to call you back?"

"You can transfer me to the barn."

Gabe explained how to send the call to the barn. Olivia hung up after she sent his on its way.

A few minutes later, Wyatt came in the back door with an angry scowl on his face.

"Why did you answer the phone?"

"What?" Olivia stared at him, not understanding why he was angry.

"Gabe thinks we're living together now. Did you tell him that?"

Olivia had never seen him so angry. "No, of course not, he was teasing when he asked if I lived here. I answered because I saw it was him on the line and thought it might be important." Her voice rose on the last word.

"Well, it wasn't and he tortured the shit out of me. Gabe won't let up. He'll just keep on me about it."

"I don't understand why you're so angry. Are you upset that Gabe knows we're seeing each other and before you answer that, you'd better remember Jake already knows we are." She was on the verge of tears.

"You just don't fucking get it. Gabe loves to

torment me and now that he thinks you're *living* here, he'll be telling everyone to expect wedding invitations," Wyatt shouted at her.

Olivia stared at him in disbelief that he would put this on her. Her entire body shook with anger. She strode over to him and stopped inches in front of him.

"God knows, we can't have that, can we?" She jerked back when he put his hand out toward her. "Don't touch me."

"You just don't understand."

"You're so right about that," she hissed out through clenched teeth.

Wyatt sighed. "I just meant that Gabe will tease me about you being here. Answering the phone as if you..." He stopped when her anger became apparent on her face.

"As if I... *lived* here?" she shouted.

Olivia marched from the kitchen and headed straight to the bedroom. She grabbed her suitcase and started packing her clothes.

Wyatt appeared in the doorway.

"Olivia, we need to talk about this."

"I think you've said more than enough." She pulled her clothes from the hangers. They swung around the bar and fell to the floor. She had to get out of here before she fell to pieces. Her heart was hurting. Snapping the suitcase shut, she lifted it off the bed and stalked toward him stopping a couple of feet from him. She raised an eyebrow at him. He frowned at her, but stepped out of the way.

Olivia practically ran down the hall and out the door to her car. She called for Punkin and after putting her in the car, she got in and started home to the B and B. Tears clouded her vision, hard sobs tore from her so she pulled off the road. She put her head against the steering wheel and cried her heart out.

* * * *

The next day, Olivia sat in her apartment working on the books. Becca had a goldmine in the B and B, and it amazed everyone how well it was doing. The little town of Clifton loved the business it brought in and it looked like Becca would have to hire more people next season. Olivia rarely sat at the front desk anymore, which was fine with her. She didn't want to face anyone right now, not even Evelyn and she loved Evelyn.

The numbers started running together. Olivia rubbed her eyes. She hadn't slept much last night. Why hadn't he come after her? Because he didn't care enough to, that was why. He'd had enough of her. She covered her face with her hands. How could she possibly have any more tears left? A knock on her door startled her, and for a moment, she hoped.

You're being silly, Olivia, it's probably Evelyn.

She stood and took a deep breath. Opening the door, she found Emma standing there holding Sophie, who squealed when she saw her Aunt Liv. Olivia took her in her arms and smiled. She carried her to the kitchen and smiled at Gabe, who was waiting there.

"What are you doing here, Emma?" she asked bouncing Sophie while avoiding looking either of the adults in the eye.

"Gabe and I were on our way home and thought we'd stop in to see you." Emma smiled at her.

Olivia knew better. "I'm fine, Emma. Don't worry about me, I'll get over him."

Gabe took Sophie from her arms and sat on the floor with her. Emma handed her daughter a wooden spoon, which she used to hit her daddy on the head. Emma laughed.

"You deserve that, Gabriel Stone," she scolded.

Gabe glanced up at Olivia. "I'm sorry, Liv. It's my fault about you and Wyatt. I shouldn't have ribbed him so much about you answering the phone."

Olivia blinked back tears. *Shit! Stop it!* You are so much stronger than this. She tried to give him a brave smile but failed. "It had to end sometime."

Gabe frowned at her. "Why..."

A sudden commotion from the direction of the front foyer stopped his words. They all hurried out to the front.

Stephanie was standing in the foyer yelling at Stacy.

"I'm sorry, Liv. She came in here demanding to see you. I told her to leave, but she refuses." Stacy stood with her hands on her hips glaring at Stephanie.

"It's okay, Stacy." Olivia looked at Stephanie. "What do you want, fluffy?"

"Hiding, are we?" Stephanie smiled with an air of superiority.

"What. Do. You. Want." Olivia narrowed her eyes at her.

"You couldn't hold onto him, could you? You had him and lost him."

"That's something that should sound familiar to you." Olivia stepped closer to her.

Stephanie's smile faded then she laughed. "Your loss is my gain. This time he won't have to beg me to take him back." She stood toe to toe with Olivia. "I'm just happy he's through with you. He never was into women who sleep with any man who comes along."

Olivia bared her teeth. "Back off before I knock you into next week."

Gabe stepped between them. Olivia glared at him. She could handle this herself. He turned toward Stephanie.

"Get out. Now."

Stephanie hesitated then turned and left. Gabe blew out a breath when Olivia turned away from him and headed back toward the kitchen.

* * * *

Three days later, Becca stopped by and had Olivia go to the feed store with her. They rode in silence for a while until Becca finally broke the silence.

"Are you all right, Liv?"

Olivia shook her head. "I can't seem to stop crying."

"I'm so sorry. I wish it hadn't ended like this."

"It's my own fault, Becs. I knew what I was getting into, but you know if he told me he wanted me back, I'd go in a heartbeat."

Becca pulled into the parking lot and shut the truck off, reached for Olivia's hand and gave it a squeeze. When they entered the store, it seemed as if everyone turned toward Olivia. She was wondering what was going on when she spotted him. Wyatt. He was standing in the back talking with a man when he suddenly turned and saw her. Olivia turned away, leaving the store without a word to Becca. She knew her friend would understand.

While waiting in the truck, she saw Wyatt walk out of the store and go right on past her. He didn't even look at her. She sighed in despair. When Becca returned to the truck, they didn't speak but simply waited while the feed was loaded into the back, after which Becca started the engine and pulled out into traffic to head home.

"Did you speak with Wyatt?" Olivia asked, breaking the silence even though it hurt even to say his name.

"Yes. I told him about Stephanie stopping at the B and B. To say he was pissed would be a huge understatement," Becca told her, glancing at her from the corner of her eye.

Olivia groaned. "Why did you have to tell him?"

"Because that crazy bitch needs to learn she can't fuck around with other people's feelings...that's why!"

Olivia's mouth dropped open for a moment then she burst out laughing, and didn't stop until tears ran down her face.

"What's so funny?" Becca asked with a scowl.

"You..." Olivia laughed. "You...said...*fuck*." She fell against the door and laughed even harder.

Becca started laughing with her. "Jake would have a heart attack if he heard me say that."

They rode home laughing. Olivia felt better than she had in days. Becca dropped her off and left to head home. Olivia walked in the back door and went straight to her apartment. Punkin snuggled up to her on the couch.

"At least you love me, Punkin girl." She rubbed the dog's ears.

She wondered how Wyatt felt about Stephanie making a scene. The woman needed help. Olivia could understand being upset over losing Wyatt but it was over two years ago, and Stephanie needed to move on. Just like she knew she needed to move on too. It was over and she had to get past the hurt. When she walked away from him last week, she'd left her heart behind.

She hugged Punkin to her.

"What am I going to do, girl? I've never loved anyone the way I love that man and I know I never will again." She choked back tears. "I shouldn't have any more tears left. I've done nothing but cry since I left him. Why hasn't he come after me? I really thought we had something, but I guess it really wasn't the same for him. It was only sex for him. He never lied to me, just like he said he wouldn't." Tears began falling. "How am I going to go on without him? I'm so angry with myself. I don't cry over men. I don't cry period. At least I never did before I laid eyes on him."

She hugged Punkin so tight that the poor dog whined and squirmed. Olivia let her go and got up from the sofa. She missed Wyatt so much. Not too long ago, she'd thought of leaving Montana, so now might be the right time. She'd forever love Wyatt, but staying in Clifton and seeing him would surely kill her. Especially if he started seeing someone else and she just knew that he would. He was a gorgeous, sexy man, and plenty of women wanted him. She'd noticed that right after she first saw him.

Olivia sighed and picked up her laptop. She could check reservations and emails to keep busy. It was her job, along with the books and the website. It would take her mind off Wyatt.

Sure, it would—right.

Chapter Eleven

Olivia couldn't take it any longer. The thought of not having Wyatt was killing her. She was becoming pitiful. She'd had enough of feeling sorry for herself so she decided to woman up and go after the man. Not having him was too hard for her and she was miserable without him. If she had to beg...well then, maybe she would. She was willing to take him any way she could get him. Before she lost her nerve, she picked up her car keys, grabbed a coat, and headed out. As she drove the road toward his ranch, she began to have doubts again. Tightening her grip on the steering wheel, she talked herself back to her goal.

"You've never backed down from anything in your life, now is not the time to start."

She pulled into his driveway and parked by the back door. She glanced toward the arena figuring he was probably in there working the horses. She got out of the car, squared her shoulders, took a deep breath, and strolled casually in that direction. As she entered the building, the heady heat from inside felt good. She glanced around for Wyatt. Her breath left her when she saw him. He had his back to her but she'd know that body anywhere.

His jeans hugged his butt deliciously, and he was shirtless. She bit back a groan at the sight of him. His shoulders and back gleamed with sweat. She slowly walked toward him. It was then she noticed he didn't have his hat on either and the ends of his hair were damp from sweat, and had started curling. He was raking wood shavings around the floor.

When he turned her way, her knees almost buckled. She loved that chest. He raised his head and stared at her. She watched a drop of sweat roll down his chest to his rippled stomach, dip inside his navel, roll back out, and disappear into the top of his jeans. She lifted her eyes again and met his. Looking at him made it difficult to breathe.

Wyatt leaned the rake against the wall, took his shirt from a nearby hook, and put it on. Olivia closed the distance between them and stopped in front of him. She took a deep breath as he continued to stare at her. One dark eyebrow lifted at her as if in question.

"You're not going to make this easy are you, cowboy?"

Wyatt leaned against the wall and hooked his thumbs into his pockets. She moved as close to him as she could without touching him. He tensed up. She hid a smile, stretched up on her tiptoes, and ran her lips along his raspy jaw. He took in a shuddering breath. She ran her tongue along his bottom lip before taking it between her teeth, and then tugged on it. She cupped his face in her hands and kissed him. She felt his entire body tense and his breathing grew heavier. She moved her hands over his chest. He grabbed her wrists. She jerked back from him.

"How long are we going to do this, Olivia, before you run off again? You can't do that every time we have an argument. Around here, we talk about it like adults."

"I'm here now," she replied repentantly.

Wyatt grunted and strode around her, heading toward the door. Olivia couldn't believe he was walking away. She ran after him, and when she reached him, she put her foot between his feet and pushed on his back. He went down like a ton of bricks. He hit the ground and she landed on his back. She sat up and straddled him. She leaned down and whispered in his ear.

"You just said we need to talk things out. Well, I'm here now so let me talk. I'm sorry I got angry over the thing with Gabe. It was stupid. I should be more sensitive to how it is with you and your brothers, but I didn't deliberately set out to cause trouble. I'm sorry, baby," she whispered. "I'm not letting you up until you agree we talk."

Wyatt sighed. "You're not letting me up, huh? Do you seriously think a little spit-fire like you can hold me down?"

"Whether you want to admit it or not, I am holding you down, cowboy."

Wyatt lifted himself up as if doing a push-up with her on his back, and then he rolled to his side knocking her off. He got up in one motion leaving her sitting on the floor. He put his hand out to help her up, but she ignored it and glared at him.

"If this," he said waving his hand between them, "is going to work at all, we don't just walk away when there's a disagreement. We talk about it. You have me dating which I don't do, so if you want to keep doing it, we talk when things go wrong. We're going to have arguments, Olivia."

"You pissed me off, Wyatt. I can't help it if Gabe took it wrong when I answered the phone and I only answered it because I saw it was him." She stood and stomped her foot.

"It's never boring with you, I'll say that," he muttered, glancing to the ceiling of the arena.

Olivia put her hands on her hips, and narrowed her eyes at him. He shifted his to meet hers and smiled at her. Her mouth twitched as she fought her own grin.

"Come here, darlin'," he said in a low tone.

Without hesitation, she leaped into his arms, wrapping her arms around his neck and her legs around his hips. He kissed her, sliding his hands up to cup her face in his hands. She moaned.

"I've missed you, Olivia."

"Then why didn't you come after me?" She pouted.

"You're the one who left over something silly. Yeah, I know I overreacted, but we should have talked about it, not walked away."

She nodded. "You're right. From now on, we talk it out."

Wyatt grinned, dropped her feet to the floor but when she frowned, he picked her up, and tossed her over his shoulder. "I need a shower."

"Need some help?" She snickered as she ran her hands over his butt.

"I might. Why?"

"There are a few parts I wouldn't mind washing for you." She laughed.

Wyatt chuckled. "As long as I get to wash some of yours too."

"I'm sure we can work something out, cowboy." They both laughed as he carried her back to the house, where he pushed the door open then kicked it closed behind them.

* * * *

Wyatt woke up, got out of bed, and moved to gaze out the windows. He gazed out over the in-ground pool, and then back at Olivia. How had this happened? His feelings for her had grown stronger than he wanted. Falling in love was not in the plan. It was just sex. That was all this was supposed to be. He sighed and went to the end of the bed to grab his jeans. He wanted to get out of here but when he saw her lying on the bed, his groin tightened. She was on her stomach with her legs slightly spread.

He dropped the jeans and crawled up behind her on the bed. He nudged her legs wider apart. She stirred a little, but didn't wake up. He ran his hand down over her ass. He swallowed hard when she wiggled slightly under his hands. *God!* He loved her ass. Mentally groaning, he leaned down, running his tongue down along her spine, and moving his hand between her thighs. She moaned loudly when he rubbed his finger over her clitoris.

Olivia glanced over her shoulder at him, and smiled, the heat blazing in her eyes.

Wyatt moved his arm under her waist and lifted her back onto his lap as he sat back on his heels, and thrust into her. Olivia's hands snaked back to wind behind his neck. Her legs straddled his. She ground back against him. He groaned and thrust hard into her and felt her breathing increase. He could feel her tightening around him already.

"Come with me, sweetheart," he whispered against her ear, nuzzling the side of her neck.

Olivia moaned out his name and bucked against him as she came. He groaned and came with her. Her head fell back onto his shoulder and he put his forehead on her shoulder. Both of them tried to catch their breath, until finally, Olivia moved off him and lay flat on the bed.

"Please, roll over," Wyatt told her. She looked at him with a frown, until he smiled.

"That," he said pointing at her backside, "is what started this."

Olivia laughed. "But do you regret it?"

He kissed her. "Never."

"I don't either, baby," she whispered.

He closed his eyes, and then looked at her. "I love it when you whisper that in my ear."

She smiled. "I love when you call me sweetheart and darlin'." She imitated his drawl.

He laughed. "I think every cowboy uses those."

Olivia sat up. "You didn't call Stephanie sweetheart, did you?"

He chuckled at that idea. "No. I didn't call her anything but Stephanie."

Olivia nodded and smiled. "Good. I call her *fluffy* because she's a nonsense piece of fluff."

Wyatt burst out laughing and wrapped his arms around her. "It suits her."

* * * *

Later that afternoon, Olivia walked into the barn to give the horses some apples. She wanted to make a habit of it so she could get used to being around them. Wyatt had gotten her on Cochise several times but she was still afraid of horses. She spotted Cochise in the corral alone and turned toward him. He put his ears back when she stepped up to the rail.

"Come here, you gorgeous beast," she said quietly. The horse whinnied and tossed his head.

She laughed. "Don't tell me no, mister. Come on." She held her hand out.

"That horse hates everyone but Wyatt."

Olivia started and glanced over to find one of the ranch hands standing beside her. He was the same one who'd informed her about Stephanie visiting

Wyatt. He grinned at her. She gave him a half-smile. He was good-looking and he certainly knew it, but she just didn't care for men with blond hair. His blue eyes ran over her, making her feel uncomfortable. She frowned.

Something about him gave her the creeps. He put his fingers to his hat.

"Ben Collins, ma'am," he said by way of introduction.

Olivia nodded. "Nice to meet you."

She didn't bother providing her name.

"My pleasure, Olivia." Ben grinned, moving slightly closer.

Olivia stepped away from him. She had no desire to have a conversation with him, not even to ask how he knew her name, and the fact that he did bothered her. She supposed he just knew it from the people in town or possibly Wyatt might have mentioned it to him. Somehow, she doubted that though. He moved beside her when she moved.

"I tried to unsaddle him once for the boss and the damn horse tried to bite me." He laughed.

Olivia laughed. Maybe he wasn't so bad after all. "I'm afraid of horses. Wyatt's had me on Cochise with him, but I'd never get on one by myself."

"You'd love it if you did. It's really exhilarating feeling all that muscle between your legs."

O-kay! He wasn't talking about horses anymore. She tossed the apple to the horse, but he ignored it. Olivia sighed and turned to leave.

"You aren't giving up, are you?" Ben asked.

"He's never going to come to me." She shrugged. "It was nice talking with you." *Not!*

"How about the other horses? You could give them apples. There are plenty of apples in the barn."

Olivia hesitated. What could he do to her on the ranch? Only, she really didn't trust him for some reason. Wyatt was around somewhere and she wished she knew where—maybe in the barn. She shrugged, nodded her head, and then followed Ben into the barn. He led her to a back stall and jerked his chin for her to go in. She glanced inside and saw a basket of apples. With a smile, she entered the stall. She had just bent over to pick up an apple when he grabbed her around the waist and tossed her down onto the hay. The breath rushed out of her when she landed, and he was on top of her in a heartbeat.

"Get off me," Olivia growled. She tried to knee him, but he had her legs trapped. He laughed and put his face against her neck. She thought she was going to be sick when he started running his tongue over her skin. She grabbed his hair and pulled as hard as she could.

"Pull all you want honey, I love it."

He chuckled, and then tried to kiss her. She bit his lip. He sat up, straddling her to keep her down, and slapped her across the face. Olivia saw stars, but when he reached for her blouse, she reached up and raked her fingernails down his face. He drew his fist back to hit her but it never landed because someone pulled him off her.

Olivia looked up to see Wyatt had him by the collar and was dragging him away from her. He hit Ben in the jaw, knocking him down. Wyatt leaped on him and pounded his fists into Ben's face. She sprang up and ran to them.

"Wyatt! Get off him. You're going to kill him," she shouted and pulled at him but she couldn't budge him. Several ranch hands came running in and succeeded in pulling Wyatt off Ben.

"Get off me," Wyatt shouted as he jerked away from them.

Lucky didn't let go of him even though Wyatt glared at him. The men lifted Ben from the ground. Blood covered his face and his nose looked broken.

"You're fired. Get the fuck off my ranch and don't ever come back." Wyatt stepped toward him threateningly. "And if you even look at her, I'll finish this."

The ranch hands made sure Ben left the ranch. Wyatt glanced at Olivia. His jaw clenched, and then he strode away. Olivia glanced at Lucky, not knowing what to think, and then she started to shake. Lucky wrapped his arm around her, shoulder giving her comfort.

"Are you all right?"

"Yes. Thank...thank you," she whispered, and then burst into tears.

Lucky put his arms around her and pulled her close.

"You just let it out, hon. You'll feel better," Lucky whispered against her hair.

She sobbed and held on to the older man. He'd always seemed distant to her but he was the only one there for her now. She glanced up at him.

"Why's Wyatt angry with me?"

"I don't think that's the case, Liv. He just needs to calm down. I've worked for him since he started this ranch and I've never seen him this angry. I'm sure it surprised him too." He rubbed her back. "It'll be all right. Ben's been a pain in the ass since he was hired. Wyatt only hired him because Ben's older brother works here. He only felt obliged because Kirk asked."

Olivia smiled half-heartedly through her tears and they walked out of the barn together. She walked slowly toward the house while Lucky headed toward the other barn. She entered through the back door and hesitated, wondering where Wyatt was. Walking through the living room, and not finding him there, she headed for the bedroom and poked her head inside. She found him sitting on the bed. He sat there bent over with his forearms on his knees. He was clenching and unclenching his fists. She could see his jaw tightening, while a muscle twitched in his cheek.

"Wyatt..." She stopped when he glanced at her.

"I'm sorry, Olivia. I should've never let him near you."

She gasped. "Good grief. Wyatt, it wasn't your fault."

Wyatt laughed without humor. "It was. I asked him to go tell you where I was. I saw you heading toward the barn and I thought you were looking for me." He stood up quickly. "I knew there was something about him I didn't trust. I wanted to kill him, Olivia. I have never felt such rage in my entire life." He clenched his jaw. "If the men hadn't pulled me off him..."

Olivia moved to stand in front of him. She put her hands over his fists. "You'd have come to your senses..."

Wyatt glared at her. "No. I wouldn't have. I would have killed him." He moved away from her. "I don't like feeling like that." He stared at her. "I can't control myself around you."

"What...what are you saying?" She blinked back tears.

"I don't know..." He took a deep breath. "I'm just so pissed right now. I could put my fist through a wall."

Olivia slowly moved to stand near him. She touched his shoulder. He jerked but didn't move away from her. She stood on her toes and kissed his cheek.

"I know a great way you can relieve that stress," she whispered in his ear, and then took the lobe between her teeth.

Wyatt pulled her into his arms and she wrapped her arms around his waist, resting her head against his chest.

"I'm sorry I walked away. I should have stayed with you...you needed me."

"I need you to make his touch go away. Please, Wyatt."

She choked back tears and looked up at him. He pulled her against him, picked her up, and laid her on the bed. He shed his clothes, stretching out beside her, and after removing her clothes, he gathered her into his arms and proceeded to make them both forget.

The next day, Olivia walked outside and headed toward the barn. She turned and saw Wyatt sauntering toward her from the arena with a smile on his face. She returned his smile and waited for him to reach her. When he did, he pulled her into his arms and kissed her.

"You smell like a horse," she told him. He laughed and pulled her against him again.

"You like my horse." He nuzzled her neck.

"Is that a euphemism?"

Wyatt laughed. "No. Get your mind out of the gutter."

"Oh, please. You like my mind in the gutter."

He reached for her hand. "Come here, I want to show you something."

"I've seen it," she teased.

"Jesus. Just come on." He led her to the barn and inside. "I want you to meet my new girlfriend."

Olivia stopped in her tracks. "You keep her in the barn? At least I get to go in the house."

Wyatt just pulled her along behind him until they reached a stall, and then he nodded toward it. She looked at him wondering what he was up to but then glanced inside. There, a beautiful brown and white horse stood.

She gasped. "Oh! She's so beautiful."

"I thought so. I bought her last month when I was in Butte. She just arrived this morning. If you'd have gotten your ass out of bed earlier, you would have seen her already."

"Excuse me, but some *cowboy* had me up half the night," she muttered.

"I didn't hear any complaints."

"And you never will." Olivia moved closer to the stall. "What's her name?"

"She doesn't have one yet."

"Coco."

"Coco?" Wyatt groaned. "Where do you come up with these names?"

"She has chocolate markings. I could've said chocolate."

Wyatt laughed. "Thank God you didn't. Come on, I need a shower."

"What does that have to do with me? I want to stay here with Coco. I can't believe I just said that."

"I knew these horses would grow on you."

"I'm still not riding one." She shuddered at the

thought. "They're so big."

"You don't have a problem being on Cochise."

"Yes, but you're holding me and I know you won't let me fall."

Wyatt stopped and stared at her. "No. I won't let you fall." She wasn't sure if he was still talking about the horse or not.

"All right," she whispered and followed him inside the house.

Later, Olivia dressed while Wyatt lay on the bed watching her. She smiled at him.

"I wish I didn't have to go yet but it's getting late and I still need to finish going through the reservations."

She put her knee on the bed, leaned down, and kissed him. Wyatt pulled her down on top of him to deepen the kiss.

"You could wait until tomorrow to do that," he said against her lips.

"I'm never going to get caught up as it is. By tomorrow, there'll be a lot more." She kissed him again. "We'll get together again on Saturday. You can wait till then, can't you, cowboy?"

"That's three days away."

"You already did without me for almost a week." She narrowed her eyes at him.

"I was pissed then. I'm not now. Come back here." He put his hand out toward her.

"I'm leaving, cowboy. I'll see you in a few days." She ran from the room, and outside where she got into her car, and quickly headed out toward the B and B before she changed her mind.

The sun glowed red as it slowly sunk behind the mountaintop, coloring the sky with pink, and yellow. It was hard to believe winter would be coming again. More snow would soon blanket the little town. Olivia smiled as she pulled into the driveway of the B and B and saw the parking area full. She walked inside and smiled as Evelyn handed her a plate of hot food.

"I saw you coming up the drive." Evelyn grinned as she wiped her hands on a dishtowel.

Olivia laughed. "I thought for a minute you were a mind reader."

Evelyn burst out laughing. "If I was, I'd be able to know what Stan's thinking." She frowned. "Then again, maybe that's not such a good idea."

Olivia laughed. "I don't think it takes much to read a man's mind. It would simply have the letters s-e-x in big red flashing letters."

Evelyn almost doubled over with laughter. Olivia joined in. She loved being in Montana, which surprised her almost as much as being in love with a cowboy.

* * * *

In less than two weeks, the B and B would close. Most of the rooms were already vacant, and only a few of the staff remained but tonight Olivia was alone at the front counter when a woman walked in. Olivia smiled at her. She looked familiar but Olivia couldn't place her.

"Hello. Welcome to the Clifton Bed and Breakfast...how can I help you this evening?"

The woman was beautiful with dark brown hair that touched her shoulders. She looked to be in her mid-forties, although Olivia really couldn't tell since the woman was wearing sunglasses. Sunglasses, of all things...it was dark outside. Olivia mentally shrugged. It was none of her business.

"I have a reservation. The name's Sharon

Winters." The woman smiled at her.

"Great." Olivia handed her a card to fill out. "Just fill this card out and I'll show you to your room."

She watched as the woman filled out the card. A strange feeling came over her. What was it about this woman that had her on edge? Olivia took the card, picked up the key to the room, and walked around the counter to pick up the woman's luggage. She had two bags. Why did she only have two bags if she was staying almost two weeks? Again, it was none of her business.

Olivia led the way up the stairs with the woman following behind her. A weird shiver ran through her, like the kind when someone claimed somebody had stepped on his non-existent grave. She stopped at the room the woman was staying in and used the key to open the door. She motioned for the woman to precede her.

Olivia set the luggage down and explained about meal times and activities, even though the woman should be familiar with everything since she'd registered online. When she was finished, she turned to go.

"I hope you enjoy your stay with us, Ms. Winters." She clasped the doorknob to pull the door closed behind her when the woman spoke.

"Oh, I'm sure I will...Olivia."

Olivia spun around. "How did you..."

Her heart nearly stopped when the woman removed her sunglasses and Olivia found herself gazing into eyes the exact same color as her own.

"Aren't you going to say hello to your mother, Olivia?" Sharon Winters smiled at her but it didn't reach her eyes.

"My mother died in a car accident seven years

ago. I don't know who you are." Olivia turned to leave the room.

"As much as you obviously hate it and want to deny it, I *am* your mother."

Olivia spun around again, and glared at her. "Why are you here?"

Sharon laughed. "To see my daughter, of course."

Olivia grabbed the doorknob, stepped into the hallway but before closing the door, she glanced back. "Enjoy your stay Missus...what was it? Oh, yes. Winters. Mrs. Winters, the staff will be in tomorrow to take care of your needs. Goodnight."

She closed the door softly when in reality she wanted to slam it so hard that it came off the hinges. Taking a deep breath, Olivia fisted her hands, walked down the stairs, and went straight to her apartment. She sat on the sofa and refused to allow herself to cry. Why was that woman here? What did she want? How had she found her? She lay down and cried herself to sleep.

* * * *

The next morning, Olivia was trying to concentrate on the books when her cell phone rang. She answered without looking at the caller ID.

"Liv?" Becca's voice came over the connection.

"Oh, hi Becs," Olivia said absently.

"Okay, what's wrong?"

"Nothing, why?" Olivia asked.

"You didn't even check your caller ID and you always do. You live by that thing. Did something happen between you and Wyatt again?"

Olivia tried to answer her but it came out as a choked sob.

"I'm on my way," Becca told her and hung up.

Olivia put the phone down and burst into tears. She'd barely slept last night trying to keep the tears at bay, and now she couldn't stop them.

A few minutes later, Becca walked straight into her apartment without knocking. Olivia went to her and cried on her shoulder. Becca wrapped her arms around her. They moved to the couch and sat down.

"Liv? What is it? I thought you and Wyatt were doing great," Becca whispered.

Olivia shook her head in an attempt to tell her it wasn't about Wyatt but couldn't get the words out.

"What did he do?"

Olivia knew Becca was getting angry but no words would come out to explain. When her cell phone rang, Becca picked it up, looked at the name on the screen, and answered it.

"Wyatt Stone, what did you do to Olivia?" Becca yelled into the phone.

Olivia shook her head again as she listened to Becca's end of the conversation.

"She's very upset about something. I assume you two had a fight or something. I can't get anything out of her."

Olivia reached for a tissue and blew her nose. When she reached for the phone, Becca held it away from her.

"Okay. See you in a few minutes." Becca hung up and looked at her. "Wyatt's on his way."

Olivia sighed and shook her head again, swallowed and cleared her throat. "It's not Wyatt. I'll tell you both once he gets here. You're not going to believe it."

When Wyatt came through the door, Olivia stood and wanted to throw herself into his arms so when he didn't stop until he was in front of her, she threw her arms around him. He took a seat on the sofa with her on his lap hugging her to him.

"What's going on, darlin'?" he asked her, caressing her hair with his large hand.

"My mother...no, that's not right. The woman who gave birth to me is here."

Becca leaped up. "Here? In Clifton?"

Olivia snorted. "Here...at the B and B."

"What?" Becca yelled.

"Why?" Wyatt asked.

"I have no idea. She said she was here to see her daughter which is a crock since she hasn't wanted to see me in twenty-eight years."

"How did she know where to find you?" Becca asked.

"I have no clue but she showed up last night. She had a reservation. Sharon Winters is what she's going by now. I remember being told her name was Charlotte, but certainly not Winters."

She began to giggle for no reason and couldn't seem to stop. She knew she was getting hysterical.

"Liv, sweetie. Calm down." Becca squatted down in front of her.

Olivia stared at her through more tears.

"I want to talk to her." She stood and started out the door of the apartment.

Olivia jumped off Wyatt's lap. "No, Becs."

But she was talking to air, Becca was already gone heading to the front desk. She ran after her and heard Becca talking to someone as she came around the corner. Surely, it wouldn't be that easy for Becca. Olivia came to a stop when she saw Sharon standing at the desk with Becca on the other side glaring at her.

"Can I help you? I'm Becca Stone. I own this bed

and breakfast."

Olivia stepped up beside her and glared at Sharon.

"I was on my way out when you stopped me, Mrs. Stone. I don't need..."

Her words faded off when her eyes shifted to the doorway behind Becca and Olivia. A grin suddenly lit her face.

"Well, hello gorgeous. Who are you?"

Both Olivia and Becca turned to see Wyatt leaning in the doorway staring at Sharon with a not so friendly scowl on his handsome face.

Olivia slapped her hand on the desk. "Do you want something?"

She watched as Sharon ran her eyes over Wyatt and it pissed her off.

"You could certainly say that, Olivia." Sharon's eyes didn't leave Wyatt.

He stepped up alongside Olivia and wrapped his arms around her. Sharon grinned.

"Well, well. It seems you've done pretty well for yourself, Olivia."

Olivia strode around the desk. "I'd like to know why you're here. For once in your life, tell the truth."

"I told you. I came to see you—my daughter."

"You don't have a daughter," Olivia screamed at her.

Sharon stepped back but straightened her shoulders. "Whether you like it or not, I'm your mother. My name's on your birth certificate."

Olivia gritted her teeth. "Oh yeah? Who's my father then, or did you forget which one it was?"

She wasn't ready for the slap but once she recovered, she raised her hand to hit her back only

Wyatt stopped her. Olivia glared up at him but then the air went out of her. He was right. Hitting Sharon wasn't worth it.

"Well. I'll be here for two weeks. So there's plenty of time for us to get to know each other again."

"*Again?* We never knew each other before and I have nothing to say to you now or ever." Olivia spun around and left the foyer with Becca following right behind her.

Chapter Twelve

Wyatt stared at Sharon Winters. She was an attractive woman and he could see where Olivia got her looks, but this woman was up to something, and he planned to find out what it was.

"Why *are* you here?" he asked her.

Sharon smiled. "She must get her good taste in men from me. If I were ten years younger, I'd give her a run for her money over you."

He smirked. "You'd never get the chance."

"Never say never, gorgeous. I usually get what I want."

Wyatt never moved. He stood with his arms crossed and didn't take his eyes off her. Then he jerked his head toward the door, telling her to go. After a slight hesitation, she turned and left through the front door. He returned to Olivia's apartment where he found her on the couch with Becca beside her.

"You can go home, Becca. I'll stay with her. You and Jake have to leave early tomorrow morning."

Becca stood. "But so do you. You're going to the sale, aren't you?"

"I can leave from here. I'll have Lucky pick me up." Becca hugged him. "You're a wonderful brother-in-law."

He chuckled and sat down beside Olivia.

"Call me if you need anything, Liv. I mean anything. Perhaps even a shotgun?" Becca grinned and after kissing Olivia's cheek, left.

"Are you really staying here?" Olivia asked him.

"I am." He kissed her forehead.

"I only have a queen size bed. It's not like your big king," Olivia teased.

He made a face. "I guess that means I have to sleep right next to you."

Olivia threw her arms around him. "If you have to, you have to."

A few hours later, Wyatt heard something in the main kitchen. Olivia was asleep beside him. He eased out from the bed and pulled his jeans on. He zipped up but didn't snap them. He crept through the apartment, opened the door quietly, and stepped into the B and B's kitchen. He flipped on the light and saw Sharon Winters standing there in her robe. She started, but then grinned when she saw him.

"You're not allowed in the kitchen. None of the guests are," Wyatt told her.

Sharon smiled at him and slowly walked toward him. "You really are something—tall, dark, and gorgeous. Those eyes are amazing."

Wyatt leaned back against the fridge and folded his arms across his bare chest. "You need to go back to your room."

"How about you? Would you like to go back to my room?"

His mouth twitched in distaste. "Not likely."

Sharon moved closer to him. "I'm really not that much older than you. I'm only forty-six—a cougar." She laughed.

"I'm not into...cougars. But I will tell you this...if you hurt her, you'll deal with me."

Sharon ran her fingernails down his chest and smiled when he stiffened. "I'd love to deal with you, gorgeous."

Her fingertip trailed through the hair

surrounding his belly button which arrowed down to disappear inside his jeans. "I'd love to follow this happy trail," she whispered.

Wyatt sneered and pushed her hand away.

"Not a chance." He straightened up and glared down at her. "Now, get out of the kitchen and don't ever come back in here again or you'll be asked to leave the B and B."

She stared up at him, and then licked her lips. Wyatt clenched his jaw and gave her a terse nod. She fled from the kitchen. He blew out a breath, turned to go back into the apartment, and almost ran over Olivia.

"How long have you been there?" he asked, hating the thought of what she'd seen.

"I came out right when she said she'd love to follow your happy trail. I wanted to filet her."

"*Shit.* I'm sorry."

"It's not your fault that you're tall, dark, and gorgeous," Olivia snickered.

Wyatt growled, picked her up, throwing her over his shoulder, and returned them to her bed.

* * * *

The next morning, Olivia stepped into the kitchen and smiled at Evelyn. She poured herself a cup of coffee and turned to go back into her apartment when out of the corner of her eye, she saw Stan outside talking with a man who had his back to her. Frowning, she walked to the door and looked out. She knew that back all too well.

She opened the back door. Wyatt turned toward the door. He smiled when he saw her. She narrowed her eyes at him with suspicion.

"What are you doing here? I thought you were going to the sale?"

Wyatt strolled over to her. "I decided not to."

"I don't need a babysitter, cowboy," Olivia snapped, knowing he'd stayed behind because of what had happened the night before.

Wyatt halted and raised an eyebrow at her. "I didn't say you did."

She glared at him before stepping back inside and slamming the door. She grumbled as she sat down at the table and scooped up some of the scrambled eggs Evelyn had made for breakfast. She was shoveling a forkful into her mouth when the back door swung open. Wyatt pulled out a chair, turned it around, and straddled it.

"Get up on the wrong side of the bed, sweetheart?" he remarked with a sneer.

"No. I got up just fine. The bed was empty and I thought you'd gone to the sale."

Wyatt reared back. "I stayed because I didn't like leaving you alone with that she-devil who calls herself your mother," he said. His voice became a growl when he said the word *mother*.

Olivia pushed her chair back, stood, and glared at him. "As I already said, I do not need a babysitter."

Wyatt stood. "It seemed like you needed one last night."

"That was low, cowboy. I was in shock last night. She is not going to run me out of here."

"Fine. I'm out of here," he said through gritted teeth.

"Good! Go catch up with your brothers at the sale." She clenched her jaw so hard it ached.

They stood glaring at each other until Evelyn cleared her throat. Olivia had forgotten about her being there and cringed at her witnessing the spat.

Wyatt narrowed his eyes at her, spun on his heel, and went out the door, slamming it behind him.

Olivia blew out a breath, and then sat back down. "Damn him. He makes me so angry. Why would I need him to stay here with me?"

"If I was your age and had a man who looked like that wanting to *babysit* me, I would definitely let him," Evelyn said.

Olivia didn't say anything but simply shook her head and returned to her apartment. She had work to do and she didn't want to think about Wyatt. She was sure that once he calmed down, he'd see her side and know he was wrong. She smiled thinking about how they'd make up. She hoped anyway.

* * * *

A few days went by but there was no word from Wyatt. Olivia didn't have the time to go see him. The B and B closed in a week, and they seemed busier than usual. She was in the kitchen helping Evelyn when Stacy came in.

"There's a woman at the front desk asking for you, Olivia," she announced. "She says she's your mother."

Olivia rolled her eyes and walked out front to the foyer. Sharon stood at the counter. A smile came across her lips when she saw Olivia.

"Were you busy?" she asked.

Olivia shrugged with annoyance. "I do have a job to do here. You know what a job is, don't you, Sharon?"

Sharon burst out laughing. "*Sharon?* You're calling me by my name now?"

Olivia leaned over the counter. "Well, I'm sure as hell not going to call you *mother,*" she said in a fierce whisper.

Sharon shrugged. "Could we talk? Somewhere private?"

Was it possible she was finally going to tell Olivia what she was really doing there? Olivia motioned for her to follow her and led her through the kitchen to her apartment. She waved a hand toward the couch, while she took a seat in the chair.

"Where's that gorgeous man of yours?" Sharon smiled, slyly glancing around.

Olivia leaned forward gripping the arms of the chair. "Is that what you want to talk about? Wyatt?"

"Wyatt." Sharon seemed to purr his name. "Sexy name for a sexy man."

"Get out," Olivia told her coming to her feet and pointing toward the door.

"You're in love with him, aren't you?" Sharon laughed. "Oh, Olivia, you're such a fool. Don't you know men only want one thing? Of course, if that man wanted it from me, I'd be more than happy to give it to him."

"I will not discuss Wyatt with you," Olivia shouted. She didn't care if every person in the B and B heard her.

Sharon waved her hand. "Fine then...I want money."

Olivia's mouth dropped open. "What makes you think I have any?"

The woman snorted. "I know the Daniels' left you money. I know your little coffee shop sold and you have a job here. You have money, Olivia, and I want some of it."

Olivia marched over to the door and opened it. "Get out. Now!"

Sharon stood and moved toward the door, stopping in front of Olivia.

"You will give me what I want. Trust me, because I can make sure you never see Wyatt again." She leaned close to Olivia. "Don't underestimate me and don't go to the police. I know all the wrong kinds of people. People who will have no problem making things happen. Do we understand each other?"

Olivia nodded, and then slammed the door behind Sharon as soon as she was in the hallway. She walked to the couch, collapsed on it, and started shaking as Sharon's words sunk in. Would she really do something to hurt Wyatt? She really didn't know anything about the woman who had given birth to her. That was, nothing other than she'd gotten herself pregnant at sixteen and two years later decided she didn't want the child around anymore.

She wrapped her arms around herself and rocked, suddenly frightened by this stranger. She didn't know how much money Sharon wanted but she was sure it was way more than what she had. Despite what Sharon thought, the coffee shop hadn't been a big payoff. After she paid off the mortgage, there hadn't been much left. The Daniels' had left her money, but she didn't even know how much. She hadn't wanted to know. All she knew was she felt she hadn't deserved it. Sure, she had loved them and they had loved her but she wasn't their blood, and she'd been terrible to them for a while.

Sitting up, she came to a decision. No. She might not deserve the money she had inherited but she wouldn't touch it, especially to satisfy this bitch. She wasn't going to let Sharon run all over her. She was going to tell the bitch she wouldn't get money from her and she wouldn't hurt Wyatt or anyone else Olivia loved. With that in mind, she pulled herself up from the couch, squared her shoulders, and went to her little kitchen to get something to eat. Sharon Winters was not going to ruin anything for her.

* * * *

Wyatt stopped along the edge of the corral when he heard a truck coming up the drive.

When he realized it was Jake's, he knew this couldn't be good. Jake rarely came over without calling first. He figured it had something to do with Olivia. He watched as the truck came to a stop but was surprised when Becca hopped out.

Shit!

He watched as she marched up to him, stopped, and then stood with her hands on her hips and glared at him. He sighed.

"Why haven't you gone back to see her?"

"She's the one who said she didn't need me. I left. What was I supposed to do, Becca?"

"You know how she is. She blows up, and then it's over. I want to tell you about her life," Becca said.

"I know all about it. She told me. It doesn't excuse the fact she threw my help back in my face." Wyatt shook his head. "I'm done, Becca. I've had enough."

"You're going to let your relationship fall apart because of her temper? Her mother has her so confused right now. She sure as hell doesn't need you leaving her," Becca said with anger.

He put his hands on his hips and narrowed his eyes. "First off, there is no *relationship* to let fall apart. It was only sex between us. Second, I'm not leaving her. She told me she didn't need me."

"Sex? You think it was just sex?" Becca grabbed his arm when he started to move away.

"Yes, damn it. It's what we agreed it would be. Otherwise, it never would have happened. I've told everyone over and over again that I'm not looking for any kind of relationship other than sex, but none of you can get it through your heads. I had a relationship and look how that turned out." He spun on his heel and stalked away from her.

"You're an idiot," Becca yelled. He turned to look at her. "Yes, you are, Wyatt Stone."

She ran toward him and halted in front of him. "You want to live alone the rest of your life and let a woman like Olivia go, then you're an idiot. She's crazy about you. She has been since she first saw you and now you want to end it. Fine. Do that, but let me tell you something, you are going to break her heart. You think *just sex* would do that?" She whirled away from him, climbed into her truck, and drove away, leaving him standing there.

* * * *

Olivia was covering the counter when Sharon walked up to it. Olivia swore under her breath.

"I'd like to take a drive. Where should I go?" the woman asked.

Olivia burst out laughing. "You don't need me to tell you where to go."

"I could always go find that man of yours and take his mind off you. I know I could get him, Olivia."

Olivia shrugged. "You'll be happy to know we aren't seeing each other anymore."

"You aren't a very good liar. You're just saying that thinking I'll leave him alone. If it really is over between you then I'd love to find him." Sharon leaned across the counter. "I don't care if you're seeing him or not. If I want him, I'll have him." She laughed. "You get me the money I want and I'll leave you both alone. Of course, that saddens me."

Olivia raised her eyebrows in shock.

"Not because of you. I have no feelings whatsoever for you but that man of yours, now he would be worth sticking around for." Sharon turned away from her even as Olivia wanted to rip the woman's hair out. "I mean it, Olivia. I want money."

"I told you. I. Don't. Have. Any," Olivia replied through clenched teeth.

Jake suddenly appeared from the hallway. "Liv? What's going on?"

Olivia wanted to groan when she saw Sharon's eyes widen at the sight of Jake. She saw her grin at him, and then it grew when Gabe sauntered in a moment later.

"Well. The scenery really is amazing around here." Sharon glanced at Olivia. "Why didn't you tell me there were more of them?"

She strode toward the men, stopping in front of them.

"You have to be related to Olivia's man."

"If you mean Wyatt, we're his older brothers," Jake informed her. "Who are you?"

Olivia snorted. "This is my...the woman who gave birth to me."

Sharon put her hand out. "Sharon Winters and you are...?"

"Jake Stone and this is my brother, Gabe." Jake didn't put his hand in hers.

"I can certainly see why you live in this godforsaken town, Olivia."

Becca and Emma arrived next and stood by their

husbands. Sharon burst out laughing.

"This is priceless. Is this your own little army, Olivia?"

Olivia strode around the desk and stood close to Sharon. "I don't need an army. I can take care of you myself." She grinned. "Want to see?"

Sharon stepped back. "I'm going for a little drive." She glared at Olivia. "You and I will talk later."

She went out the front door without looking back.

Everyone breathed a sigh of relief when she disappeared.

"I hate that woman," Olivia cried. "I need to see Wyatt. I think I'll go...what?" she asked when she saw a look pass between all of them.

"Nothing," Jake told her.

"Bullshit, Jake. You are a horrible liar." Olivia glanced at Becca. "There's something you're not telling me. Is he all right? Did something happen?" Her voice rose as panic began to set in.

"Let's go to your room and we'll talk." Becca led her away.

Once in the apartment, Becca told Olivia about the conversation she'd had with Wyatt.

Olivia jumped up from the sofa and clenched her fists.

"What?" she shouted at Becca. "He's breaking things off with me? *Through you?*"

"Liv, just give him time to think about what it's like without you," Becca suggested.

"No. I'm going over there right now. He's not breaking it off with me through his sister in-law," Olivia muttered as she grabbed her car keys and ran out the door.

* * * *

Wyatt was riding Cochise around the arena when the door opened. He glanced over and swore under his breath as he reigned in the horse and dismounted. Cochise put his ears back.

"We just can't get rid of her can we, buddy." Wyatt rubbed the horse's neck and led him to the stall where he wiped him down, fed, and watered him.

"You can't just ignore me, Wyatt."

"I can sure give it a hell of a good try, Stephanie." He glanced at her. "I thought I told you not to come back here."

"I heard you weren't seeing your little slut anymore, so I decided to come over and see you." She smiled at him.

He glared at her.

"I don't want you talking about Olivia that way and I sure as hell don't want you here." He strode away from her but she grabbed his T-shirt in her hands and stopped him.

"Wyatt. I forgive you for seeing her. We can be together now."

Wyatt clasped her arms in his hands. "Look, I know this is all an act with you but I can't figure out why. You don't want me back any more than I want you back." He gave her a small shove. "Go away."

He moved past her and headed out of the barn. That's when he saw Olivia pull up in her SUV. He groaned thinking he must be in hell. He watched her march across the yard to him and come to a halt in front of him. Those beautiful eyes of hers were shooting flames at him.

"You can't break it off with me in person? You

had to have your sister-in-law tell me?" Olivia had her hands on her hips, and her lips tightened into a flat line.

Wyatt opened his mouth but Stephanie came up behind him. "This is why you're telling me to leave? Because your...*she* was coming here?"

Wyatt didn't shift his gaze away from Olivia but instead watched as her mouth dropped open and her eyes widened, and then narrowed—dangerously.

"Fluffy? Really?"

Olivia folded her arms over her chest as she stared up at him and then she moved her eyes to Stephanie, who was staring right back at her. He had a bad feeling about this. He saw Stephanie swallow and nearly laughed because she was not quite as tough as she wanted to appear. He ran his hand down over his face.

Christ, why me?

"You want him? You got him," Olivia exclaimed as she spun around to head back toward her car.

Wyatt moved fast and wrapped his hands around her waist, pulling her close to put his mouth next to her ear. "Do you seriously think I'd have her here?"

"She doesn't want you, Wyatt. She said so." Stephanie stepped up beside them.

Olivia jerked out of his arms. "You didn't even have the balls to break it off with me in person."

He sighed. "I was upset. You told me you didn't need me. How was that supposed to make me feel?"

"You were upset because you thought I didn't need you?" Olivia asked.

"You *didn't* need me. You told me you didn't need a babysitter but I wasn't being a babysitter, I was there for you because Sharon was here." Wyatt stared into her eyes and hoped she could see he was telling her the truth. He had missed her so much.

Stephanie huffed. "You're going to come crawling back to me one day, Wyatt Stone. When your little slut's done with you and moving on to the next cowboy, you'll come back to me."

"That's it," Olivia growled and reached out to grab Stephanie.

Wyatt quickly grabbed her around the waist, picking her up so her feet dangled off the ground.

"Put me down," she hissed.

"I think it's time you got the hell out of here. I'm not sure how long I can hold her," he told Stephanie. When she hesitated, Wyatt shrugged and started to lower Olivia to her feet.

"This is just great. You told me to come here, Wyatt, then she shows up and you act like I don't even exist," Stephanie shouted at him.

"Are you still here?" he asked Stephanie.

Wyatt kept his hold on Olivia as Stephanie ranted. Finally, she stormed away from them and left. He blew out an exasperated breath.

"Christ, she's a pain in the ass," he muttered.

"Put me down. Now," Olivia told him.

He slowly lowered her to her feet. She turned and glared up at him. Wyatt tilted his head as he gazed down at her. When her mouth twitched, he reached out and pulled her close to him.

"I've missed you, sweetheart," he whispered in her ear. He grinned when she shivered.

"You know, you could be married to her right now," Olivia told him.

"That shit's not even funny," he muttered.

Olivia laughed and wrapped her arms around him. "I'm so glad you're not."

She squealed when he threw her over his shoulder and headed for the house. "Must you always carry me this way, and just where do you think you're taking me, cowboy?"

"I seem to recall you saying something about me not having any balls. I need to prove that I do and I like carrying you this way. It gives me great access to your fantastic ass." Wyatt ran his hand over her jean-covered ass while carrying her into the house.

Sometime later, Wyatt woke up with Olivia's head on his shoulder. He knew the minute she woke up because she blew out a breath.

"What was that for?" he asked in a sleepy voice.

Olivia jerked. "Sorry, I didn't mean to wake you up."

Wyatt moved away from her and sat up. "It's fine. I'm hungry."

"Me too." Olivia smiled up at him.

"You're always hungry."

Olivia sat up and wrapped her arms around his neck. "Always hungry for you, cowboy," she said with a laugh that made him feel great.

Wyatt wrapped his arms around her.

"I'll fix us something." He stood up.

Olivia flopped back on the bed. "Are you sure? I can wait a little longer."

He gazed down at her and shook his head. "I can't. If I get back in that bed with you, I'll die of starvation. You wouldn't want that, would you?"

She laughed with a naughty glint in her amazing eyes. "No. You need your strength, cowboy."

"I sure as hell do where you're concerned."

* * * *

Three days later, Olivia was sitting at the front counter when Sharon came striding in. She halted at the desk, and glanced around as if to make sure they were alone then leaned forward.

"I want seventy-five thousand dollars, and I want it within the week. I'll stay in town until you get it for me then I'll leave, and you'll never hear from me again."

"Are you out of your fucking mind? I don't have that kind of money," Olivia exclaimed, trying to keep her voice down.

Sharon smiled slyly. "You might not, but I bet that hunk of yours does."

Olivia gasped. "I can't ask Wyatt for that kind of money."

"I guess we'll be seeing quite a lot of each other then. Until you give me the money, I'll be staying right here in Clifton." Sharon turned away from her with a grin, and glided up the stairs to her room.

Olivia blinked tears from her eyes. She knew she had no choice. To get rid of Sharon, she'd have to give her money. She marched to her apartment and found the number for the bank where the Daniels had deposited money into an account in her name. She groaned at the thought of doing this. Becca could never know about it. It would be the end of their friendship if she found out Olivia had used the money to pay off Sharon.

She was heading back through the main kitchen but turned toward the foyer when she heard the front door open. She watched as Wyatt walked toward her and for the first time ever, she was wishing he hadn't come by—not right now anyway.

"Hey darlin'," Wyatt said with a smile.

She glanced away and didn't respond. She felt

his hand at her chin lifting it to force her to look at him.

"What's wrong, sweetheart?" he asked as he moved his hand up to cup her cheek.

She leaned into his hand. It would be so easy to tell him what Sharon wanted, but she didn't want to burden anyone else with her problem.

"Nothing. I guess I'm just tired," she whispered.

Wyatt frowned at her. "Tired, huh?" He smiled. "Then I guess that means I'll be sleeping alone tonight."

"I said I was tired cowboy, not dead." Olivia glared at him.

He chuckled. "Will you come over later? I'll fix dinner. God knows, I know you'll be hungry."

She swatted at him and laughed. "I'll be there. I get off at four."

Wyatt gave her a wicked grin. "I'll make sure you get off again after dinner."

This drew another chuckle from her. "You are so bad, Wyatt Stone."

He leaned down and kissed her fast and hard. "Later, darlin'."

Olivia sighed as she watched him saunter away. She was so in love with him and in way over her head. She was going to end up with a broken heart yet. It was already beginning to crack, but if she didn't get rid of Sharon soon, she was also going to go insane.

Chapter Thirteen

Wyatt, Jake, and Gabe sat at a table in the diner having lunch when Sam sauntered toward them. Wyatt pushed a chair out with his foot.

"Have a seat, Sam," he said with a nod of his head.

"Thanks. I *was* just going to pick something up, but Betty Lou's driving me crazy today," Sam said with a smirk.

The men chuckled. Betty Lou Harper was sixty-five years old and the sheriff's dispatcher slash secretary. Sam hired her because his mother asked him to and soon discovered Betty Lou could drive a crazy person sane, but he loved her.

"What's she on you about today, Sam?" Gabe asked.

"That I should be married by now. She's not getting any younger, she says." Sam rubbed his chin. "My own mother doesn't get on me like Betty Lou does."

Wyatt chuckled. "You're like a son to her, Sam. Of course she wants to see you have kids."

Sam snorted. "I have to have a woman first."

After they finished their lunches, they all headed outside onto the street. Wyatt nudged Jake. "Look over there." He jerked his chin toward the sidewalk across the street and heard Jake swear.

"What's going on?" Sam asked, curious and looking in the direction of their gazes.

Wyatt couldn't believe what he was seeing. Sharon Winters stood on the sidewalk talking with Stephanie as if they were old friends. He saw

Sharon glance their way, and then she crossed the street toward them. She stopped in front of them.

"It must be my lucky day." She smiled at them.

Wyatt watched as she boldly ran her eyes over Sam. "What makes you think it's your lucky day?" he scoffed.

"I'm going in for lunch. Maybe one of you gorgeous men could join me." She glanced at Wyatt. "Or all of you."

"I don't believe I've had the pleasure," Sam said smiling at her.

Wyatt laughed. Jake coughed. Gabe swore. Sam frowned.

"This..." Wyatt muttered, "is the woman who gave birth to Olivia."

"Hello, Sheriff," Sharon purred.

"She's up to no good," Wyatt informed Sam none too quietly.

"Is that so?" Sam's mouth tightened as he looked at her.

"I'm just here to see my daughter." Sharon glared at Wyatt.

"That's a damn lie. Why would you suddenly want to see her after twenty-eight years?" Wyatt was pissed and not worrying about hiding the fact.

"I just want to get to know her..."

"Bullshit," Wyatt growled. He jerked his eyes to Jake when his brother gripped his bicep.

"Let it go, Wyatt. Eventually, we'll find out why she's really here," Jake told him.

Sharon huffed, tossed her hair back, and proceeded into the diner. Wyatt blew out a breath.

"You want to tell me what's going on? Do I need to look into this woman?" Sam asked them with a scowl as he watched her walk away.

"I wish you would," Gabe said. "Liv says she goes by Sharon Winters now but that isn't the name she remembers her by. She thinks it was Charlotte something."

Sam was writing down what Gabe said. He nodded. "I'll let you know what I find out."

Sam left them and strode down the street, waving to someone who yelled a greeting.

Wyatt glanced behind him to stare into the diner where he could see Sharon had taken a seat and was watching them.

"She's here for no other reason than to hurt Olivia in some way," he said, turning toward his brothers.

"I agree." Jake nodded. "Why would she be here after all these years? And how the hell did she ever find Liv?"

"I'm sure we'll find out what she's up to with Sam looking into her." Gabe glanced over his shoulder into the diner.

Wyatt wanted to know why she was talking to Stephanie too. Did Stephanie have something to do with her being here? He suddenly turned on his heel and headed back into the diner. Jake and Gabe followed him as he weaved his way through the tables to where Sharon was sitting, stopping alongside her table.

"Why were you talking with Stephanie?" Wyatt asked through clenched teeth.

"Who?" Sharon blinked up at him with an innocent expression or as innocent as the viper could look.

Wyatt grumbled. "Don't give me that shit. You were talking with Stephanie Taylor before you came across the street."

Sharon's eyes widened. "Oh, I only asked her where I could get something to eat. I don't know her."

"I don't believe you," Wyatt said.

"I really don't care what you believe, gorgeous. It's the truth. Now, if you don't mind, I'd like to eat my lunch."

Wyatt's jaw clenched. He was about to say something when Jake stepped forward.

"We'll find out what you're doing here and if you're here to hurt Liv, we will run your ass out of town." Jake glared at her.

Wyatt watched as she shifted her eyes around the diner. Everyone was looking at them. He nudged Jake and nodded for them to leave. The brothers left the diner and headed for their trucks. Wyatt drove home wondering what Sharon Winters was up to, and he knew in his gut that she was up to something no good. He just needed to find out what.

Two days later, he walked through the door of the B and B and almost ran over Sharon. He instinctively put his hands on her hips to steady her. She gazed up at him with Olivia's eyes. He mentally shook his head. No. They weren't Olivia's eyes. Sharon's eyes were cold and calculating whereas Olivia's were warm, and sparkled when she gazed up at him.

"Thank you, Wyatt," Sharon said in a husky voice.

He gave her a terse nod and stepped back from her. She stepped closer.

"You know, anytime you change your mind, I'm just up the stairs," she whispered as she put her hand over his fly.

Wyatt jumped back from her as if her touch had burned him. Olivia chose just that moment to enter the foyer. Sharon didn't take her eyes off him. Olivia moved beside him and wrapped her arms around his waist. He put his arm around her shoulder.

Sharon looked over at Olivia and met her gaze. "Remember what I told you." Then she walked out the front door.

"What is it you're supposed to remember?" Wyatt asked looking down at Olivia.

"Nothing," she whispered glancing away.

Not believing her, Wyatt took her hand and led her back to her apartment. Once inside, he insisted she sit on the couch, closed the door, and then joined her there.

"Tell me, sweetheart."

Olivia burst into tears. He wrapped his arms around her and waited for her to calm down. When she finally quieted, he tilted her chin up and kissed her tenderly.

"Tell me," he whispered against her lips, and then listened as she explained everything to him. What Sharon wanted and how she threatened to harm Wyatt if Olivia didn't comply.

Anger tightened his body so much that he had to get to his feet. "You are not to give her any money." He put his hand up when Olivia started to object. "No. I mean it, Olivia. Do not give her one red cent."

Olivia stood, wearing an expression of defeat. "I don't have a choice, Wyatt. It's the only way she'll leave and get out of my life." She put her hand on his arm. "I saw her touching you."

"*Shit!*" He closed his eyes wishing she hadn't seen that. "It shocked the hell out of me too."

"She's one crazy bitch and I want her out of my life."

"That doesn't mean you give her money in the hope of getting rid of her. She's the kind to keep coming back for more. Sam is going to check into her. Do you remember what last name she used when she was going by Charlotte?"

"I think it was Mitchell, but I'm not positive about that." She shrugged. "It could've been Roberts, since that's mine."

He nodded. "I'll let Sam know."

"What are you doing here anyway?" Olivia gazed up at him.

Wyatt grinned. "I was just heading back from town so I thought I'd stop in and see how you're doing."

Olivia wrapped her arms around him, pulled his head down, and kissed him. He wrapped his arms around her, lifted her up, and deepened the kiss.

"I want you, darlin'," he murmured against her lips.

"I want you too." Olivia smiled.

They sprang apart when a sudden knock sounded on her door.

Wyatt groaned and set her down, but raised his hand when she started for the door. He strode over to it and opened it to find Stacy standing there.

"Oh...hi, Wyatt, I just wanted to let Liv know I'm leaving. She needs to cover the desk until seven tonight."

He heard Olivia swear behind him. He glanced back at her. "You have to work?"

"I forgot. Stacy told me yesterday she was leaving early today." She shrugged and stuck her bottom lip out in disappointment. She wasn't the only one disappointed by the news.

Wyatt nodded and sighed.

"Okay, I'll call you later then." He smiled then kissed Olivia quickly on her mouth, and moved around Stacy to make a fast exit.

* * * *

The next day, Olivia met Becca for lunch at the diner. As they sat there enjoying their lunch, the door opened and Sharon came striding in with Stephanie. Olivia almost choked on her drink.

"Are you all right, Liv?" Becca asked.

"Sharon just walked in with Stephanie," Olivia whispered.

Becca glanced around. When she spotted them, she turned back to face Olivia. "Why are they together?"

"Two people I can't stand most, together. Imagine that."

"I think we need to let Sam know about this. Sharon is here for a reason and Sam needs to know she's buddies with Stephanie." Becca turned to look at them again.

"They're not sitting together. They went to separate tables," Olivia said as they stood to leave. She noticed Sharon looking her way but Olivia refused to look at her.

After leaving the diner, Olivia and Becca crossed the street and walked the few blocks to the Sheriff's department. Betty Lou Harper smiled up at both of them.

"Hi, girls," she said with a big smile.

Olivia smiled. "Hello, Betty Lou. How are you?"

Then she mentally groaned when Betty Lou proceeded to tell her exactly how she was. Becca nudged her as they tried not to laugh.

"Liv? Becca? What are you two doing here?" Sam asked as he sauntered toward them.

Olivia bit back a sigh. Sam was so hot. Those baby blues were absolute killers. *If I weren't so crazy about Wyatt...*

"Hi, Sam." Olivia grinned up at him.

"Can we talk in your office a minute?" Becca asked.

Sam gave a worried frown but had them follow him. He nodded for them to take seats and then he sat behind his desk. They sat in the chairs opposite him.

"Olivia's birth mother is in town and we're sure she's up to no good. We just saw her and Stephanie Taylor talking," Becca told him.

Sam nodded. "I know. It's not the first time either. Wyatt, Jake, Gabe, and I saw them talking the other day."

"Could you check into her for me?" Olivia asked.

"I'm on it. I already called a friend at the U S Marshals' Office in Butte. He'll get back to me in a few days, I'm sure."

"Is it possible Stephanie had Sharon come here to mess with me?" Olivia asked.

"Anything's possible, Liv. With the Internet the way it is today, just about anyone can be found," Sam told her. "Stephanie's made it clear she's not happy about you and Wyatt so nothing would surprise me, but what does she hope to gain? Wyatt's not going back to her no matter what she does."

"I agree, but Stephanie won't give up. I'm sure she's behind Sharon being here," Becca said.

After talking a little longer with Sam, and confirming all the information she had on Sharon,

Olivia and Becca thanked him and left the office. She felt Becca boring a stare through her.

"Spill it, Liv."

"She wants money from me. I told her I didn't have any, but she knows your parents left me some." She glanced at Becca, feeling guilty about it all. "I don't know what to do. Wyatt said I'm not to give her a single penny—"

"He's right. Don't you dare give her any money," Becca exclaimed.

"Becca, she threatened to harm Wyatt."

Becca gasped. "You need to march right back in there and tell Sam that."

"It'll just be her word against mine, Becs."

"I don't know...I suppose you're right. We'll talk about it later. You're still coming tonight for Jake's birthday party at the town hall, aren't you?"

Olivia smiled.

"Of course, I am. Wyatt's picking me up." She hugged her friend. "I'll see you tonight. I love you, Becs."

Becca waved goodbye, got into her vehicle, and drove away. Olivia headed home as well and since she had a few hours before Wyatt was picking her up, she decided she'd work on the website a while longer. Only a few more days and the B and B would close and Sharon would be out of her hair. But sadly, not out of Clifton.

Olivia bit her bottom lip with her teeth. If she gave Sharon the money she could be rid of her, and she definitely wanted her gone and out of her life, which made her ponder how Sharon had found her at all. As Sam had reminded her, the Internet was full of information but why show up all of a sudden? Becca's parents died seven years ago and the coffee shop sold months ago, so why had Sharon shown up now? It all seemed to come back to when Olivia started seeing Wyatt, and that was why she suspected Stephanie had something to do with it.

Too distracted to work, she returned to her apartment, fed Punkin, took a shower, dressed, and sat down to wait for Wyatt to pick her up. She was so anxious to see him. They hadn't had much time together lately and she missed him terribly. When someone knocked on her door, she jumped up and ran to open the door, only to groan aloud when she saw Sharon standing there.

"What do you want?" Olivia demanded folding her arms across her chest.

Sharon pushed her way in, and then spun around to stare at her. "You know why I'm here. I'm getting tired of this one-horse hick town. I want to leave, and I want my money."

"Well, you sure as hell aren't getting any."

Wyatt surprised them both when he strode in before Olivia could shut the door.

"So, she told you, huh?" Sharon waved her hand. "No matter. If you want me out of your lives, you'll give me the money I want."

Wyatt folded his arms across his chest and glared at her. "Then I guess you'll be staying in Clifton for a while because it'll be a cold day in hell before you get any money from either of us."

"You'd better give that some more thought, gorgeous. I can make your life a living hell," Sharon shouted.

"Are you threatening me? Because if you are...bring it on. I can take anything you dish out." Wyatt clenched his jaw. "You will get nothing from us."

Sharon's eyes widened, and then she smiled. "It looks like we're going to become a family after all, Olivia." She narrowed her eyes at Wyatt. "Think about it."

She marched through the door, slamming it behind her.

Olivia let out a breath and sat down. She was shaking. Wyatt crouched in front of her and took her hands in his.

"She's bluffing. Once she finds out we're not giving her the money, she'll leave. She hates it here."

"I hope you're right. I can't live in the same town she does." Olivia shuddered.

"All the more reason to get rid of her since I sure as hell don't want you going anywhere, darlin'."

She grinned at him. "You're so getting lucky tonight, cowboy."

Wyatt laughed. "Let's go celebrate Jake's birthday and just put the bitch out of our minds."

He stood and put his hand out to her. Olivia placed her hand in his and they set off together to Jake's birthday party.

As usual, the citizens of Clifton had packed the town hall. Anytime there was a reason to celebrate, just about the entire town turned out. When Olivia and Wyatt entered, people waved and called out to them. She laughed in delight.

"This is such a tightknit community. I love it." She gazed up at Wyatt, and he grinned.

"Tightknit, as in knowing everyone else's business, you mean."

Olivia was about to reply when Becca and Jake walked forward to meet them.

"I was wondering where you were," Becca said

with far too much worry in her voice.

"I had a lovely visit from Sharon, but I don't want to talk about it right now." She grinned at Jake.

"Happy Birthday, handsome," she exclaimed before kissing Jake's cheek.

"Thanks, Liv." Jake grinned and shook Wyatt's hand. "Come sit with us. Gabe and Emma are already here."

A few hours later, Olivia sat in her seat holding Sophie as she gazed around the room. She noticed Sam Garrett sitting alone. She watched as his eyes swept the room. She glanced in the same direction where his gaze had stopped, and spotted Sharon. What in the hell was she doing there? Olivia noticed how Sam watched her.

"Who are you looking at, Liv?" Emma asked as she reached for her daughter.

"Sam Garrett."

Emma laughed. "I know...nice scenery. He can arrest me anytime."

Olivia smiled. "He's hot, isn't he? I just noticed he's sitting alone but he's watching Sharon."

"Sharon is here?" Emma asked with raised eyebrows glancing around.

"Yep." Olivia jerked her chin toward where Sharon was sitting.

Emma turned to look. She whipped her head back around, and then slipped into the seat next to Olivia.

"She has no business being here. Let's ask Sam to sit with us. I hate seeing him sitting alone anyway." Without hesitation, Emma was back out of her seat and Olivia watched her stride across the floor to speak with Sam. He stood when she reached him, towering over her.

Olivia grinned when Sam took Sophie from Emma. A gorgeous guy who had no problem holding a baby, how much sexier could one man get? She watched as Sam followed Emma back toward her.

"Hey, Sam." Olivia smiled at him.

Sam grinned at her. "Hi, Liv. How are you?"

"Great. Are you here alone?"

"I have to work tonight to cover for Brody. He's out with the flu. I just stopped in before I have to go into the office." He took a seat at the table and bounced Sophie on his knee. *Yeah, sexy!*

Jake and Becca were on the dance floor dancing to a slow song and looking completely in love. Olivia scanned the crowd for Wyatt but couldn't find him, which didn't surprise her since the place resembled the inside of a sardine can. When she finally spotted him, she stood up and glared at him. She saw him frown at her as he came toward her.

"What?" he asked.

"What's that?" She pointed to the cupcake in his hand.

"It's called a cupcake, darlin'." He grinned at her.

"A cupcake?" she repeated.

"Yes. It's like a cake, only smaller," he teased.

Olivia put her hands on her hips. "I know what a cupcake is, Wyatt. Why are you eating it?"

"Because I like them?" He was looking at her as if she was crazy. She took it from him.

"What the...?"

"It's chocolate," she said clenching her jaw. Wyatt nodded. "You don't like chocolate."

His eyebrows shot up. "I don't?"

Olivia moved closer to him until she was almost touching him. "I remember a day when I had chocolate all over me and I asked you if you wanted to lick it off. You specifically told me you didn't like chocolate."

Wyatt stared at her for a long moment, and then suddenly burst out laughing. He pulled her tight against him. "Sweetheart, if I had licked the chocolate off you that day, we'd still be on the kitchen floor."

Olivia tapped her fingers against his chest. "So...you lied to me?" She watched as his lips twitched.

"Yes. Yes, I did."

"You, Wyatt Stone, are in *big* trouble."

Wyatt ran his lips along her jaw. "How can I make it up to you?"

She moaned when his teeth nipped her neck. "I'll have to think of something."

He ran his lips to her ear. "You do that, darlin', and let me know. I'd do anything to make it up to you."

Olivia moaned again.

"For now, just kiss me, cowboy." He did.

As a group, they all sat at the table chatting, laughing, and enjoying the music when Olivia felt Wyatt stiffen up beside her. She glanced around expecting to see Sharon but instead, she saw Ryder Wolfe approaching them. She hid a grin as he took a seat beside her.

"Hi, Liv," he said to her.

"Hi, Ryder, how are you?"

"I'm good." He glanced around her to look at Wyatt and nodded. "Wyatt."

"Wolfe," Wyatt practically growled.

Olivia chuckled when she heard Ryder laugh. "Something wrong, Wyatt?"

"Not a thing, Wolfe. Are you alone?"

"I came alone, if that's what you mean."

Wyatt muttered under his breath and Olivia swore she heard him say something about not getting any ideas about leaving with her. She snickered, and then covered it with a cough when he glared at her. She batted her eyes at him. Ryder stood and grinned at them.

"You two have a nice evening." He put his fingers to his hat and chuckled as he walked away.

"Do you have a problem with Ryder?"

"I don't want to discuss Wolfe with you," Wyatt told her.

She nodded. "Sure."

She grinned at him and let the subject drop, but she knew Wyatt didn't like Ryder talking to her. He had seemed jealous of Ryder ever since they'd gone on a date together. Olivia stopped herself from laughing. One date, it had been one date. She leaned over and kissed Wyatt's cheek.

* * * *

Later in the evening, everyone seemed to be winding down a bit when Becca went up on the stage and called for everyone's attention.

"I want to say happy birthday to my wonderful, gorgeous, sexy husband, Jake. I gave him his present earlier."

Everyone laughed.

"No! Not that." Becca giggled. "But I have one more for you, Jake." She took a deep breath. "I'm pregnant."

The place went silent until Jake let out a whoop then the place erupted with good cheers. Olivia watched Jake pull Becca off the stage and hug her. Olivia got tears in her eyes. She glanced at Emma to see her crying too. Wyatt and Gabe were congratulating their brother. Olivia ran over to Becca, and hugged her.

"I can't believe you didn't tell me," she scolded Becca.

Her best friend hugged her and smiled with pure happiness. "I didn't want to tell anyone until I told Jake. I'm two months along and I'm due in May."

Olivia hugged her again. "Jake must be over the moon happy."

Becca laughed and cried at the same time. "If it's a boy, I'm sure he'll have those Stone good looks."

Her face went all dreamy when her husband came striding toward her. He scooped her up into his arms and carried her toward the main doors.

"Goodnight everyone," Jake yelled as they left the town hall, leaving everyone behind them grinning, applauding, and cheering.

* * * *

Wyatt smiled as his oldest brother carried Becca from the building. His gaze roamed the room and landed on Olivia. She stood talking with Sam. Wyatt frowned. He liked Sam but there wasn't a woman in town who didn't think the sheriff was the best-looking thing on two feet. He'd heard it enough from his sisters-in-law. He headed over to where they stood and wrapped his arms around Olivia from behind.

"Who's behind me, Sam?" Olivia asked. He and Sam grinned at each other.

"It sure as hell better be me, sweetheart," Wyatt growled in her ear.

She laughed and leaned her head back to kiss his jaw.

"That's my cue to leave. You two have fun." Sam

laughed.

Wyatt noticed how Olivia watched Sam move through the crowd but then when she sighed, he frowned. "What was that for? You like Sam?"

He tightened his arms around her when she laughed.

"I was just thinking Sam needs a woman."

"Matchmaking? Seriously, Olivia?"

She turned in his arms and wrapped her arms around his waist. "I can't be a matchmaker if I don't have a woman in mind for him—yet."

"Maybe you should just let Sam find his own woman."

Olivia huffed. "Men. Sam just needs a good push."

"Not our problem, darlin'." He kissed her when she opened her mouth to say something, and then pulled back. "Let it go, Olivia. Sam has no problem getting women and you have a more pressing thing to worry about."

Olivia leaned back in his arms. "Oh really, and what would that be, cowboy?"

"Me." Wyatt took her hand, and led her from the town hall and out to his truck.

Chapter Fourteen

The Clifton Bed and Breakfast closed for the winter, and Sharon moved into a motel in town. Olivia was happy she was gone but in reality, she knew Sharon would show up again. Olivia had no idea how to get her to leave and never come back other than give her the money.

She exhaled a long breath as she finished answering emails and setting up reservations for next May. It still amazed her how well the B and B had done. The little town of fifteen hundred was thrilled it was doing so well because if the B and B did well, the town did well too. People seemed to love visiting the little town of Clifton, since so many guests were repeat customers.

When someone knocked on the back door, Olivia frowned and felt a little apprehensive since the B and B was closed, and she was here alone. She cautiously opened her apartment door and peered around the refrigerator to look to the back door. She smiled when she saw Wyatt, and quickly ran to let him in. He pulled her into his arms and kissed her.

"Hi, darlin'," he said against her lips.

"Hi, yourself. What are you doing here?"

"I came to get you. Come home with me. I've missed you."

Olivia reared back. "Seriously?"

Wyatt nodded.

"Go pack some clothes. Not too many though. I

like you naked," he said grinning at her.

She didn't argue with that request but hurried back to her apartment. She threw some things quickly into a suitcase, hollered for Punkin, and ran back to the kitchen. Wyatt was leaning against the counter with his arms folded and his booted feet crossed. His head was down. She couldn't contain a moan. He was so hot. She'd seen him like this before and it always turned her on. His head snapped up and he grinned at her with pure sex appeal.

Olivia set her suitcase down, stepped up to him, pushed up on her tiptoes, and kissed him. His arms went around her as he deepened the kiss. When his tongue entered her mouth, she groaned and ran her hands under his T-shirt and up over his chest. Her nails scraped his pecs.

Wyatt moaned low in his throat as he moved his lips across her cheek to her ear. He took her lobe between his teeth and tugged on it. She felt him grin when she shivered. His lips moved down her neck. He lightly bit her making her gasp. All of a sudden, he straightened up, picked up the suitcase, grabbed her hand, and pulled her out the door. Olivia grinned.

"In a hurry, cowboy?" she asked with a laugh as he pulled her along.

"Yes. Get in your car and I'll see you at the ranch." Wyatt shut the door on her SUV after she and Punkin had settled in, and then he ran to his truck with her suitcase.

Olivia laughed as she started her car and pulled out behind him. She followed him to his ranch with a big grin on her face the entire time. Once they pulled up to the house, they parked the vehicles and entered the house together. She barely made it in the door before Wyatt spun her around, pushing her back against it and leaning into her. Both of them moaned when their lips met.

She grabbed his hat off and threw it to the floor, and then pulled his T-shirt over his head. Her nails scraped down his chest, and over his rippled stomach to the snap on his jeans. She pulled the zipper down, snaked her hand inside, and wrapped her fingers around him. He pushed into her hand and groaned when she tightened her grip. After a moment, his hands went to her sweater and pulled it over her head.

Olivia reached behind her back, unhooked her bra, pulled it off, and tossed it. Wyatt's hands went to the snap of her jeans and opened them. He pushed them down, along with her panties. She stepped out of them. Wyatt dropped to his knees in front of her. His mouth roamed over her stomach and down to her curls. He pushed his tongue through them to her clitoris, and in response, Olivia grabbed a handful of his hair. Wyatt lifted her leg over his shoulder, holding her hips in his hands while his tongue moved over her, and he scraped his teeth against her.

Olivia threw her head back against the door and shuddered as her orgasm shook her. She cried out his name as she came. Wyatt slowly moved up her body and lifted her other leg to encircle his waist, and thrust into her hard. He pressed his lips to hers as he moved against her.

Her arms wrapped around his neck and she held onto him tight.

"Come with me, sweetheart," he whispered against her lips.

She moaned. "Yes."

He moved against her faster and harder. "Now, Olivia."

She moved her hips against him and groaned as she came. Wyatt growled her name out as he joined her. Spent, he rested his forehead against hers as they both tried to catch their breath.

"That's twice you've had me against a door," she said between breaths.

Wyatt chuckled. "Any splinters this time?"

Her breath rushed out in a laugh. "No."

Her let her legs down and swore softly. "Damn. I wanted to pull them out for you."

He caught her when her knees began to buckle. "You all right, darlin'?"

"I'm wonderful." She kissed his lips, and then picked up her clothes heading toward the living room.

"Where are you going?" Wyatt asked.

She smiled over her shoulder.

"To take a shower." She laughed when she heard him following her and knowing he was watching her naked ass.

Two days later, Olivia sat at Wyatt's kitchen table answering emails for the B and B. The phone rang, but she shook her head. There was no way she was answering it—not after what happened the last time. Wyatt must have answered it since it quit ringing. She knew he was in his office working, so she headed that way. She could hear his deep voice as he spoke on the phone. She shivered with arousal remembering his voice whispering in her ear.

She stopped in the doorway. Wyatt glanced over to her and signaled for her to come in. She walked slowly around his office. One wall was nothing but glass. It had a gorgeous view of the back pastures. She knew the room opposite the office was his bedroom because there was a matching wall of glass in his bedroom too, but it had a view of the large in-ground swimming pool. Heated, with underwater lights, they'd spent a lot of time in it, swimming until all hours. Olivia loved the time they'd spent in it together.

As she strolled around the room, her gaze landed on a picture sitting on the bookshelf behind Wyatt. She moved closer and picked it up. It was an image of Wyatt sitting on Cochise in a competition. His hat sat low on his forehead and his hands were holding onto the saddle horn. Cochise had his hooves buried in the wood shavings as he stared down a calf. It was the sexiest picture Olivia had ever seen. She ran her finger over the image of man and horse. Smiling, she set it back on the shelf and another image caught her eye. This one was of the Marine symbol. The same one Wyatt had tattooed on his bicep.

Olivia gasped when Wyatt grabbed her around the waist and pulled her onto his lap.

"I didn't know you were off the phone." She laughed.

"I've been off the phone for a few minutes," Wyatt said against her neck.

"What does Semper Fi mean? I know it has something to do with the Marines, but I'm not sure what."

"It's short for Semper Fidelis, which is Latin for *Always Faithful.* It's the code of the Marines and means a Marine can always count on a fellow Marine."

"Were you in combat?"

"I was in Afghanistan for eighteen months. I was a sniper, which you already know. I was the best." He shrugged. She knew he wasn't bragging, but just stating a fact.

Olivia knew just how good he was. He'd saved Becca from being shot by Steve Harris, and then again at Becca and Jake's wedding reception when the brother of Harris tried to kill her family. Wyatt saved a good many people that night. The man was shooting at anyone and everyone, and someone had to stop him. She hugged him and stood.

"I love this picture of you and Cochise." She smiled picking it up again. "Who took it?"

"A local newspaper...I think it was about three years ago. They sent me a copy."

Olivia nodded and put it back on the shelf but she couldn't stop looking at it.

Wyatt wrapped his arms around her and kissed her neck.

"I'm hungry," he said nuzzling his face against her neck.

"I'm not going to say I am. You'll just make fun of me." She pouted.

Wyatt laughed. "I wouldn't do that, darlin'." He led her toward the kitchen.

Later that evening, Wyatt touched a match to the wood in the fireplace then they sat on the couch, curled up together to watch television. They no sooner got comfortable than they began arguing over what to watch. Wyatt wanted to watch a football game and Olivia wanted to watch a movie. He grabbed her and pulled her onto his lap.

"If we can't decide what to watch, we may as well go to bed," he said.

Olivia frowned. "Are you sleepy?"

"I didn't say anything about sleeping, sweetheart."

She pulled out of his arms and got to her feet. "Well in that case, let's go cowboy."

She ran down the hallway and started laughing when she heard him running behind her. He caught her and tossed her over his shoulder.

"Must you always carry me like this?" She grunted even as she smiled.

Wyatt chuckled as he carried her down the hallway to the bedroom. He kicked the door closed behind them, carried her to the bed and slowly lowered her to it. He lay down beside her, kissing her. She shoved him to his back and pulled his T-shirt off over his head. Her hands went to the snap of his jeans, and then she slowly lowered the zipper before pulling them down his legs. She threw them across the room and then reached for his boxer briefs. She could see his hard shaft straining against them. Giving an evil grin, she pulled them off him.

"You have too many clothes on, darlin'." Wyatt reached for her.

"Keep your hands to yourself, cowboy." Olivia grinned as she ran her tongue around his nipples and down his hard abs. He hissed in a breath when her tongue touched the tip of him. His hands clenched in her hair. She pulled her hair back over her shoulders. Her tongue ran the length of him, up and down, around the rim, and then down the length again. She covered him with her mouth and sucked hard.

She heard him groan long and low in his throat. His hips jerked and his hands let go of her hair to move to the bed where they fisted in the sheet. She heard his breathing growing heavier.

"Olivia...you have to stop, sweetheart," he panted.

"Give me a minute."

Wyatt's breath rushed out in a rough laugh. "I don't have a minute."

Olivia grinned. "Sure you do."

He growled and tried to pull her away from him. She tightened her grip on him.

"Behave, Wyatt. Just relax and enjoy, cowboy." She continued until she felt him stiffen and she heard a groan tear from deep in his chest as he came. His head went back and his fingers tightened in her hair again. She didn't let up until he lay completely spent trying to catch his breath. She climbed her way up his body, kissing every bit of hot skin her lips met until she reached his mouth. She kissed him.

"You all right?" Olivia asked him, and then laughed when all he could do was nod his head.

Wyatt lifted his head to look at her. "Wow."

She laughed again. "Yeah, wow. Didn't we have this conversation before?"

He joined her laughter. "I believe so." He rolled her to her back and moved over her. "You didn't have to do that."

"Why not? You do it for me." Olivia frowned up at him.

Wyatt grunted. "I know but..." He shrugged.

"I know what you're saying and know that I wanted to do it for you." She raised her eyebrow. "You didn't like it?"

He kissed her. "Are you kidding? I loved it!"

She wrapped her arms around his neck. "I'm

glad."

"Now, let me return the favor," he whispered as he began moving down her body.

"You don't have to do that." She moaned when his tongue circled her nipple, and then moved lower.

"I know I don't. I want to. I love the way you taste, Olivia." His mouth moved down over her stomach and her excitement increased. Then his tongue moved lower to touch her clitoris.

Olivia gasped as he pulled her legs over his shoulders and feasted on her. Her hands clenched fistfuls of his hair as she screamed out when her orgasm hit her. Wyatt moved up her body and nudged her legs further apart.

"I can't seem to get enough of you," he said as he thrust into her while she was still shaking from her orgasm.

"I see no problem with that." Her breath rushed out in a low satisfied moan.

Wyatt grinned at her and made love to her slowly and thoroughly. Completely sated, they fell asleep in each other's arms.

* * * *

Olivia returned to the B and B to help Becca, Emma, and Stacy clean it up and ready it for the winter months. Working as a team, they dusted, ran the vacuum, and tossed sheets over the furniture. While having lunch in the kitchen, they all frowned when the bell at the front desk rang. All of them strode to the foyer and halted in unison when they saw Sharon standing there. Olivia made a face of apparent disgust.

"We're closed. What are you doing here?" Olivia watched as Sharon's eyes scanned the women then she smiled at them.

"You know why I'm here, Olivia. We need to talk," Sharon told her.

Olivia moved toward her. "We have nothing to talk about. I told you and Wyatt told you.

You will get no money from us." The women behind her gasped loudly.

"You're here for money?" Emma practically shouted.

Olivia smiled knowing her friends had her back. "She wants seventy-five thousand dollars. Extortion, I believe it's called."

Sharon smiled at her. "That's not true, Olivia. I simply want to *borrow* it."

Olivia snorted. "Like anyone is ever going to believe that crap."

Sharon shrugged. "We need to speak in private."

Olivia glanced over her shoulder to her friends and nodded. "It's fine. She won't be staying long."

After a slight hesitation, the women left Olivia and Sharon alone. Olivia turned to stare at Sharon.

"I want that money, Olivia. Did you get it?" Sharon asked.

"No. I told you I'm not giving you any money. You may as well leave Clifton."

"You really shouldn't give me an attitude, Olivia. I want that money and I want it now."

Olivia leaned in close to Sharon. "Not going to happen."

Sharon jerked back. "What do you mean? You really have no idea what you're doing by not giving me that money. I know how crazy you are over Wyatt. Do you really want to see him hurt?"

"Wyatt can take care of himself." Olivia shrugged. "He does dangerous things every day."

She hoped Sharon wouldn't call her bluff. Inside, she was terrified Sharon would make good on her threat. All of a sudden Sharon laughed.

"Oh, you're good, honey, almost as good as your mother but not quite. The thing is you *are* scared I'll have him hurt, or take him away from you. You just want me to think you don't care."

Olivia shrugged again. "Think what you want."

Sharon chewed on her bottom lip. "You're in love with him. I know you wouldn't want him hurt." She leaned closer. "But know this, daughter of mine I will do anything I can to get that money. *Anything.*"

"What the hell are you doing here?" Wyatt growled as he strode into the foyer.

Olivia watched as Sharon's eyes shifted toward him. Olivia did the same. His hair was damp on the ends as if he'd just stepped from the shower. She wanted to groan because he looked so good. His eyes moved to her and then back to Sharon.

"I came to speak with my...Olivia," Sharon said.

"I'm sure Olivia's not interested in anything you have to say."

He glanced over to Olivia and raised a brow. She nodded in agreement.

"We'll talk again, Olivia," Sharon muttered.

Olivia watched with relief as the woman who had given birth to her spun on her heel and left the premises. The breath whooshed out of her as she sat back on the stool behind the counter. She put her hands over her face. What was she going to do? She was her mother yet all she could think of was that she had to get Sharon to leave. If it took money to accomplish that then Olivia would give it to her...anything, anything at all to get her out of her life.

"Are you all right, darlin'?" Wyatt put his arm around her.

"I should just give her the money so she'll go away."

"No." Wyatt's voice booked no argument.

She gazed up at him. "If it will make her leave—"

"No," he said through clenched teeth. "Let Sam do his job. Maybe he'll find something on her. Just give him a little more time, sweetheart."

Exhaling on a loud huff, she nodded. "All right, I'll wait for Sam."

Wyatt kissed her. "How much longer are you going to be here? I'm lonely for you," he whispered against her lips.

She wrapped her arms around him as he deepened the kiss, but then they sprang apart when someone cleared her throat.

"You two need to get a room." Becca grinned at them.

Wyatt laughed. "I think you're right." He glanced at Olivia. "Let's go, darlin'."

She grinned happily as he took her hand and began leading her across the foyer. She glanced over her shoulder and waved goodbye to Becca, Emma, and Stacy standing in the doorway.

When they arrived at Wyatt's home, Olivia headed straight for his bedroom with him on her heels. She spun around to face him once inside the room. He strode up to her, took her face in his hands, and kissed her.

"I need you so much, sweetheart," he said before pressing his lips to hers.

Olivia smiled. "I need you too."

Wyatt pulled her sweater off over her head then

unhooked her bra. He groaned when he gazed at her breasts. Her nipples were already distended and eager. He placed his hands over them and rubbed the pads of his thumbs against them. She moaned and felt her body come alive.

Wyatt quickly disposed of her jeans and then chuckled. She pulled back to stare at him.

"What's so funny, cowboy?"

Wyatt chuckled again as he gazed at her panties.

"You don't like my little hearts?" She laughed.

Wyatt rested his forehead against hers. "Sweetheart, you could wear pajamas with feet in them and I'd think they were sexy."

Olivia laughed then hissed in a breath when he pushed them down her legs and his hand moved between her legs. He lowered her to the bed, and then stood again to pull his clothes off. She watched his every move until he was naked, then she lowered her eyes as she took in every bit of his beautiful body from his broad chest, over his rippled stomach, and finally, to his hard shaft. She scrambled to her knees and wrapped her hand around him. He closed his eyes enjoying the feel, and then pushed her down on the bed before stretching out alongside her.

His hands slowly roamed over her, making her squirm. Unable to resist, she ran her hands over him until she wrapped her hand around him tightly again. Wyatt groaned and pushed into her hand making her slide her hand up and down the length of him until he put his hand over hers to stop the action.

"I can't wait, Olivia. I need you now."

He moved over her and slid into her inch by inch until he could go no further. Her legs wrapped around his waist while Wyatt moved slowly in and out of her. Suddenly, he pulled out, making her whimper. Grinning, he rolled her to her stomach then lifted her hips until she rested on her knees. Then he thrust into her hard, making her cry out his name. He repeatedly pulled out and thrust back into her hard.

Feeling the rhythm, Olivia lifted up on her hands and moved back against him, meeting his every thrust. She groaned as her orgasm grabbed her so she began moving against him harder and faster. She felt his body stiffen when he groaned her name and came.

Olivia fell forward with Wyatt on top of her, rewarding her with kisses to the back of her neck even while both of them fought to breathe, their bodies slick with sweat. He rolled off her but rubbed his hand down her back. She suddenly felt overwhelmed, tears stinging at the back of her eyes. A feeling of panic washed over her, as if her world was suddenly ending.

"Olivia?" When she didn't answer him, he put his hand on her shoulder and rolled her toward him. "What is it? Did I do something wrong, sweetheart?" She shook her head. "Then tell me what's wrong."

"I can't," she whispered.

Wyatt scooted up to sit against the headboard and pulled her against him.

"Why can't you?" When she tried to get out of the bed, he grabbed a hold of her.

"I think you need to tell me what's going on in that beautiful head of yours."

She pushed against him. "Let go of me, Wyatt."

He quickly let go of her. She got out of bed and went into the bathroom, closing the door behind her. She sat on the closed toilet and sobbed. How could she tell him what was going through her head when she knew if she did, he'd want out of this relationship, which wasn't a relationship according to him. Wiping her wet eyes dry and taking a deep breath, she stood, exhaled even as tears threatened again, and turned on the shower. Even with water running over her tear-stained face, she heard him enter the bathroom. She could see his reflection in the mirror. He leaned against the counter and folded his arms across his broad chest. He had only his jeans on.

"Olivia, I need to know what's going on with you."

She shut the shower off and reached for a towel and quickly covered her nakedness. She raised her eyebrow at him.

"Do you mind?"

Wyatt straightened up. "Do I mind? What the fuck does that mean?"

They glared at each other. With a surly grumble, he turned and left the bathroom. Olivia let out a ragged breath. *How do you tell a man who doesn't want a permanent relationship what you just shared was the most fantastic thing you've ever experienced?*

It had been mind-blowing sex. The best she'd ever had. He was a fantastic lover and she was going to lose him because of it. She'd never have that again with any other man. Wyatt would walk away and she'd be in hell. A hell she knew from the very beginning would eventually happen. She stared at her reflection in the mirror and shook her head. She knew there was no way she could tell him, *Well, you see, my gorgeous sexy cowboy, you just gave me the most amazing orgasm I've ever had and now I want to spend the rest of my life with you because I'm crazy in love with you.*

Yeah, that would go over real well, about as well as walking through church with a cow paddy on your heel. She entered the bedroom a few minutes later only to find it was empty. Dressing quickly, she walked down the hallway, glancing into the living room, only to find it was empty too. She took a deep breath and headed to the kitchen. It was also empty. Where was he?

Olivia strode to the back door and peered out just in time to see Wyatt riding Cochise out of the barn and heading toward the north pasture. They were moving at full speed. That was her obvious cue to leave. He made it clear by not sticking around that he didn't want to deal with her anymore. Blinking back tears, she returned to the bedroom and packed her suitcase. After calling for Punkin, she got into her vehicle and drove back to the B and B. Once inside, she collapsed on her sofa and sobbed until she had no tears left and fell asleep.

* * * *

Wyatt rode Cochise into the barn and wiped the horse down. He shook his head thinking of what had happened earlier. There was no way he'd ever understand a woman. They'd just had fantastic sex and she acted as if she wanted nothing to do with him afterwards. He swore aloud.

Cochise turned his head to look at him.

"What are you looking at? It's not my fault she's mad," he grumbled when Cochise snorted.

He led the horse to his stall then as he was coming out, he almost ran over Kirk.

"Sorry, boss. I didn't see you," his ranch hand mumbled.

Wyatt sighed. "No problem. Hey, are you doing all right?"

Kirk blew out a breath. "Not really. I'm real sorry about Ben."

"Did you and Ava talk? Is she still leaving?" Wyatt asked, changing the subject away from Ben Collins. He placed his hand on Kirk's shoulder. "You can tell me anything. It goes no further than right here."

"Yes, she is."

Wyatt was shocked. "You have no idea why?"

Kirk sighed and shook his head. "I still have no clue. We've always gotten along great. I've had to move to a motel since Ben took off."

"Why didn't you say something?"

"I didn't want you thinking I was just worming around for a raise."

"Christ, Kirk. I wouldn't think that. I know you well enough." Wyatt took his hat off, ran his fingers through his hair, and then resettled his hat.

Kirk glanced away. "I'm just staying at the motel until I find a place."

"Let me know if you need anything. I'll help you any way I can," Wyatt told him.

Kirk nodded and strolled away. Wyatt blew out a breath, headed toward the house, and halted when he saw Olivia's vehicle was gone. His heart hit his stomach. If that didn't shout out she was finished, nothing did. He was sure they'd talk about what happened and work it out, but apparently not.

Olivia wasn't a fickle woman. When she wanted something, she went after it. Hell, he knew that better than anyone else ever could. She'd been after him since they first met two years ago. So what in the hell was her problem now? *Son of a bitch!* He couldn't let this go. He was going to find out exactly what her problem was and if she wanted to end this, she needed to tell him to his face.

Wyatt drove his truck to the B and B. Snowflakes swirled in the headlights. It was late October after all. It wouldn't be long before the weather would get much worse. He wanted Olivia at his home with him. Shaking his head, he couldn't believe he'd even pondered the idea. He never had women at his place but he couldn't stand being there without her. *Shit!* He was in trouble now. From the very beginning, going into this with her, he knew he was taking a big risk with his heart. It was why he didn't want to get involved with her in the first place.

"Think with the head on your shoulders, not the one between your legs," he muttered.

When he pulled up to the back door of the B and B, he noticed the place was dark. She usually had a light on since she was there alone now. He glanced around and sighed with relief when he saw her vehicle. She was home—unless she'd gone out with someone. Still, Olivia would've left a light on. He hopped down from his truck, took the steps to the back door two at a time, and knocked. When no one answered, he tried the knob and found it unlocked.

"Olivia," he called out and saw the door to her apartment open slowly.

"Wyatt? What are you doing here?" Her voice sounded raw.

"I want to know what the hell's going on. I thought we'd talk about it when I got back from my ride, but you were gone." He strode toward her. "You have something you want to tell me?"

"Like what?"

"If you're walking away from this, then you need to tell me now—to my face."

Olivia's eyes widened. "I'm not."

Her response made him swear as he pushed his way into her apartment.

"Then what the fuck was that about, Olivia? You left and I thought we'd talk about it when I got back," he practically shouted.

"You were the one who left, Wyatt."

"I went for a ride to cool off. You knew I'd be back."

"How was I supposed to know you didn't want me to go?"

"How were you supposed to know? Because I didn't say I wanted you to go," he shouted.

"I..." She shook her head.

"I need to know what you want to do."

"I'm not walking away," she whispered.

Wyatt stared at her then nodded. "All right then. I still don't understand why you left or why you were upset but if you'd rather not say, that's fine. Just know that I'm not going to put up with these tantrums of yours. We do this or we don't. I'm not going to chase after you the next time."

"One of us is going to end up hurt, Wyatt."

"It's not going to be me, and if you think you'll be hurt then maybe you *should* walk away."

"I can't. Not yet." Olivia sighed and moved to take a seat on the sofa. She patted the spot beside her. Wyatt sat in the chair opposite her instead, stretched his long legs out, and clasped his hands across his flat stomach. When she didn't say anything, he raised an eyebrow at her.

"I'm sorry, Wyatt."

He leaned forward. "Sorry?" She nodded. "Sorry

for what? What exactly are you apologizing for?" He leaned back in the chair when she waved her hand at him.

"I, uh..." She cleared her throat. "I thought that was the most amazing sex ever."

He frowned at her. "Then why...?"

"It was just so mind-blowing. It just..."

Wyatt came to his feet. "Do you plan on getting this out some time tonight? I have things I need to do."

Olivia got to her feet and glared at him. "I didn't know how to react to it. It was fantastic and I wanted to tell you how great it was but I was afraid that if I did, it would scare you away.

How do I tell you something like that without making you bolt and run?"

Wyatt glanced away, exhaled in a huff, and then looked at her. "You just did. Am I running?"

"No."

"I thought it was amazing too, darlin'. I don't have a problem with you saying you thought so too."

"You thought it was amazing too?"

"Yes. Now go pack and come home with me. I'll make us dinner."

"I am hungry."

He burst out laughing. "Why am I not surprised?"

She stuck her tongue out at him, and his eyes dropped to stare at her mouth.

Olivia groaned. "You keep looking at me like that, cowboy, and dinner will be very late."

Wyatt grinned, kissed her quickly, and headed for the door. As he passed through, he glanced over his shoulder. "You'd better hurry up then."

Chapter Fifteen

The next evening, Olivia sat in the living room watching television while waiting for Wyatt to come in from the arena. She knew he was out there with a client but she needed to talk to him, and had grown tired of waiting for him. Impatient, she got up and after putting her coat on, she headed over to the arena. Snow pelted her in the face and it was cold so she pulled her hood up and stuck her hands in her pockets.

She opened the door to the metal building and gratefully entered the warmth. She saw Wyatt talking with an older man. He grinned at her when he saw her and put his hand out toward her. She practically skipped to him she was so giddy. Wyatt pulled her tight against his side and kissed her temple. She shivered and put her arm around his waist. She smiled at the other man, only he didn't smile back.

"Olivia, this is Blake Taylor. Blake, Olivia Roberts," Wyatt said, introducing them.

She stuck her out hand. Blake shook it but dropped it almost immediately, and told Wyatt he needed to go. Olivia frowned watching the man leave.

"He wasn't very friendly," she said to Wyatt after they were alone.

Wyatt laughed. "Not to you, anyway."

She narrowed her eyes at him. "What's that supposed to mean?"

"He's Stephanie's father."

Olivia gasped. "Oops." She laughed then sobered. "Does he want you and Stephanie to get back together?"

Wyatt nodded. "I told him it wasn't going to happen. It was over and I've moved on, and she should too, but he thinks we can work it out."

"What about you? Do you think you can get back together?" Olivia asked.

Wyatt's eyes widened. "Are you out of your mind?" he practically shouted.

Olivia burst out laughing. "That was the right answer, cowboy."

"Let's go inside, darlin'." He put his lips to her neck.

She pulled back from him. "Um, I have to make a trip back to the B and B."

"Now? It's snowing."

"I need to get some...uh, personal items." She pulled her lip between her teeth feeling embarrassed.

"What personal items?"

"I'm on my period, okay? I need to get some...things." She was sure her face was beet red.

Wyatt stepped away from her and Olivia laughed. "It's not contagious."

Wyatt chuckled. "I'm sorry."

"It's all right, cowboy. I'll just run over there and be right back." She started to move toward the door, and then stopped when a sudden thought came to mind. "Unless, you'd rather I stay there?"

Wyatt's brows shot up and he closed the distance between them.

"Do you want to stay there?" She glanced away from him, but Wyatt turned her face back toward him. "Olivia? I'd love for you to stay here but if you think you'd be more comfortable there, I totally understand."

She wrapped her arms around him. "I want to stay with you."

"I was hoping you'd say that. Do you want me to take you?"

"No. I'll be right back. I'm sure you want to shower." She wrinkled her nose at him as a hint.

Wyatt laughed. "Yeah, I know. I smell like a horse." He kissed her. "Be careful. This light snow can make the roads slick."

Olivia kissed him. "I won't be long."

Not wanting to be gone too long, she hurried to her car and made the trip to the B and B in good time despite the snow. She retrieved the items she needed, and began the trip back to Wyatt.

As she drove along, the snow started coming down heavier. She slowed down in case any animals jumped out in front of her. Reaching into her pocket, she pulled her cell phone out to call Wyatt to let him know she was on her way back when suddenly another vehicle, most likely a truck, pulled up behind her. The headlights were reflecting in her rearview mirror almost blinding her, and it was obvious the driver was following too close. She tapped her brakes lightly to get him to back off. If anything, he moved closer.

Feeling nervous, Olivia slowed down and pulled off the road, hoping the truck would go around her. It didn't. It pulled off the road behind her. She started trembling as a bad feeling descended on her. She pulled out onto the road again, and for a minute, the truck didn't follow her. Sighing in relief, she drove on but she hadn't gone too far before the truck came barreling up behind her, and then pulled alongside her. Again, she slowed down, but the truck slowed down too. Olivia sped up and the other vehicle did too.

Suddenly, the truck raced around her. Olivia stopped her car, and watched as the truck's brake lights came on, water from the road spraying up from the tires when it spun around, and faced in her direction.

Olivia nervously dialed Wyatt.

"Hey, sweetheart, are you on your way back?"

"Wyatt," her voice trembled uncontrollably.

"Olivia. What is it? Where are you?"

She started to tell him what was happening when the truck suddenly started toward her.

Olivia screamed instead.

* * * *

Wyatt yelled into the phone, but she didn't answer him. He could hear her car radio playing. He ran out of the house and got into his truck, dialing Jake as he drove down the drive. Turning toward the B and B, he pushed the accelerator to the floor. Not seeing her SUV anywhere in sight along the route, he drove on to where he knew she'd been. When he pulled up to the back of the B and B, he could see it was dark except for the small lamp burning in the foyer. He jumped out of the truck, ran to the back door, but found it locked—just as it should be with no one there.

He wasn't taking any chances though, so he took out his spare key and opened the door. Entering the kitchen, he strode back to Olivia's apartment and pounded on the door. As he figured, there was no answer. She wasn't here.

Wyatt swore. Where in the hell was she? He ran back to his truck and glanced around. Her vehicle was nowhere around. Driving back toward his place, he traveled the road slowly and scanned the road ahead looking for any sign of her. Then headlights came toward him, he slowed down and then stopped when he saw it was Jake's truck. They stopped beside each other and put their windows down.

"Did you find her?" Jake asked.

"No. I checked the B and B and it's locked up tight." Wyatt noticed Becca sitting beside Jake with tears on her cheeks. "I'm going to check along this side...you check your side, Jake. I was in such a hurry that I didn't check that side real well."

Wyatt glanced down the road and saw flashing red and blue lights heading toward them.

"I called Sam," Jake told him. Wyatt nodded.

The Sheriff's SUV cruiser came to a stop behind Jake. A pickup truck stopped behind it. It was Gabe. Wyatt watched as both men strolled forward. He explained what he'd heard. Sam slowly walked along the road, shining his flashlight in search of clues.

"There are skid marks over here," Sam yelled out.

Wyatt ran to where he stood. He saw them too. Then he ran to the side of the road calling out for Olivia. She couldn't have just disappeared. Jake walked beside him.

"I shouldn't have let her go alone," Wyatt muttered. "I offered to take her but she said she wouldn't be long. *Damn it.*"

"We'll find her, Wyatt," Gabe told him.

Wyatt nodded absently and walked along the road. He spotted tracks in the freshly fallen snow and followed them, calling her name. He stopped and listened. That was when he heard her. Her voice was faint but he heard her. Running along the tracks with his flashlight shining, he saw her SUV. He made his way down the bank to her and opened her door. She was sitting inside with her hands clenched around the steering wheel. Wyatt touched her shoulder.

"Olivia? Sweetheart, are you all right?" Wyatt asked. Her face was wet with tears when she turned her head and stared at him. Her bottom lip trembled. He reached in and unhooked her seatbelt. He barely had time to react before she threw herself at him. Catching her in his arms, he held her tightly against him. He kissed her forehead. "What happened, sweetheart?"

"Do I need to get an ambulance out here for her, Wyatt?" Sam called down to him.

Wyatt pulled back to gaze into her eyes. "Are you all right? Are you hurt anywhere?"

Olivia shook her head. "I'm not hurt. I drove my truck down here to avoid being hit." She stared at him with glossy eyes. "He ran me off the road, Wyatt." Her voice ended in a sob.

"Who did?" Wyatt growled. He was more than pissed.

"I don't know who it was. It was a big, dark pickup truck." She shivered.

"I'm bringing her up," he called out. "No ambulance, Sam."

Wyatt held her hand as they walked up the bank. Once at the top, Becca reached for Olivia and held onto her as they comforted each other. The men stood off to the side until finally, Sam stepped forward.

"Olivia? Are you sure you don't need to go to the

hospital?" he asked in a worried tone.

"I'm fine, Sam. Just scared."

Sam nodded. "Tell me what happened."

Olivia told them what had transpired. Becca kept her arm around her. Wyatt got angrier and angrier as Olivia went into detail.

"He spun around in the middle of the road and sat there pointing right at me for about a minute, then he gunned it and came straight at me. I sat there frozen, until for some reason, I looked to the right and saw the embankment. I drove over the side and went down the hill." Trembling, she hugged Becca.

"I doubt he would've hit you, but you did the right thing," Sam told her.

Wyatt stepped close to Sam. "Why do you *doubt* he would've hit her? Obviously, he wanted to hurt her," he said through clenched teeth.

"Back off, Wyatt," Sam growled. "Think about it. If whoever it was actually hit her, they could've been injured too, and even if not, they would certainly be easy to find due to the damage on the truck. No, this was to scare her, not kill, or hurt her."

The two men stared at each other until Wyatt gave a terse nod of agreement, and stepped back.

"Look, I know you're pissed, we all are, but someone wants to scare Olivia for some reason, and I'll find them," Sam said.

"Try looking at Dalton's Motel. That's where Sharon's staying," Gabe added. Olivia and Sam both shook their heads.

"It's too obvious to be her," Sam said.

"She wouldn't have the balls," Olivia said at the same time.

Sam smiled at Olivia. "Nonetheless, I will check her out, and find out where she was when this happened." He started toward his SUV then stopped and glanced back. "She may not have been driving but she could still be behind it."

"Sam..." Wyatt called to him. Sam turned in response raising an eyebrow. "Thanks."

Sam nodded and began calling in for his deputies to get to the scene, take pictures, and get measurements. Wyatt huffed and put his arm around Olivia moving her toward his truck.

"Sit in here where it's warm."

Olivia latched onto his arm. "Please don't leave me."

"I'm not leaving you. I'm just going to look around. You can see me." Wyatt tried to console her so when he saw Becca heading toward them, he relaxed a bit.

"I'm going to get in the truck with her," Becca told him when she reached the truck.

"Thanks. She's a mess right now," Wyatt said.

Becca smiled up at him. "I'll hold her hand until you can."

Wyatt smiled. "I'd appreciate it."

He leaned down when she crooked her finger at him. She kissed his cheek. Wyatt grinned, glanced up at Olivia, who nodded. He stepped aside to allow Becca to get into the truck then walked down the road to where Sam stood.

* * * *

Olivia sat in the truck staring out the windshield. A small smile lifted her lips when she saw Becca kiss Wyatt on his cheek. She scooted over in the seat so Becca could get in with her. Olivia reached for her best friend's hand. Becca squeezed it. Olivia watched Wyatt walk to stand next to Sam. She kept her eyes on him. She released a shuddering breath.

"The only time I've been more scared was when Steve took you, Becs," Olivia whispered. She felt Becca squeeze her hand. "I don't know who would do this. But like Sam said, Sharon may be behind it, only it doesn't seem like her style. Scaring me won't get her the money any faster."

"She needs to leave this town," Becca muttered.

"Yes, but she's determined to get money from me and she says she won't leave until she gets it."

"I hope Sam finds something on her. He'll take care of things," Becca said with conviction.

Olivia sighed. "I know he will."

Wyatt strode toward the truck and opened the driver side door, dropping her bag of essentials she'd needed, which had started this scary night, behind the seat. Olivia moved over to give him room to climb in too. He wrapped his arms around her and held her tight, making her feel a bit better. Neither paid much attention to Becca getting out of the truck. Olivia shivered against him and he hugged her tighter.

"Let's go home, darlin'. You need to get some rest. Sam called a tow truck to bring your SUV up. They'll tow it to my place."

"All right, Wyatt. I want to take a long bath in that wonderful Jacuzzi of yours."

He chuckled. "I think I can arrange that."

Olivia grinned and stayed close to his side as he drove them home.

* * * *

The day of Thanksgiving was cold with snow falling. Olivia had slid into a funk and she knew

Wyatt had no idea what to do to get her out of it. She lay on the couch waiting for him to come in from working, and eventually, drifted off. A little while later, she felt someone touching her hair. She opened her eyes to see Wyatt squatting in front of her. He made her smile.

"Hi, darlin'," he whispered.

"Hi, cowboy."

"I'm going to take a shower, and then we can head to Gabe and Emma's."

She nodded at him and closed her eyes again. "All right," she murmured.

Olivia waited until she heard the shower running before she headed in to join him. She knew he was wondering what was wrong with her and she honestly didn't know. But she knew she needed to get out of her slump, and taking a shower with Wyatt seemed like a good start.

After undressing in the bedroom, she silently opened the bathroom door and stepped inside. She walked toward the shower and gasped. Wyatt stood with his hands on the wall and his head under the showerhead. Water sluiced down over his big body. Good Lord, the man should be illegal. Her gaze roamed over him taking in every glistening inch, but when her eyes shifted back to his face, she moaned. He was staring at her, water droplets glistening on his long eyelashes.

Taking a deep breath, she opened the shower door.

"Can we save water and shower together, cowboy?" she asked smiling at him.

"Sure thing, sweetheart, come on in."

He straightened up. She stepped in front of him and faced him with her back against the wall. She ran her hands over his chest and teased her fingers down through the hair trailing down his stomach to the thick thatch surrounding his hardening shaft. Her fingers wrapped around him, he groaned and reached for her. Olivia wrapped her arms around his neck and lifted her legs to encircle his waist. Wyatt slid inside her as she pressed her lips to his.

"I've missed you, baby," she whispered against his hot mouth.

He moved out of her then thrust back in making her gasp.

"I've been right here, sweetheart."

Wyatt caressed her lips with his tongue before ravaging them. His hands cradled her ass as he continued to move in and out of her, going deeper with each thrust.

She dropped her head to rest against the wall as she thrust her hips against him. The groan that tore from her came from deep inside. She lowered her forehead to his.

"Kiss me, Olivia," Wyatt moaned against her lips.

She ran her tongue along his lips and moved it inside. He took control of the kiss. His tongue entered her mouth, tangling with hers. When he started moving harder, and faster against her, she tightened her legs around him crying out his name as she came. Wyatt followed her over the edge.

Olivia caught his groan with her mouth, making her moan low in her throat.

"That was some shower, cowboy." She laughed.

Wyatt chuckled. "You're telling me."

She started to put her legs down but it was slippery and every time she tried, she'd start laughing.

"Let me get us out of here, Olivia. Hold on."

Wyatt tried to step from the shower but she was laughing harder. He glared at her.

"You're not making this any easier."

"Just let me put my feet down, Wyatt." She giggled and tried to get her footing but he was too close to the open shower door and the next thing she knew, they were falling onto the floor. Wyatt took the brunt of the fall with her landing on top of him. They laid there a minute when she lifted her head to gaze at him. He had his eyes closed.

"Wyatt?" she whispered. When he opened one eye and gazed up at her, she lost it. She put her head against his chest and laughed until she cried.

"Get off me, woman," Wyatt growled, sending her into another fit of laughter. She could feel him laughing too. Finally, she was able to get herself up to sit on the lid of the toilet. He still lay on the floor chuckling.

"I'll have bruises tomorrow," he muttered.

Olivia grinned. "Not me."

"That's it," he said as he got up from the floor and grabbed her, tossed her over his shoulder and entered the bedroom. He tossed her onto the bed, and she put her arms out to him. They were very late for Thanksgiving dinner.

* * * *

When Wyatt woke up early the next morning, he glanced over at Olivia. She was still sleeping. He smiled and gently kissed her forehead. Not wanting to disturb her, he moved quietly to get out of the bed. She muttered in her sleep and rolled away from him. He reached for his jeans and pulled them on. After another glance at her, he left the room to make coffee since he hadn't gotten around to it last night. Once they got home from dinner at Gabe and

Emma's, they had headed straight for the bedroom. Sex with Olivia was amazing—always amazing. Keeping his hands off her was almost impossible. He leaned back against the counter, folded his arms across his bare chest, and waited for the coffee to brew. His thoughts went to the sexy woman asleep in his bed.

Wyatt was startled when someone knocked on his front door. Most of the people he knew came to the back door. He strode through the living room to the door, opened it, and loudly groaned when he saw Sharon Winters standing there grinning at him.

"What the hell are you doing here?" he asked.

Sharon brushed past him and entered his home. Her eyes roamed over his bare chest and down along his stomach. She grinned at him. "You have a gorgeous...home, Wyatt."

He pushed the door closed because it was cold. "Nice to know you think so. Now you can leave."

"I'm not going anywhere...yet." Her eyes landed on his fly. "You really are sexy." She stepped closer to him, put her hands on his chest, and gazed up at him. "I could do so much for you. Some things you've only dreamed about." She smiled up at him, and then moving toward his living room, she glanced around.

"I don't think so." Wyatt opened the door again. "Go."

Sharon slowly strolled back toward him. "Have you ever been with an older woman, Wyatt?" He glared at her. "I bet you could teach me a few things too." She ran one finger down his chest to his unsnapped jeans. "Let's go to your bedroom."

He smirked. "Your daughter is in my bedroom."

Sharon glanced around. "How about the couch then?"

He laughed at how pushy she was. "You're really something." When she laughed, he narrowed his eyes. "It wasn't a compliment."

He heard a sound in the hallway and glanced over his shoulder to see Olivia standing there in nothing but his T-shirt. She walked up to him and put her arms around his waist.

"You lost, Sharon?" Olivia asked.

Sharon stepped back from Wyatt. "Damn you. I almost had him, Olivia. I told you I could get him. I would've had him on his knees in a few more minutes."

Wyatt burst out laughing. "You'll never see me on my knees for any woman."

Sharon grinned as she looked at Olivia. "I told you men only wanted one thing. He just admitted he certainly wouldn't get on his knees and beg you to stay if you wanted to leave him, Olivia. What does that tell you?" She spun on her heel and headed out the door, slamming it behind her.

Astonished by the trap he just fell into, Wyatt turned toward Olivia, only to see her striding down the hallway. He went after her. She was pulling her suitcase from the closet.

"Olivia..."

"As much as I hate to admit it, she's right. You don't care enough to beg me to stay if I wanted to end this."

He stepped in front of her. "Do you want to end this?" She didn't answer him. "Olivia? Do you?" She shook her head as she continued to pack. "Then it doesn't matter, does it? If it isn't going to end yet, why worry about it?"

Olivia gazed up at him with tears rolling down her face. "You just said why."

He frowned. "What?"

"You said, *yet*." She raised her hand up when he started to speak. "I know I agreed to it in the beginning, but...I can't do it anymore."

"Olivia..."

"No. I don't need to hear that it was what we both agreed on, Wyatt. I'm...I'm walking away."

When she lifted the suitcase off the bed and moved to go past him, he wrapped his fingers around her arm. "Olivia, I..."

"Let me go...please." Her voice caught on the last word as she pushed past him, and left.

Chapter Sixteen

Two weeks had passed since Olivia walked out on him and he felt worse than when Stephanie had broken their engagement. A pain surrounded his heart and he was sure it would never go away. He loved her, and he'd fucked it up. What an idiot he was. How was he going to go on without her?

Wyatt swore when he saw Gabe enter the barn and head toward him. They glared at each other. Gabe halted in front of him. They stood eye to eye.

"You look like shit," Gabe told him.

"Yeah, well it's not the first time, but it sure as hell will be the last." Wyatt led Cochise to his stall. Gabe was on his heels. Wyatt spun around. "Don't you have something to do? A wife to go home to? A little girl to take care of?"

When Gabe shrugged, Wyatt clenched his fists. "Go home Gabe. Leave me the hell alone or I'll put you in your truck."

Gabe laughed and Wyatt stepped toward him. "You think I'm joking?" he warned as he clenched his jaw. Gabe threw his hands up in surrender.

"I'm going. I just wanted to make sure you were all right."

Wyatt snorted and turned away but apparently, Gabe wasn't done yet.

"Why the hell can't you just admit you love her? I don't understand what the problem is. You'd rather be alone than have her in your life," Gabe shouted at him with his arms folded across his chest.

Wyatt spun back around, strode toward Gabe,

and punched him in the face. Catching him off guard, Gabe stumbled back but then he smiled at Wyatt.

"Is that the best you can do, little brother?"

Wyatt growled, reached out and grabbed Gabe's shirt, and hit him again. This time, he left Gabe with a busted lip. His stubborn brother swiped his arm across his lip and smiled at him again. Wyatt growled and charged at him, grabbing him around the waist, and taking them both to the ground. Gabe pushed Wyatt off him and quickly stood. When Wyatt tried to get up, Gabe put his booted foot on his chest and held him down, making Wyatt even angrier.

Wyatt grabbed Gabe's ankle, twisted it, and took Gabe back down onto the ground. Wyatt jumped up and stood over him. He was about to reach for Gabe again when someone grabbed his arm from behind. Wyatt spun around, swinging his fist and hitting Jake squarely on the jaw, knocking him to the ground. When he realized he'd just belted his oldest brother, he swore, and stormed off. He'd only gone a few feet when someone spun him around and punched him on the chin, knocking him down to the ground. This time, it was Jake, not Gabe, who stood over him.

"I owed you that," Jake told him as he put his hand out to help Wyatt up.

Wyatt stared up at him, and then gave him a terse nod before accepting his brother's hand. Once on his feet, he narrowed his eyes.

"All good, but get him the hell away from me." He jerked his chin toward Gabe. Jake nodded.

"Are you all right?" Jake asked rubbing his own jaw.

"I'm fine. He didn't hurt me."

Jake grunted. "Like I'd think he would. I meant, are you all right, since you and Olivia..."

Wyatt held a hand up. "I'm fine. I'll get past it." He tightened his jaw, turned and walked away through the barn.

* * * *

Sheriff Sam Garrett pulled into the parking lot of Dalton's Motel. Sam was pleased with what he'd found out. It seemed Sharon Winters was, in fact, Charlotte Roberts and had an impressive criminal record. He shut off his SUV cruiser and got out. Scanning the doors, he found room sixteen and knocked. A few seconds later, she opened the door. Sam saw a flash of fear in her eyes but she quickly recovered and gave him a come-hither pose.

"Well, if it isn't the gorgeous sheriff. What can I do for you?"

"I'd like to come in and speak with you," Sam told her.

She hesitated and then opened the door wider, allowing Sam to step inside. He moved to the small table and nodded for her to take a seat. After she sat, Sam pulled a chair out, turned it around, and straddled it. He reached into his shirt pocket and took out a small writing tablet. Sam was old school. He wrote everything down on paper—no iPad for him. Finally, he glanced up at her.

"Who had you come here, Ms. Roberts?" He noticed her blink when he used her real name, but she kept a calm expression.

"I don't know what you mean, Sheriff. I came here to see my daughter."

He smirked. "And to extort money from her."

Sharon gasped. "I did no such thing. If she told

you that, she's lying."

He folded his arms across the top of the chair and leaned toward her. He knew she was feeling cornered because she wouldn't meet his eyes. "We can talk here or at the station. It's up to you." He shrugged.

Sharon laughed, but it was forced. "We don't have anything to talk about."

He grinned. "Oh, I think we do...Charlotte. You see, I know all about you, except why you're here, so you may as well tell me. You're not getting any money from anyone. I know you're wanted for embezzling from your last employer, and you've been hiding under assumed names for the past three years."

Sam watched the blood drain from her face. If he hadn't been so pissed about what she'd put Olivia through, he might have felt sorry for her. He sighed in impatience.

"All right, Charlotte. Let me tell you what I know. You, as Charlotte Roberts, embezzled over one hundred thousand dollars from your employer so you disappeared, and got a new identity. Then someone found you, and enticed you to come here to try to run your daughter out of my town." He narrowed his eyes at her. "I don't know why yet, but I want you to tell me what I'm missing." Sam shrugged. "It may help your case of extortion, if you cooperate. As far as the embezzling, you'll be fully prosecuted."

He watched her put her hands over her face and burst into tears. Sam didn't move. He knew tears and these were real. She was scared. He handed her a tissue. She blew her nose and stared at him over the tissues. He raised his eyebrow.

"Let me ask you this. Was Stephanie Taylor involved?"

Sharon shook her head. "No. I introduced myself to her the day you all saw me talking with her on the street. I just wanted to see what was so special about her then anytime I saw her after that, I spoke to her."

"What made you want to see what was so special about Stephanie? How would you even know who she was?"

"Because of her father, Blake Taylor. He hired me to come here and run Olivia off so Stephanie could get Wyatt back," Sharon whispered.

Sam reared back. "It was Blake? You're sure about this?"

"Of course, I'm sure. I met with the man. He paid me fifty thousand up front and once Olivia moved away, I'd get another fifty thousand. Only, I underestimated my daughter. She didn't run away." She took a deep breath. "Blake Taylor hired a private detective to find me, and once he found me, Taylor made me the offer."

"Was Blake behind running Olivia off the road?"

Sharon nodded. "Yes. He hired a man who used to work for Wyatt. Ben...something or other."

"Collins?" Sam asked.

"Yes, that's it. Ben Collins. He said he owed Wyatt." She sniffed. "Now what, Sheriff?"

Coming to his feet, Sam reached for his handcuffs. "Now you stand up and put your hands behind your back."

Sharon gazed up at him and blinked. "Isn't there something I could do to change your mind?"

Sam glared. "No, there isn't." He snapped the cuffs on her wrists. "You have the right to remain silent..."

* * * *

Blake Taylor's arrest shocked the entire town. He'd wanted to give his daughter what she wanted and she'd wanted Wyatt. Even his daughter was in shock. The townspeople stood outside the courthouse watching as Sam escorted Blake inside.

Olivia, Becca, and Emma stood across the street in front of the diner when Stephanie approached and stopped in front of them.

"I'm so sorry, Olivia. I know this was my fault. I never should have gone on about how much I didn't want you and Wyatt together," Stephanie said, and by her expression, with sincere apology.

"He did achieve what he wanted though. I'm leaving Montana," Olivia said, and then entered the diner with Emma and Becca following her without giving Stephanie a chance to gloat.

She had no other choice but to leave. As much as she loved this little town and her friends, she couldn't stay here so close to Wyatt. Seeing him without being able to be with him would destroy her. Both Becca and Emma had begged her to stay, but Olivia stood firm.

"You're going to go get the rest of my things from Wyatt's place, aren't you, Becs?" Olivia asked after they settled into a booth.

"Yes." Becca sighed. "I hate to see him since I may just have to give him a piece of my mind."

Olivia touched her hand. "Please don't. I knew going in it wouldn't last. I have no one to blame but myself." She choked back tears. "It's not Wyatt's fault. He made it clear from the beginning what kind of relationship it would be."

They ordered lunch. Olivia had no appetite and

only picked at her salad. The sooner she got out of this town, the better.

* * * *

Wyatt was sitting in his living room when he heard the back door open. He stood and headed toward the kitchen, half hoping it was Olivia returning. It was Becca standing in the center of the room wearing a surprised expression.

"What are you doing here, Becca?"

"Me? Jake told me you were going to Butte, otherwise..."

"I'm going tomorrow. Why?"

"I came to pick up the rest of Olivia's things."

Wyatt nodded and turned away from her. He should have known Olivia wouldn't want to come back for any reason. She had sent Becca instead. He knew Becca was following him.

"Her things are in the bedroom. You know where it is." He waved his hand toward the hallway.

"It's too hard for her to come here, Wyatt."

He nodded. "You can tell her she's welcome to come by and get whatever you miss. I'm sure she wants to see Coco once in a while too. She loves that horse."

"She won't be coming at all, Wyatt. She's leaving Montana."

"What?" he asked, shocked. He hadn't expected her to leave town completely. He didn't like that idea at all.

He listened as Becca told him how Olivia had decided to travel, and then settle down somewhere. He fell back into a chair and put his hands over his face. He felt Becca touching his knee. He opened his eyes and stared down at her as she kneeled in front of him.

"I really messed up this time, Becca. I should have told her how I felt a long time ago. Now, it's too late."

"How *do* you feel about her?" Becca asked him.

Wyatt took a deep breath. "I'm in love with her."

Becca jumped up. "Well, then you have to tell her." He started shaking his head.

"Yes, Wyatt! You have to. Can you really just let her go? Can you live like this the rest of your life?"

"No, but I hurt her."

"Yes, you did and it won't be easy getting her here but I have an idea. Do you have to go to Butte tomorrow?"

"Not really."

"I'll convince her to come here to see Coco and check for any of her things I might've missed. In fact, I'll deliberately miss something so she has to," Becca said smiling.

Wyatt frowned. "And then?"

Becca swatted at him. "Then she'll come over here and you'll be here. You can tell her how you feel and convince her not to leave."

He shook his head. "She won't listen to me. I hurt her too badly."

"Wyatt, she loves you. You have to try, at least. Don't let the best thing you've ever had disappear from your life."

"I suppose it's worth a try," he muttered. Becca hugged him and smiled happily as she headed back to the bedroom.

He wished he were as enthusiastic about it as she was. *What if Olivia doesn't come over? What if she does and tells him she doesn't want him anymore? Jesus!* What in the hell was he going to do if she told him she didn't want him anymore? He ran his hand down his face, groaned, leaned his head back, and closed his eyes. Becca had better know what she's doing.

* * * *

Olivia pulled her car into Wyatt's driveway and parked near the back door. She blew out a breath. How was she going to do this? How could she go into that house? Enter that bedroom? That bedroom with the bed they'd shared and not fall apart? She glanced around and didn't see anyone. Had they all gone to the sale?

She shook her head thinking it didn't really matter. Nothing would ever matter to her again. She blinked back tears as she got out of her vehicle. Once she entered the kitchen, she took a deep breath and headed toward the living room. She halted in her tracks when she saw Wyatt leaning against the wall, his arms folded across his chest. Olivia blinked, thinking it was her imagination, but he raised an eyebrow at her.

"What are you doing here?" she asked, her insides suddenly turning into a flock of butterflies fluttering around at the same time.

"I live here. What are you doing here?"

"I came to get the rest of my things," she said, her voice ending on a sob.

Wyatt straightened up, moved toward the living room, and took a seat in the recliner. Olivia stared at him like a woman stranded in the burning hot desert and he was a sparkling cool swimming pool. She wanted to jump in. Gathering her pride, she headed back to the bedroom where she put the rest of her things in the bag she'd brought with her. As she left the bedroom, she glanced into his office. After a quick glance toward the living room, she entered the room and took the picture of Wyatt and Cochise. She stuffed it into the bag before entering the living room again.

"Weren't you supposed to be in Butte?" she asked in curiosity, but grateful he was here so she could see him one last time, imprinting his gorgeous face on her mind so she never forgot it.

"I changed my mind," he said without looking at her.

Olivia bit her lip to keep from gasping at the pain shooting through her heart. She blinked the tears back while heading out through the kitchen, pausing a moment to wish things were different but knowing they weren't, and then left.

* * * *

Wyatt swore when he heard the door close softly behind her as she left the house. He'd have felt better if she would've slammed it. He jumped up and hurried through the kitchen. As he gazed out the back door, he saw her hesitating about getting in the car. Was she going to come back in? She closed the door of her vehicle and headed toward the barn. *Coco.* She was going to see Coco.

Do something, you idiot! If he didn't do something quick, she was going to walk out of his life—forever. Wyatt put his coat on. He was about to go out the door when he saw her coming back from the barn, wiping tears away from her cheeks with her gloved hands. She started toward her vehicle, but then suddenly changed her course and headed for the metal building. *Cochise.* She wanted to see him before she left.

Son of a bitch! He couldn't let her leave. Not now. Not ever. Wyatt went out the door and strode across the yard, and quietly entered the building behind her. She was petting Cochise. Other than him, Cochise only let Olivia touch him. She'd stolen his heart, too.

He leaned against the doorjamb, folded his arms across his chest, and crossed his booted feet at the ankles. To anyone looking at him, he looked completely relaxed but in reality, he was strung tighter than a bow. His eyes never left her and he was ready when she turned to leave. The minute Olivia spotted him, she faltered in her steps. Then her chin went up and she strolled toward him. He pushed himself away from the doorjamb and stepped into her path. He stopped and waited for her to reach him. She hesitated only slightly as she came forward, and then she moved around him.

Wyatt closed his eyes for a second, and then turned to watch her walking away.

"Olivia..." He cleared his throat. She didn't stop. "Olivia," he said louder and watched as she slowed her steps, but still she didn't stop. Wyatt blinked his eyes quickly as tears made it difficult to see.

"Please..." He was willing to plead for her to stay. She stopped and turned to face him. He dropped to his knees. "I've never begged for anything in my life, but I'm begging you now. Please, don't leave me." Wyatt lowered his head.

Olivia slowly moved toward him. "What are you saying?"

He raised his head and heard her gasp. He knew she saw the tear rolling down his cheek.

"I'm begging you to stay with me, darlin'. I'll crawl if I have to."

"Why? Why do you want me to stay, Wyatt?" Olivia asked him, and he knew what she needed to hear.

"I can walk away from anyone but you, Olivia." He shook his head. "I can't walk away from you."

"Why?" She repeated her question.

"I'm in love with you." He swallowed hard. "I love you so much. You're the only woman I'd ever be on my knees for." When she didn't say anything, he thought he'd waited too long. He lowered his head and took a deep breath. "I blew it, didn't I?"

"You hurt me, Wyatt." He heard her whisper and the words were like a knife through him.

He despised himself for hurting her.

He gazed up at her. "I swear I'll never hurt you again if you'll stay with me. I don't want to be without you. I *can't* be without you in my life. Please."

She stared down at him with tears rolling down her face. "You love me?"

"More than you could ever know." Another tear rolled down his face. "Please. You're all I want in my life. I'd give up everything I own to have you back. Nothing matters to me as much as you do. Name it. If you want to leave Montana, we will. It doesn't matter as long as we're together."

"Cochise?"

He nodded without hesitation. "Yes."

Olivia gasped. "You love him."

"I love you more."

"I love you too, cowboy," she whispered, her voice filled with emotion, and her beautiful, amazing eyes glistening with accumulated tears.

"You do?"

"Oh, Wyatt, I've loved you since the first time I saw you."

He smiled. "I want to spend my life with you, sweetheart. I want to marry you."

Olivia squealed and leaped into his arms, causing them to tumble onto the floor laughing. Wyatt rolled her onto her back catching her head in his palms, and kissed her deeply.

"I love you, darlin'. I'm going to tell you every day so you'll never doubt it, and if I have to get on my knees to prove it, I will—every day."

"I don't want you on your knees, Wyatt. I never did. I just wanted you to love me."

"I do. I love you so much it scares the hell out of me but if you ever leave me, I'll come after you."

"You'll never have to worry about that. You're stuck with me. Now let me up, cowboy. I have a wedding to plan."

Wyatt burst out laughing and lowered his head to kiss her again. It was a while before they got off the floor.

Epilogue

June was unmercifully hot, but the bride and her party didn't care. They sat in the living room of Becca and Jake's home sipping champagne. Olivia gazed at her two best friends. Their gowns matched the color of their eyes. Becca wore green and Emma wore blue. Olivia had stolen Becca's idea for the color of the gowns. In her wedding, Olivia had worn purple and Emma had worn blue. They looked so beautiful, making Olivia smile.

She set her flute down and picked up her gown. She stepped into it and pulled it up. The gown was strapless and hugged her like a second skin with a beautiful train flowing out behind her.

"Will one of you zip me?" she asked her best friends.

"Oh my God, Liv, you're so gorgeous," Emma said as she stood and quickly moved behind Olivia to help her.

Olivia glanced over to Becca, who was grinning like it was her own wedding day with tears glistening in her happy eyes. "Don't cry, honey. You'll ruin your make-up."

Becca waved her hand in front of her eyes. "I'm trying not to but you look so amazing."

Olivia smiled. "We can't have the matron of honor with runny mascara."

Emma laughed. "Yeah, you'll look just great in the pictures." She laughed aloud when Becca stuck her tongue out at her.

"You're not nervous at all, are you?" Becca asked as she fussed with Olivia's hair.

"No. I have no reason to be nervous. I'm marrying the man I love. The one I wanted the minute I saw him. A *nasty cowboy*," she said wrinkling her nose, and then laughing.

Olivia remembered how she'd told Becca before she moved to Montana that she thought cowboys were nasty but after meeting the Stone brothers, and every other cowboy in Clifton, she had quickly changed her mind.

Just then, Stan entered the living room to tell them it was time to go to the church. Just as he had for Becca's wedding, he was giving Olivia away. Taking a deep breath, she headed out through the kitchen with her matron of honor and bridesmaid following behind her. She was so ready to do this.

* * * *

Inside the church, Wyatt paced, and his brothers grinned at him as they watched him.

"You're not nervous are you, little brother?" Jake asked with a sly grin.

Wyatt stopped pacing, and grinned at him. "Nope. I'm so ready to do this." He moved to the window and gazed out.

"You know, they claim it's bad luck to see the bride before the wedding," Gabe told him stepping up beside him.

Wyatt laughed when he heard the crowd outside cheering. The entire town had shown up.

Those who couldn't fit in the church stood in the street. They had done the same for Jake and Becca's wedding, as well as Brody and Madilyn's wedding.

"Sounds like your bride's here, little brother." Jake slapped him on the back.

Wyatt smiled. "I had no doubts."

The Reverend entered the room and told them it was time. The men followed him out and moved to stand at the altar. When the music started, Wyatt kept his eyes on the door at the back of the church. He smiled when Emma started down the aisle. A moment later, Becca stepped into sight and followed behind her. The music suddenly changed to the wedding march and when his gaze shifted to the doorway, Olivia was standing there with Stan.

His breath whooshed out of his chest at the sight of her. She was stunning. Her white dress was skintight, showing off that gorgeous body of hers, and she had pinned her silky hair up, leaving her neck and shoulders open to his eyes. There was a purple rose behind her left ear and around her neck, she wore the infinity necklace he'd given her two days ago. Her hands clutched a bouquet of purple and white flowers with baby's breath and ivy. She was beyond beautiful.

Wyatt almost burst out laughing when he heard Gabe whisper a *holy shit* upon seeing Olivia. Wyatt was sure there wasn't a man in the church who wasn't slack jawed, but she kept her eyes only on him as she moved gracefully down the aisle. He grinned with pride, and took her hand when she stopped beside him.

When the Reverend asked who gave this woman in marriage, Stan cleared his throat and announced proudly that he did. He kissed her on the cheek and stepped away. He seemed to look around instead of taking his seat right away, and then walked to the end of pew. There he smiled at Evelyn Robinson before taking a seat next to her. Wyatt swore he saw the sweet lady blush when she scooted over to make room for him, and then she smiled at him. *Good for them!* He wished them the same good fortune he now had.

He and Olivia listened to the Reverend say the words joining them in marriage but never took their eyes off each other. When Wyatt slipped the ring on her finger, he raised it to his lips and kissed the back of her hand. He thought he heard the women in the church let out a collective sigh, but it was possible he'd only imagined it. When the Reverend pronounced them husband and wife, Olivia grabbed the lapels of his tuxedo, jerked him forward, and kissed him soundly.

"I've got you now, cowboy," she said against his lips but loud enough for everyone to hear, and make them laugh.

He laughed along with everyone else, and then gave her a wicked grin before he picked her up, tossed her over his shoulder, and carried her down the aisle. Their guests applauded, and laughed. When he stepped out into the sunshine, the crowd outside cheered too. He could feel Olivia laughing against his shoulder as he walked toward Cochise, and put her up on the horse.

He vaulted onto the horse's bare back behind her.

"We have to have pictures taken, Wyatt. Where are you taking me?" Olivia kissed him.

"Just a little trip around the block. We'll be right back for pictures. Jake and Gabe knew I wanted to do this, and arranged to have Cochise here waiting." He kissed his wife. "We've come so far, you and me, just as you have when it comes to getting on a horse."

She laughed and stroked his cheek, gazing up at him. "I love it."

"This is just the beginning, sweetheart. I love you."

"I love you too, cowboy, and I can't wait to see what the future brings." Wyatt grinned, nudging Cochise through the crowd.

"Only happiness, darlin', I promise...only happiness."

The End

About the Author

Susan was born and raised in Cumberland, MD. She moved to Tennessee in 1996 with her husband and they now live in a small town outside of Nashville, along with their two rescued dogs. Although, writing for years, it was a year ago she decided to submit to publishers and she chose Secret Cravings Publishing. When SCP closed their doors, Susan decided to publish on her own. She is a huge Nashville Predators hockey fan. She also enjoys fishing, taking drives down back roads, and visiting Gatlinburg, TN, her family in Pittsburgh, PA and her hometown. Although Susan's books are a series, each book can be read as standalone books. Each book will end with a HEA and a new story beginning in the next one. She would love to hear from her readers and promises to try to respond to all.
She would also appreciate reviews if you've read her books.
You can visit her Facebook page and website by the links below.

https://www.facebook.com/skdromanceauthor

www.susanfisherdavisauthor.weebly.com

susan@susanfisherdavisauthor.com

Made in the USA
Monee, IL
23 March 2022

93395998R00144